LOVE ON THE RUN

A PINE HARBOUR NOVEL

ZOE YORK

WWW.ZOEYORK.COM

Bodyguard. [Noun]
A person hired to escort and protect another person.
Escort and protect. **Definitely no flirting, kissing, or testing the bounds of third base.**

Dean Foster has nearly two decades experience being calm, cool, and collected. His first gig in his new private security contractor role should be more of the same, but Nashville superstar Liana Hansen blows all that out of the water in one breathy hello.

Liana isn't sure how she feels about the straight-laced cop shadowing her everywhere she goes, but there's no denying the chemistry between them. Too bad he insists on keeping his clothes on. And then there's the pesky matter of feelings. Neither of them likes *those.*

With only a dozen stops left on the tour, one of them is going to have to bend. Or the other is going to wind up breaking something.

to flying high and being free

*For everyone who has chased their dreams, and discovered
themselves in the process*

PLAYLIST

All of these songs are available at your favourite retailers

Unlove You - Jennifer Nettles
We Can't Be Friends - Joanna Smith
Enough - Reba McEntire (featuring Jennifer Nettles)
Crash and Burn - Thomas Rhett
A Woman Like You - Lee Brice
Good News, Bad News - George Strait and Lee Ann Womack
Girl Next Door - Brandy Clark
Grandma's Garden - Zac Brown
Riser - Dierks Bentley
Faded Gloryville - Lindi Ortega
Outside Your Door - Dolly Parton
Marry Me - Martina McBride

LIANA HANSEN 2016 TOUR

THE SUMMER DATES

Savannah - June 27
Washington - July 4
Raleigh - July 5
Charlotte - July 6
Knoxville - July 7
Louisville - July 8
St. Louis - July 9
Memphis - July 10, 11
Tulsa - July 16
Denver - July 18
Bozeman - July 19
Mountain Home - July 20
Salt Lake City - July 22
Portland - July 25
Humbolt County - July 27
Los Angeles - July 30, 31
Los Vegas - August 2
Phoenix - August 3
San Diego - August 5

CHAPTER ONE

HIDING from her problems wasn't a great plan.

Not a long-term one, anyway. In the short term, Liana Hansen had a pitcher of fruit tea and a shady tree under which she could read. Or at the very least, hold a book and stare into the distance without worrying that someone might notice and ask her what was wrong. For the first time in two days, there was no hovering best friend doing her darnedest not to ask why Liana had shown up in Pine Harbour.

She was finally alone.

Still numb, still confused. Solitude wasn't an easy fix, either.

Deep down, a voice whispered that she could try talking about it. But she wasn't ready to confide to anyone that for the first time in her adult life, she'd given her career the proverbial middle finger.

Not even to Hope, who would understand completely.

She didn't want to voice any of it out loud, because she didn't feel good about what she'd done. But she couldn't let that gross worry in the pit of her stomach take over.

When your career was all you had, and the livelihood of others rode on your reckless, spur-of-the-moment decision to run away, she imagined nausea and regret were pretty par-for-the-course side effects.

And bigger than those feelings was the intense, unexpected relief at having escaped.

It couldn't last.

She knew that.

But it felt weirdly, dizzyingly right at the moment, even if it created a host of messy complications.

She'd arrived at Hope's house mid-morning two days earlier, dropped off by an airport limo driver who'd appreciated that she'd doubled his fee. And she'd in turn appreciated that he treated her as a totally anonymous customer.

Didn't mean that she wouldn't get outed at some point. There was no such thing as guaranteed privacy, not when the tabloids would pay top dollar for any embarrassing anecdote or photo or, better yet, both. Not that coming up to Pine Harbour wasn't a dirty secret—as long as nobody knew why.

Nothing wrong with a celebrity gallivanting off to cottage country, right? It kind of worked for her image most of the time. People loved it when she shared pictures with her bestie. She hadn't done that yet this trip, though, and wouldn't until it became necessary. Until she knew what her next step was and she needed to set that stage.

And since Hope and her family were out shopping right now, she didn't need to think about that for at least another hour or two. Tomorrow was a national holiday in Canada, so they'd all gone shopping since the stores would be closed the next day. Pine Harbour and the Bruce Peninsula were a lot like Nashville in that a celebrity— even a movie star like Hope Creswell—could hit the supermarket to stock up for a long weekend grill out and nobody looked twice.

She'd bowed out of going with them, as she always did. She wasn't in a hurry to be found out just yet, and had no desire to tempt fate. As far as her fans knew, she was on tour. Nobody knew that she'd had an anxiety attack in Savannah, and instead of heading home to Nashville for a few days before their next gig, she'd taken the last flight to Toronto.

She'd come to her safe space. Hope's house, in the middle of Canadian nowhere-ville, surrounded by pine trees and a glittering blue lake.

She glanced at her cell phone.

Thirty unread messages glared back at her.

Her tour manager and her agent hadn't accepted her weak-ass story. She winced. She owed them more details, but right now, she didn't have anything reassuring to tell them.

What she needed was a sign from the universe. Something that would bolster her up, renew her ability to be The Liana Hansen when deep inside she felt like she'd been stripped back to little Leigh Anne Hansen, eighteen years old and willing to do anything to get heard by the right person.

What had the last eleven years done for her?

So much. Everything, really.

So why wasn't she more grateful for what she had?

Why did she want to cry when she thought of stepping on to that stage in Washington?

From the front of the house, tires crunched on gravel, a sharp, unexpected popping sound that made her heart race. It hadn't been that long since Hope and her family had left, and they'd planned to drive down the peninsula to the larger city at the base of the bay.

She swung her legs down from the lounge chair, but before she could stand up and slide into the house like a ghost, a tall man in a dark blue uniform, big and broad and serious looking, strolled around the corner of the house.

For a second, panic seized her chest. Why was a cop here?

He stopped at the bottom of the steps leading up to the deck and gave her a nod as he looked at her, then past her, clearly checking out the property. He rolled his shoulders, which only dragged her attention to his solid, heavy arms, which matched the rest of him. Definitely tall. Definitely big. And definitely serious. "Good afternoon."

"Hello." Lord, she sounded like a breathy pin-up caricature of herself. Why was that her default response? Charm was only her defence mechanism. She was a one-trick pony.

He swivelled his attention back to her, a frown pulling between his clear, dark-grey eyes as he cleared his throat. "I'm looking for Ryan."

Her heart hammered against her ribs in relief. "Oh." She straightened up. He was a friend of Ryan's. He wasn't there to arrest her for hiding. Of course not. Hiding wasn't a crime, not even in Canada. She tossed her hair and gave him a smile. So what if it was practiced? Nobody noticed the difference anyway.

A muscle twitched at the corner of his mouth and he looked at her again, more closely this time.

She looked right back at him. At those eyes, and the fall of light brown hair above them, a little long in the front, but regulation short on the sides. At his square jaw and long, muscled limbs. He was *built,* a very distracting combination of strength and leanness through the middle that made her wonder if he had six-pack abs or just one long, hard flex of muscle there. *No ogling,* she tried to tell herself, as she dragged her attention back to his face, and back up to that very distracting lock of hair teasing his forehead. She couldn't tell if the lighter strands in his hair were blond or grey, and it didn't matter.

Big, serious, and hot.

She felt her smile widening on its own. Not being arrested made her a wee bit more generous with information. "They're all out. Shopping for the party tomorrow."

"Ah." He crossed his arms, the short sleeves of his uniform highlighting the flex of his thick, corded forearms. "Shouldn't have assumed. I'll give him a call."

Was he looking for an invitation to stay?

Sexy arms aside, she hadn't been looking for company for the afternoon. Even if those arms were attached to movie star good looks she couldn't ignore now that her flight or fight response had faded.

Okay, maybe some company wouldn't be a bad thing at all.

"I'm Dean, by the way." He uncrossed his arms, as if he was thinking about offering his hand to shake but then thought better of it. He propped his hands on his lean hips, right next to a gun on one side and what she imagined were handcuffs on the other.

Hello, Dean.

— —

IT HAD TAKEN him a minute to place the woman standing in front of him, because he'd never seen her in person, and the country music star was always made up in photographs.

But it was an open secret in Pine Harbour that Hope's best friend visited from time to time, and always kept to herself.

Now he understood why. Liana Hansen was drop-dead gorgeous. The kind of pretty that scrambled brain cells and made grown men stupid. Maybe even more so right now, without any makeup or fancy outfits.

He couldn't stop looking at her, cataloguing the very real, very sexy woman in front of him. Her dark, wavy hair was tousled and shoved haphazardly over one delicate shoulder. Her grey t-shirt and black yoga pants were as ordinary as could be. But the grey also made her clear blue eyes pop out of her face, and the pants seemed to highlight tight, compact curves that went on for miles.

And when she'd said hello in that breathy way, her eyes big and her voice husky, turning up at the end, his body had reacted in a completely unprofessional way. Now he jerked his gaze back to her face, only to have his eyes trip over her bare pink lips, full and lush as she parted them.

Finally he remembered the flash of alarm she'd given him when he walked around the corner. Shit. "Is something the matter? Because—"

"Everything's fine." She smiled as she cut him off, but it was locked down and controlled. Didn't go anywhere near her eyes.

He lifted his hands into the air in a universal *easy there* signal. "As I said, I just popped in to catch up with Ryan.

But if you wanted me to take a look around the property for some reason..."

She blinked at him, then groaned and shook her head. "No. Oh, God no. I'm just..." She winced and her lower lip caught between her teeth.

Lush.

Inappropriate, he told himself.

But it wasn't every day he stumbled across a woman like this.

Of course his sub-conscious had a retort for that, too. *High-maintenance, high-profile, high-drama.*

And when Liana let out another breathy sigh and finished that thought, she reinforced all of that. "I'm on a little break from reality, okay? And I wasn't expecting anyone to show up, so you caught me off guard is all."

A little break from reality? Must be nice.

She gave him another one of those not-quite-to-the-eyes smiles and glided closer. "Of course, now that you're here..."

Whoa. Dean wasn't sure which he was more surprised by—the one-eighty spin on her personality or his body's willingness to take her up on the blatant offer. Because as her purred words dropped off into a pregnant pause, his gut tightened and his thighs clenched, like a thoroughbred chomping at the bit.

Hell yes. Except his brain caught up, a second behind but always in control.

He could add *complicated little games-player* to the list of reasons why he shouldn't, couldn't find the woman in front of him captivating. But actually slamming that cell door shut on his libido was easier said than done, because even as his mind struggled with how to phrase the rejection—politely, of course, because she was a guest in his community and he was wearing the uniform, and she was also just a human being deserving basic courtesy—

"Cat got your tongue?" She laughed, a little too brightly.

"Uh..." Yes, obviously. He cleared his throat. "I'm afraid I'm on duty."

She pressed her lips together and nodded, even though they both knew he'd stopped in for a social call of another kind. She turned toward the house. "Well, I'm going inside. If you want a glass of iced tea or something, just let me know."

He didn't say anything else, even as he watched her shoulders roll in and her head duck down, just a fraction, as she pulled open the glass sliding door and disappear into the shadows of the kitchen.

He shook his head, either at his own confusion or maybe to clear the cobwebs, he wasn't sure. But either way, his afternoon had just gotten a bit weirder. And he had the sinking feeling that somehow he'd missed something important.

—— ——

LATE THE NEXT MORNING, Liana lay in bed after trying and failing to sleep in. She told herself that today was the day she figured shit out and made a plan. Like going to the Canada Day BBQ with Hope and pretending that was her reason for visiting all along.

But then she got up and caught sight of herself in the mirror over the dresser.

Nope. No selfies or public appearances today.

Shit, she looked like she'd been wrung through her Meemaw's ringer washer.

Well, it was just Hope and her family who would need to see the horror, she thought, and then did a double take at herself. "Who are you and what have you done with the real me?" she whispered, horrified. She grabbed her brush and smoothed out her hair, then dabbed on a bit of lip gloss. Her hand shook as she hovered over the mascara, though. *You're just going to give yourself raccoon eyes.*

With a deep breath, she backed away from her makeup bag and pulled open the bedroom door.

Hope was standing on the other side, her face twisted in worry. "You want to come with us?"

Out in public? Not a chance. "No. You go. I need to have the world's longest nap. I didn't sleep well last night." Her dreams had been filled by an oversized cop with a decided lack of interest in her. *Didn't sleep well* was an understatement.

"I could stay."

No, God no. "Really, that would be boring. And creepy, watching me sleep."

"You sure you don't want to talk about why you're here?" Hope softened her voice. "Even in broad strokes, Li. I'm a good listener."

"I know. But no. Thank you." On the bedside table, her phone vibrated. Again. She pointed to it. "I need to respond to some messages."

She followed Hope downstairs. The kids were all dressed in red and white t-shirts, the two boys wearing cargo shorts that matched their dad's and the youngest, Maya, wearing a white tutu with hers. Hope and Ryan had matching t-shirts, too, and Liana's chest ached as she watched the new family bustle about, getting ready.

She loved the Howard family, because they loved Hope. And Hope was so good for them, too, Liana could tell.

She had no right to be jealous, and she wasn't exactly. But she was something.

It was bittersweet, maybe. Probably something to do with her thirtieth birthday coming up and her being painfully alone.

Jeez, if this entire anxiety episode was just about that, she'd slap herself silly. She settled on the couch, then, fingers shaking, and sent a faux-breezy text message to her tour manager. **Sorry about the radio silence, I lost my phone charger. I'm fine.**

Brad Harrison fired back an immediate response. **Anything I need to know?**

A careful question. She appreciated that he wasn't asking any of the other questions he could have: *Where the hell are you, are you coming back, will you be at our next stop in Washington, are you in breech of contract?*

She didn't know the answers to any of those. But this one she could handle. **Nope. I'm up in Canadian cottage country visiting my best friend.** A little gimme of truth so he wouldn't think she was hiding anything.

Okay. Let me know what time your flight will get in to Washington.

She didn't respond to that one, because she didn't know what the answer was, and she felt more than a little guilt that he trusted that of course she'd show up.

But would she? She didn't have a flight booked, and the way her heart started racing at the mere thought of it… she wasn't sure she'd make it to Washington.

You have to go. This is your career. Be a professional. She knew all the things to tell herself, but none of them were ringing true.

She had the entire house to herself. And she just wanted to go back upstairs to the guest room, climb under the covers, and cry for reasons she couldn't even name.

Big, dark, ugly feelings loomed over her. So big they were like storm clouds or monsters, terrifying in their enormity.

She'd never felt like this before. Like her heart might rip out of her chest and flee just to get away from her.

In a desperate attempt to ground herself, she scanned the room, settling her attention on the bookshelves around the fireplace. She ran her fingers over the spines, most of them broken. Books that people actually read.

A weird mix, as she made her way down the shelves. Proof of the happy, odd family that had blended together under this roof. Some she recognized as series that Hope had raved about, with demons and vampires and female protagonists that kicked ass. Others she was pretty sure her best friend would never read—dry historicals about military generals and man-against-the-elements type of adventure books. Ryan's, probably. And then the bottom four shelves were all children's books. Chapter books and Lego reference volumes. Skinny picture books about bright pink ponies and chunky board books that had been chewed on.

She'd fallen to her knees as she made her way down the shelf. Now she rose roughly, her legs shaking, and she grabbed a thick novel with a woman on the front, surrounded by swirling mist. She had a giant dagger in her hand.

Maybe if she imagined herself a fantasy heroine she

wouldn't be scared of the boogyman her ex-fiancé represented.

Washington wasn't just another stop on her tour. She'd been invited to perform on the nationally televised A Capitol Fourth concert, with many other performers—including Track Gantley.

Why had she said yes to the concert?

And now that she'd admitted to herself that she was freaked out, how was she going to get back onstage after what happened in Savannah?

CHAPTER TWO

three nights earlier
Savannah, Georgia

SHE TUGGED her signature black t-shirt over her head and settled the snug, soft cotton over her curves. The v-neck showed just enough cleavage to be sexy, but the cut stayed on the conservative side, guaranteeing there would be no wardrobe malfunction while she was on stage.

"Ten minutes, Ms. Hansen!" the tour manager called out after knocking on her dressing room door.

She reached for her water bottle and took a small sip, careful not to mess up her makeup.

When he knocked again, she frowned at the door. He knew she wouldn't holler back. Top of her short list of concert day requests was not talking too much before the show. Limes instead of lemons with her water and cucumbers on the veggie tray—she really wasn't that demanding.

So seriously, W.T.F.?

She pulled the door open, about to snap at Brad that she'd heard him the first time, and the smart remark died on her lips.

It had been a few years since Track had stopped coming by her dressing room to play his little mindfuck games before a show. A chill rippled through her body and she struggled not to show her long-ago ex-fiancé any glimpse of fear.

It was entirely ridiculous, because he wasn't going to say anything that bad. She knew that without a doubt.

Track was smart enough to stay on the subtle side of manipulation. To stay in the grey zone of "wow, that felt super weird and gross, even though the individual words weren't far from appropriate."

She stepped aside, letting him into her dressing room. He left the door open, and she could just imagine how that would be spun in the gossip blogs.

Track is well known for mentoring other performers on his label. That's a little awkward because one of them is Liana Hansen, the hussy who broke his heart and selfishly put her career ahead of the family he wanted. Of course, Track still self-lessly reaches out to her, but he's careful not to let her get her claws into him. Even when she invites him into her dressing room, he leaves the door open…

Or maybe that was just her own fear of how it would look.

"Track," she said smoothly. "I didn't realize you were here tonight."

"Thought we could get together for drinks after the show and talk about the album," he said, sitting on the edge of the counter that ran along one wall. He stretched his long, denim-clad legs out in front of him, and crossed his ankles. He was wearing his brown cowboy boots tonight, the ones with the extra half-inch heel.

Someone feeling small, Track? Need to bully me to make yourself feel like more of a man? But she didn't say that. She just smiled coolly and shook her head. "I can't talk about the album without my agent, unfortunately. I'm sorry you came all this way."

"We're visiting Amber's parents. Not that far." He hooked his thumbs into his jean pockets. "Don't make this harder than it needs to be."

He didn't need to spell out the reason for his visit. He didn't like the songs she'd cut for the new album. And he'd shown up before her show to make sure she knew that as she went onstage. White hot anger slammed through her. "Definitely a conversation to have with my agent."

"I don't want this to turn into a big thing just yet."

"Bless your heart for thinking of me, Track." She slid past him, shaking now.

He snapped his arm out and hooked his fingers around her elbow. "Hang on."

"I don't have time for this."

"I'm doing a cover of 'Forget Me Not' with Gina Bellingham. We're going into the studio after the show in Washington on the fourth of July."

She physically recoiled, stumbling into the door. "What?"

She hated that song. But it was *still her song*.

"You took it off your set list for this tour. The label thinks we can revitalize it with a fresh sound." He sighed and pushed himself upright, sliding his thumbs into his pockets. Pretending he was casual about this conversation.

Neither of them were ever casual about a conversation

between them. Ever. Eight years of tension and anger and resentment still simmered hard beneath the surface.

"Then I suppose that's your prerogative." She shrugged, a quick jerk of her shoulders that she regretted because it revealed just how much he affected her. She hated that she'd let him get under her skin.

"I took a look at your set list—"

"Okay, we're done here."

"'Cravings' isn't the right tone for you, Liana." He gave her a look that anyone else would read as concerned.

She saw the judging sneer. Heard the censure in his voice. *Don't be slutty*, he meant.

"I have to get out there," she said instead of all the things she wanted to say.

"Have a good show." He smiled, and the coldness of it hurt so much she wanted to cry.

Good thing she was starting with a sad song. All the feels, delivered straight to the Savannah fans courtesy of Track Fucking Gantley.

America's favourite singer.

Liana's private enemy—and her boss for at least one more album.

She grabbed her gargle bottle and swept out into the hall before Track could say anything else. Her band members were already milling around, and she gave them all a quick smile.

Let's do this.

Jackie Billings, her lead guitar, narrowed her eyes as she glanced over Liana's shoulder. Shit. She didn't need her worrying. She gave Jackie a wink to say, *it's all good*. It wasn't. This tour had been a terrible idea. They were six weeks into it and each night she was getting progressively wound tighter.

She was pretty sure Jackie was the only one who noticed or cared. The older woman didn't have a lot of love for Track, either, but Liana's drummer and bass player both did, so the women kept their opinions on the down low.

The only thing worse than Liana being miserable on tour would be tensions flaring in other directions as well.

Jackie might think that Track was a pig, but she was a professional. And it wasn't like the rest of their industry was made up of sensitive feminists, either. Nashville was a hard town to be a woman in, which was ironic, because it was a town that celebrates female singers in a way that rock never had.

But the hoops those vaunted stars needed to jump through…

Liana had learned the hard way that sometimes it just wasn't possible to please the kingmakers.

Didn't mean she didn't have a career.

Didn't mean she wasn't still blessed.

Speaking of which… She set her gargle bottle down on a ledge and wiggled her fingers. Jackie took one hand, West Jackson took the other, and her bass player, Andrew Yoast stood across from her, completing the circle between Jackie and West.

Liana let Andrew lead the prayer. He was most devout. It was enough that she pulled them together.

With a whispered *amen* at the end, they broke apart, and as the lights fell, Andrew and West took their spots on stage.

Liana swished her mouth rinse, vocalizing a bit in the back of her mouth as she did the secret, super gross routine that nobody wanted to see. Jackie snickered at her as she spit it out, and that little secret laugh pushed away the darkness Liana had been feeling.

Fucking Track.

But *this*? She loved performing. Loved connecting with a crowd, watching them sway back and forth as she brought tears to their eyes, or have them jumping for joy as she sang to the rafters about living in the moment, no matter what the cost.

She'd belt that particular song out no problem today.

But first she had to tear some hearts out.

Jackie plugged in her electric guitar, and while they still stood in the dark of the side stage, she played the first three, slow notes of 'River Bed Lullaby'.

The crowd went wild, and warm, welcome relief poured into Liana's heart.

It would be a good show.

Jackie walked onto the stage, the spotlight following her all the way across to the far side, then split into two, the second light tracking back to pick up Liana as she walked into view.

The song, her first hit, when she was only eighteen, was about a young woman knowing that she was losing her mother to the bottle. A fearful prophesy that her mother might one day kill herself. A plea not to hurt them both. Begging her to let her daughter help.

It was Liana's favourite song, still, and Jackie played the part of the wounded mother well, pouring soulful agony into her guitar as Liana sang to her from the other end of the stage.

It was an ugly song, and Savannah brought up a lot of ugly feelings for Liana.

It was where Track had proposed.

Where she caught him cheating on her a year later.

America's golden boy. Ha.

No, every time she played here, she took the crowd to the dark, ugly parts of her soul first. It gave decent cover to the raw edge of her voice when she finally hit centre stage and held out her hands, offering the crowd a figurative circle of connection just like the one she'd shared with her band before they came on stage.

"Hello, Savannah!" she called out. "You are looking beautiful tonight, I gotta say. Yes, you. Stunning."

She grinned, then pressed her hand to her chest. "Anyone feeling a little sad right now? I know. Me too. But there's joy to be found in music, right?"

That was West's cue, and behind her, he started into the next song.

And on they rolled, through some of her favourites, and all of her hits—and the two columns didn't always match up, but there was enough to make her and the crowd and the band all happy, so by the time they hit the last song, "Craving", she was flying.

Until she glanced over at Jackie, whose head was bowed over the guitar, riffing hard, and behind her stood Track.

The mocking look on his face was a punch to Liana's guts, like he was laughing at her. She stumbled over the bridge, missing the beat where she should have started singing. Her band just looped a few lines again, and this time her voice took flight where it should.

I've got cravings that
Would shock you
Desires I can't
Speak of

She tore her gaze away from the wings because fuck him, but the damage was done. The heart of the song, her heart, had been squashed like a bug, and when her voice dropped low and slow at the end, she knew she didn't have the crowd with her.

They applauded when the lights went down, but it wasn't deafening.

She hated that she needed that roar to drown out her doubts.

Jackie took one look at her face and made sure she was between Liana and Track as they exited the stage.

"Liana!" he called out to her, but she was into the hallway that led to the dressing rooms, and Andrew and West were making enough noise behind her that she could pretend she didn't hear.

Jackie was talking to her, but her friend's voice was coming from a distance. A dull roar thundered inside her head as she yanked out her in-ear monitor and handed it to one of the roadies.

She shook her head. She just needed a minute alone.

Somehow she made it to her dressing room and shut the door, sliding down it as the tears started to fall.

What the hell was going on?

When did she start losing her mind?

She scrubbed the heels of her hands against her eyes, cursing at herself under her breath. Her palms were covered in eye makeup and her face was almost definitely a mess.

She shoved to her feet and found her makeup bag, fixing as much as she could as her heart rate sped up.

It was time to go.

She shoved a few things in a bag, grabbed her purse, and headed for the door.

The hallway was full of people, but she made noises

about heading to the tour bus, then kept on walking, finding a cab on the app on her phone.

The last thing she did before she told the driver to take her to the airport was send a text message to Jackie. **I'm taking off for a couple of days. Going to see Hope. Don't tell anyone where I am.**

CHAPTER THREE

Canada Day
Pine Harbour, Ontario

DEAN FOSTER KNEW BETTER than to worry about his brothers.

They were all grown-ups, after all.

Gainfully employed.

Jake was even having a baby. Matt and Sean weren't anywhere near being that adult, but they worked hard and played hard and Dean hadn't had to take care of either of them for nearly a decade.

But you never turned off the worried older brother instincts. Not when you were all they really had.

And the tightness at the back of his neck told him something was wrong with Sean—more than the usual emotional shit that stewed in the twenty-six-year-old's head.

He'd tried to find out what was going on when they

went for a run early that morning. Sean blew him off, swore up and down it was just work stuff. So Dean asked Matt if he knew anything as they set up tables in the Pine Harbour Park for the annual BBQ.

"He's just being moody," Matt said, his attention on their task at hand.

"More than usual."

"Maybe he's getting his period."

"That's not funny."

"Only because you don't have a sense of humour."

That wasn't true at all. Or not completely, at least. "He's hiding something."

"It's not drugs."

Dean rolled his eyes. "I didn't think it was, but thanks for telling me where *your* head is at."

Matt flipped him the bird. "Eff you, too."

"So you do know what's going on."

"You should talk to Sean."

"I tried."

"Okay, you should try to talk to him like a brother, and not a father."

"I don't—" But he did worry about them like a parent. Not a father, really. They had one of those. More like the mother they lost way too young.

Turned out, Dean wasn't as naturally nurturing as they'd needed.

He'd tried, damn it. But times like this, he failed pretty hard. "Maybe I'll get Dani to talk to him."

"That's a good idea. Stress out the pregnant woman."

Shit. Right. Hey… "So it's something stressful?"

Matt laughed. "Seriously, it's your first day of being your own man. Take a knee. Have a beer. Trust that whatever Sean's stewing about is going to be there tomorrow and you can enjoy the bloody holiday like the rest of us."

That didn't sound like a feasible plan at all. "I'll talk to Dani in a non-alarmist way."

"Whatever. Good luck. Remember to try and have fun."

That was Matt's motto in life: have fun. Dean's motto… well, until yesterday, it had been the motto of the provincial police, where he'd worked for eighteen years. A personal motto?

Dean didn't have one. He didn't really have a personal anything.

He had work, and his brothers, and carefully constructed relationships that allowed him release and escape when he needed it—and ensured zero extra responsibility, because he sure as shit didn't need *that*.

A pang of guilt lanced through him. His brothers weren't a responsibility he resented. He watched Matt amble toward the tent where the Legion ladies were setting up cold drinks and bowls of potato chips.

For all his muttered concern, he was damn proud of the men his brothers had grown into.

And he knew he needed to let go of the irrational worry that brewed deep in his gut when it came to them. But it was hard. He'd basically raised them for six long, anxious years. And when he'd made the agonizing decision to go to Police College and leave Pine Harbour for a year—that turned into four when his first OPP posting had been further up north—he'd done so only after making sure that every adult member of their tiny community was watching out for his brothers.

Because their father sure as shit hadn't been.

The Colonel had only been there for them in the

strictest sense. A financial provider. Someone to pay the bills. But he'd never made a school lunch or read a bedtime story. Never really given two shits about what time Matt came home, or Sean woke up.

Part of Dean had hoped that when he went south for college, their father would step up and fill the gap. Instead, it'd been Jake who'd taken a turn at parenting the youngest two Foster brothers.

When Dean left Pine Harbour, his next younger brother had been a gangling teenager. When he'd come back, Jake had sprouted into a young man, intent on a career in construction and ready to join the army reserves just like Dean had.

And when Matt and Sean each turned seventeen, they did the same. Following in the Colonel's footsteps, despite everything.

How would their lives have been different if their mother had lived?

Across the park, Jake's familiar green pick-up truck pulled into the lot. Jake wasn't that much like their father, actually. He'd be an amazing, hands-on dad to the baby his wife Dani was currently carrying. As sappy as it was, even Dean could say that Jake had managed to figure out how to have a healthy, fulfilling relationship— something Dean had never even tried, Matt skillfully avoided, and Sean…well, who wanted to fall in love with an asshole?

Jake was also the only one out of the four of them that had what could be called a good relationship with the old man.

Matt would probably say he did. Dean would beg to differ—avoiding all conflict was not the same thing as not being in conflict.

And Sean made Dean's strained relationship with the Colonel look downright cozy.

The similarities between Dean and his youngest brother pained him. It was one thing to be a fearful, mistrusting jerk at twenty-six. It was another at thirty-seven. There was a reason Dean avoided psychoanalyzing himself—he never liked where it took him.

— —

THE PARTY WAS WELL under way by the time Dean made it to the coolers to grab his first beer. Almost everyone was there. Rafe and Olivia Minelli with their daughter Sophie, Ryan's entire family—which reminded Dean he still hadn't explained to the other man about stopping there the day before. Jake and Dani, and Dani's older brother Zander, Dean's new business partner. They needed to sit down at some point today, too, since it was Dean's official first day on the new job.

But right now, Zander was otherwise occupied, one arm wrapped around his fiancé and the other clasped firmly on the shoulder of his future step-son.

Another man who'd found the kind of love that terrified Dean to his very core.

He looked at these women that his brother and friends had fallen for, and he saw the worst case scenario—illness, loss, grief so intense it would immobilize them. It didn't matter that it was completely irrational.

He looked at a man in love and saw his father, broken-hearted and useless. Then later, cold and removed.

Dean knew that he'd go down that same road, if he let himself. And that wasn't worth the risk.

But he admired Zander—and Jake, and Rafe, and Ryan—for putting their families first. He could identify with that, if in a different way. For the last twenty-five years, since his mother passed when he was twelve, he'd been putting his siblings first.

And he always would.

But there was a limit to how much responsibility one man could bear and still keep a sense of self. Dean knew his limits.

He strolled over to the back of his pick-up truck and hopped onto the tailgate.

Zander materialized in front of him.

"Speak of the devil," Dean said, grinning at his partner. "I was just thinking about finding you."

"We've got a potential client." That was fantastic news. But Zander's voice was full of wary caution, and he was glancing around the party like he was looking for something—or someone.

"What's the catch?" His pulse thudded with anticipation. What did it say about him that he was relieved to have the distraction of work on what should have been a day off?

Zander grimaced. "It's complicated."

"How so?"

"The client is expected to be reluctant."

"How reluctant?"

"She wasn't the one who hired us."

"Ah."

"Aren't you going to ask me who it is?"

"I figure you're drawing this out for a reason."

Zander snorted. "Yeah." He scrubbed his hand over his

jaw. "Liana Hansen."

Dean's eyebrows shot up, probably all the way to his hairline. Shit.

She'd be a seriously A-list client…if she wanted them to work for her. And the way their accidental meeting had gone the day before, he wasn't sure about that in the least.

He'd been thinking about her ever since.

Something had been missing yesterday. Like she was a puzzle and he only saw some of the pieces.

Which made sense, because he didn't really know anything about her. Of course the town whispered, but he didn't pay any attention to gossip.

Most of the time.

So yeah, he'd heard things. People could be mean, and her ex-fiancé was a superstar. In their break-up, she'd gotten the blame, apparently.

All of that was hard to reconcile with the woman who'd looked at him, eyes wide and face pale, like she was scared—and maybe needed a bodyguard.

Another puzzle piece, maybe.

"So Hope has hired us?" He re-focused his attention on Zander. His partner looked like Dean felt—ready for this. "What's the plan?"

"She wants us to meet with Liana."

"Okay. I can do that." *Tomorrow*, he told himself. He lifted the beer again and tipped it against his mouth. Boundaries needed to be maintained so he didn't burn out of this career like he had the last one.

"Zander snatched it out of his hand. "Can't wait. She needs to be on a plane tomorrow. Day after at the very latest. She's got a concert in Washington, D.C. on the fourth of July, and a dress rehearsal for it on the third."

Well, that sounded like a problem. And she was reluctant...yeah, this would take some time.

Dean took a deep breath. He never could say no to someone needing his help.

Even if that someone was distractingly gorgeous and he'd had an awkward encounter with her that nobody else knew about.

It didn't matter. He was in. "Where will I find our new client?"

"She's hiding at Hope's house."

———

ON THE EIGHT-MINUTE drive out of town to the Howard-Creswell home, Dean tried to think of all the possible ways this meeting could go. None of the ways it played out in his mind went that well, to be honest. They all stumbled around the point in the conversation where they either acknowledged or ignored the elephant in the room of her having invited him inside for an entirely different reason.

But that was off the table now, so he needed to focus on why she needed security consultants.

Did she just need muscle? It wasn't the long-term business vision he had, but he was tall and wide and knew how to look menacing. He could work with that.

Maybe she'd been threatened. He certainly knew how to run an investigation. But so did others...why come all the way up here if that was the case? And she shouldn't be traveling alone if she was in danger.

He frowned.

Why *had* she come up here?

He hopped out of his truck and walked up to the front door and knocked. Only one way to find out.

The front curtain shifted, and he stepped back, letting her get a good look at him. He might not be wearing his uniform, but the same instincts kicked in.

It took her long enough to open the door that he figured she'd given *not* opening it a solid consideration. The handle turned, slowly, and then his client stepped into view.

"You again," she said softly.

"Yes."

"To what do I owe this pleasure?" He didn't miss that her foot had nudged behind the door so he couldn't push it open.

He'd made a great impression the day before, clearly. "Hope asked me to come out and speak to you."

"About what?"

"Security of some description."

"You're a cop."

"I freelance."

"There's been a misunderstanding. I don't need any security."

He stepped back. "Maybe you should call Hope?" Her gaze flicked past him, over his shoulder, and he turned around. Hope's car pulled into the drive. "Ah, okay, there she—"

Behind him, the door shut with a firm click.

"—is," he finished to himself. He crossed his arms and waited for Hope to join him on the porch.

"Hey," she said as she jogged up to him. "I'm sorry I didn't get here before you."

"No worries. But ..." he jacked his thumb over his

shoulder, pointing at the front door. "I take it she wasn't expecting me?"

Hope gave him an apologetic smile that probably worked wonders on Ryan. It didn't move Dean in the least. "Possibly yes."

He crossed his arms over his chest. "What's going on, Hope?"

Her smile shifted to something more sheepish. "Let's go inside." She reached for the door handle, but the door didn't open when she turned it. She tried again, then started to laugh.

Dean didn't see how it was funny. The woman on the other side was quickly proving to be difficult.

"Liana!" Hope raised her voice and knocked. "Don't be like that!"

Thud. Something heavy hit the other side.

Great. Now she was resorting to violence to make her point that she wanted to be left alone.

Too bad being left alone probably wasn't an option, because he was down with turning around and heading back into town.

He sighed and rubbed his jaw. Not the right attitude in the least. Giving them some space, on the other hand… "You want me to come back later?"

Hope shook her head. "We don't have a lot of time."

"So Zander said."

She nodded, a worried look rippling across her refined features. "She needs to be on a plane to Washington tomorrow."

"This is for a concert, right? Can she get out of it?" Maybe the woman was unhinged. She'd said she wanted a break from reality. Maybe she needed a trip to one of those fancy-people rehab centres, if only to hide from the world for a bit. "Call it exhaustion. Make up some excuse."

"It's complicated." Hope rubbed her fingers against the furrow that had taken up residence between her eyebrows.

That was becoming a standard refrain. "I'm not sure what we can do here if she won't even talk to me. What's the problem, exactly?"

"I think she just needs to know that she's got someone watching her back."

"Is she in danger?"

The door swung open, Liana standing in the triangle of open space. Hope stepped in and gave her a quick hug, whispering something that made Liana scowl. Her hand was braced on the edge of the door, like she planned to slam it in his face any second.

He held out his hand, trying again for the introduction they didn't get through the first time. "Ma'am, I'm Dean Foster."

She glared at him. "Don't call me ma'am, seriously. And don't talk about me on the other side of a door. I'm not deaf or stupid."

Right. "My apologies on every count. As I was just saying to Hope, I'd like to help."

"I don't need a bodyguard."

No, you need a shrink, he wanted to retort. Instead he said, "Sure, of course not."

"So go away."

Something about her made him want to do battle. Not against her, exactly, but since she was poking at him…"Aren't you the one who's supposed to go somewhere?"

She slammed the door in his face.

Well, at least he'd called that one accurately.

CHAPTER FOUR

"WHAT...WHY...HOW did you think it would be a good idea to bring that man into my business?" Liana asked, her pulse racing as Hope approached her across the living room—much like one would approach a cornered wild animal, she imagined.

Great, her best friend thought she might be rabid.

But Hope had looped a total stranger in on Liana's freak-out, and that wasn't cool.

"That's Dean," her best friend said softly. "He's worked with Ryan in the army reserves for a long time. He's a good guy."

He was a cop, and a soldier? And he did "freelance security?" Ryan had some badass friends, apparently. Liana frowned. But that didn't make them trustworthy.

If it were any other day, any other year, she'd have been all over "meeting" Dean. He was tall and broad and good-looking in that will-only-get-better-with-age kind of way. Classic, rugged outdoorsy kind of hot.

Exactly her type.

She narrowed her eyes at Hope, who didn't seem to notice. "What exactly are you doing?"

"I thought you might need protection or something…" Hope trailed off, worry dripping off her words.

Liana's mouth dropped open. Oh. Was concern for her safety better than matchmaking? Yes, probably. But way more complicated. "You think I need a bodyguard?"

"Sweetie, you showed up out of the blue, when you're supposed to be on tour. And you're about to do a concert with Track. And I'm not an idiot, right?"

With a frustrated huff, Liana puffed out her cheeks and started pacing. "I don't think you're an idiot."

"So you wanna tell me what's wrong, exactly?"

"No." And not because she didn't trust Hope. They were practically sisters. The actress had come to Nashville to research a part, eight years earlier, and they'd clicked hard. Liana had been fresh out of her break-up and had a big empty house. Hope had needed a place to crash.

They'd bonded over shared secret loves of science-fiction television and caramel corn. Preferably consumed together, late at night, with a bottle of champagne.

She squeezed her fingers together, then stretched them wide, trying to ease the stress-ache in her knuckles. She felt awful not being able to explain this properly to Hope, but how could she when she didn't understand it completely herself?

"I mean, I can't tell you because I don't really know," she said slowly. That was the truth after all. "I freaked out after the show the other night. Took a cab to the airport and came straight here. And yes, it's also that I don't want to see him, I guess, but that's not the only reason I needed to get away all of a sudden."

"You went to the airport straight after the show?"

"Yes."

"You just happened to have your passport in your purse?" Hope gave her a disbelieving look.

Yeah, she had. Ever since the tour started. The realization made her stomach roil. "I know it sounds crazy."

"No, not crazy. But concerning, yes. That's why…" Hope pointed at the front door. "Just…talk to Dean. He's the most level-headed guy Ryan knows. Is taking a security detail with you such a terrible idea? Lots of people do it."

It wasn't a terrible idea, but she really didn't need it.

She took a long, slow breath in, then let it out. "I'm fine."

"Are you going back?"

Damn Hope. Damn her for seeing right through the lies. "I'm fine," she repeated.

"Okay. Well, I'm going to invite him in for a cup of coffee."

"Please don't."

Hope's forehead furrowed as she knitted her brows together. "I know I'm pushing you, but…"

But they didn't have time for niceties.

Hope was just as much a professional as Liana was. She understood the timeline. And she understood Liana, too. *Maybe better than I do myself.*

"I thought for a second you were introducing us for a personal reason."

"God, no." Hope gave her a look of alarm. "I mean, you don't need… but no. I wouldn't, anyway, and definitely not when you show up so freaked out."

Freaked out. An understatement if there ever was one. "I didn't come here so you could fix this."

"Is there something that needs fixing?"

She winced. She couldn't *lie* to her friend. But she didn't want to answer that question, either.

"Okay. Then he's coming in for a cup of coffee."

Liana could feel hot, splotchy patches of embarrassment creeping over her chest and up her neck. "Give me a few minutes," she whispered, blinking back tears she'd thought she'd fought off successfully.

This wasn't at all what she'd meant to make happen. But that was the thing about impulsive, emotional actions, wasn't it? The chain reaction that spilled forth was entirely out of your control.

———

HE WAS HALFWAY through an are-you-fucking-serious text message to Zander when Hope opened the door and ushered him inside, apologizing profusely.

With a weak, worried laugh, she waved him into the kitchen. "Liana's just gone upstairs for a few minutes. Let's have a cup of coffee. If you're still willing?"

Willing, yes. Skeptical that Liana wanted his help… absolutely. But this might be his new normal. He was in, no matter what.

"We're willing and able." He accepted the mug and sat on one of the barstools in her kitchen.

"I promise, she's usually lovely."

He had no doubt. He could still feel the tug in his gut from when she'd blinked up at him from under her thick eyelashes. Lovely was an understatement. It was also beside the point.

"So what's going on that she's—" He glanced around. *Batshit crazy* was probably the wrong thing to say. "Like that?"

"I'm not entirely sure, but she's not herself," Hope said quietly. "It doesn't help that her ex is going to be at this concert. Track Gantley."

The pieces were starting to come together. "They broke up quite a while ago, right?"

"Eight years ago. But they still have a professional relationship. It's mostly handled through her manager and the staff at his label, but from time to time they need to be in the same place and that's awkward. She's usually more level about it. Something else is rattling her right now."

He filed that away in his mind. "Okay. But he's going to be at this concert."

"Exactly." Hope's phone rang and she excused herself with a quick apology.

Dean didn't mind. It gave him a minute to do a quick internet search on Liana and Track's history. It didn't take him long to get the gist of what she was dealing with. An awful lot of judgement for breaking up their relationship eight years earlier. Tabloid stories still to this day that she wanted him back, the kind of screaming headline that immediately made him doubt their veracity.

Photos of her on dates, judging her outfits. Those same photos pasted beside photos of Track and his wife, who seemed to be pregnant more often than not.

Rumours of… And he'd read enough.

He tucked his phone away as Hope came back into the room.

"Nearly a decade and he still has an upsetting effect on her?" Dean tried to soften the question, but Hope still bristled and he held up his hand. "I'm not saying that to be critical."

"She's not a delicate flower," the actress said, steel in her voice. "But Track messes with her head. It's subtle, and he's American's golden boy, so nobody else sees it. He's won artist of the year three times. He's got a gorgeous wife and three kids with another on the way. Why would he care about what Liana does? That kind of bullshit."

There were key words that jumped out during an investigation, and Dean might not wear the badge anymore, but he was still a cop. And *nobody else sees it* set off all kinds of red flags for him. "Has she ever explicitly said anything to you about it?"

Hope shook her head. "Never. Everything I know, I've figured out in the disconnect between the stuff you see in the media and what I know of my best friend."

"Maybe you should tell me more about her."

"She's amazing. Vibrant and smart and talented. Funny and sexy. If you ask me, Track's the one who's never gotten over her."

"He's married."

She snorted. "Like that ever stopped anyone. I think he's still punishing her for breaking up with him. Punishing her for not accepting that men play by a different set of rules. But it's not just about hurt feelings. I'm talking about *him*. He isn't nice to her, he never was, and he's hurting her because she stood up to him. He probably does it now just because it hurts her, no other reason."

He leaned forward. "You don't need to convince me. I believe you."

She looked up, startled. "Really?"

Jesus. He shouldn't be shocked by her reaction, not

after fifteen years on the force, but he was. Somehow, he'd hoped that wealth and worldly experience would have made this easier for these women. Apparently not. "Hope, I've had this conversation before. The first dozen times, I said some bonehead things. Doubted that a reasonable man would do such things. All the shit we're taught from early age, like you said…subtly. But after a while you see a pattern. Of course it's not news to women, because you've been taught something different from an early age. So it took me longer than I'd like to admit to come around to it, but when a woman says something is wrong in a relationship, I believe her. Without question."

She examined him closely, slowly, looking him in the eyes, then down at his mouth. His hands. He'd seen this before, too. The search for something to hang on to, some sign that it was okay to trust him.

He had an advantage here. Hope knew him as a friend of her fiancé, and he hoped maybe she saw him as a friend herself. That would help.

Finally she relaxed. Her shoulders sagged as she dropped her guard and she shook her head. "It's so hard to tell you about something that I only see the edges of. I'm not sure what is real and what I'm imagining. The same for her too, I bet. But I'll tell you this: she was in a good place last spring, when she came to visit me, and I saw her in the fall and she was fine, then, too. Something serious has happened since the start of this tour. Something that has to be Track's fault. Even if he didn't orchestrate it, she's not in a good place right now, and having to see him on the fourth is going to be really hard for her."

"She could…develop laryngitis."

Hope shook her head. "Not for just one concert. And she lives for performing on stage. She wouldn't want to risk the rest of her tour. The label might get involved, or the tour promoter, with the insurance companies…Too risky. Besides, Track's not just the label's biggest star. He's also part owner."

"Her ex is also her boss?"

"Yeah. And he makes her life a nightmare before an album gets approved. There's a reason she's only had two out in the last six years."

Dean clenched his jaw. Zander had been right to pull him out of the party. This was fucked up. And it might be his first day on the job, but he wasn't new to sticking up for what was right and fair. "Then let's see what we can do about convincing your friend that maybe I can be on her side."

— —

LIANA LAY on her back and counted backwards from ten, telling herself to get a grip. When that didn't work, she tried a hundred, but she petered out somewhere around seventy.

The problem was, she really *had* lost it in Savannah, and when she walked off stage, she wasn't sure that she hadn't made a bad decision to keep on walking.

Officially, it was fine. The tour had taken a four day break. It wouldn't be unusual for her to fly home to Nashville. Coming up north to see Hope was acceptable.

Unofficially, she'd felt the emotional break coming even as she waited for the cab that night. So she wasn't sure she could get a grip.

And there was a stranger downstairs that Hope had thrust into the middle of Liana's breakdown. She wanted to murder her best friend, and that wasn't great, either.

On the other hand…she was losing it.

Of course Hope had taken one look at her and gone into career-salvage mode.

Too bad Liana wasn't sure she cared about salvaging anything.

She got up and went to the washroom. Splashed cold water on her face, then paced back and forth a few times in the hallway, her mortification growing with each step.

No. She did care about salvaging her reputation.

And first step in that direction would be going downstairs and apologizing.

"Go on now, make your peace," she could practically hear Meemaw saying. So like a good southern girl, she squared her shoulder, checked her hair in the mirror, pursed her lips so they'd have some decent colour, and marched off to do the right thing.

She found them in the kitchen, and the man—Dean—was sitting with his back to her. She paused in the doorway, waiting for them to finish talking. Somehow he was even bigger when sitting down. He looked like he could take Track.

He looked like he could take an ox.

"Just give her some time," Hope said. "I've handled this badly."

"It sounds like an unexpected situation for the both of you. And we're at your service. Really, it's fine."

"It's not fine," Liana said, moving forward. He turned around, pivoting quite gracefully for a giant. She gave him a smile that felt more natural than most she'd given in the last while. Not quite happy, but authentic at least.

"Hello again," she said with a sigh. "I'm sorry about before."

He stood up—and up, and up. She wasn't wearing any shoes, which made her five feet and a couple inches. She liked to pretend she was five and a half feet tall, but that took serious heels.

And he had at least a foot on her.

Yes, he would more than suffice as a bodyguard.

If she was willing to go that route.

He nodded at her and gruffly but quietly returned her greeting. "Hello. I think the apology should be mine to make. I shouldn't have been talking about you. I was just trying to get an understanding of the situation."

She glanced at Hope. "What did you tell him?"

Her best friend gave her an unhappy smile. "Not much. I told him I don't like Track and…I think you've been stressed since the start of the tour."

Liana let out a quiet, unhappy laugh. "Yeah. I don't like Track either."

She didn't answer the bit about the tour stress, because she didn't feel like she had any right to complain about the best job in the entire world. Her newfound anxiety was a weakness she'd get a quiet handle on all by herself.

Dean sat back on his barstool, equalling out the height difference between them. He had an air of calm around him that belied the organic threat of his do-you-play-football? size, and his eyes were pretty gentle for a guy that looked like the rest of his face had been chiseled out of granite. And to his credit, he was focused on the here and now, and not the fact she'd hit on him the day before. "Let's go back a few steps and introduce ourselves, maybe. I'm Dean. I'm a security guy, and Hope can vouch for me."

"I'm Liana. I'm neurotic."

He laughed, like for real. An out loud, straight teeth flashing chuckle that kept going and she found herself smiling again, too. This time not quite so ruefully.

"I'm sorry you've been dragged into this."

"No worries. You want to tell me what's going on?"

"It's complicated."

He rocked his thumb over his shoulder, pointing at Hope behind him. "That's what she said. Complicated doesn't scare me. How can I help?"

"I…" She trailed off.

Behind Dean, Hope stood up. "I'm going to go sit outside."

"You don't need to," Liana said, her voice dropping to just above a whisper.

"How about I step outside for a minute?" Dean offered. He held up his phone. "I need to call Zander, anyway."

Hope waited until Dean closed the front door behind him, then she held up her hands. "Look, I know you don't really need a bodyguard. But you could use a friend—one you don't also employ," she added, clearly anticipating Liana's protest that she had Jackie, her lead guitarist and closest friend on tour. "Think of Dean as my proxy."

He was friendly, and kind, but there was something about him that unsettled Liana. She wrinkled her nose. "It would be easier if you could just abandon your family and come with me on tour."

Hope laughed.

Liana wasn't kidding. She sighed. "He won't have anything to do."

"He'll be learning to be a bodyguard. Think of it as Bodyguard Bootcamp."

"My tour is not the place for some country boy to play at—"

"I'm thinking of taking Ryan and the kids with me on a film shoot next summer. I'll need bodyguards, and I'll need to know they'd do anything to protect our children. These guys might be the only option Ryan would accept."

Oh. Well, when she said it like that…Ryan's first wife had been killed in a police raid, and to say he was overprotective of his children was an understatement. "Okay."

"So if you need to think of it as a favour to me…"

"I said okay." She smiled to soften the snap in her words. "You're the only family I've got beyond my band. It's not a favour. I'll hire him. But I'm not going to bare my soul to him."

"I'd never ask you to do that. But you can trust him, should you need anything. I'm sure of that."

As they hugged, a dull regret settled in Liana's chest. What would it be like to share Hope's trust in people?

CHAPTER FIVE

WHEN DEAN CAME BACK INSIDE, Hope excused herself to read on the deck, and Liana waited for him to ask her something. Say something. Do anything to guide the conversation, because she was at a loss.

She listened to the hum of the fridge, the tick of the clock on the wall, and drew herself up to the full extent of her height.

Nope. Still no words came to her.

Dean just waited.

She walked across the kitchen and got herself a glass of water. "You want a drink?" She stumbled over the offer, because *she* hadn't forgotten the other day, but he pretended not to notice.

"Sure."

She passed him the same, and he downed a quarter of it before giving her his undivided attention again.

That prickled at her, so she gave him *her* attention, too. She looked him over again. "You're wearing jeans."

He gave her a bland look. "I am."

"It's hot outside."

"What should I be wearing?"

"I don't know. Shorts." She was wearing jeans, too, although hers ended just below her knees. He didn't point that out. And she was wearing a tank top, where he was wearing a long-sleeved shirt, albeit rolled up, over another shirt beneath that. It was the middle of summer for goodness sake.

"I'm used to wearing a bulletproof vest over a heavy navy blue uniform, as you may recall." He gestured at his cotton shirt. "This is light compared to that. And we get nasty blackflies at night."

"How perfectly reasonable." Man, she was grasping at straws here. She moved across the room again, restlessly roaming for a place to sit. She finally settled at the kitchen table, and Dean moved over there with her, sitting on one of the chairs kitty-corner to hers.

When she didn't push that conversation any further, he gave her a quiet, patient smile and called a spade a spade. "Are you always this petulant?"

She laughed despite herself. "Only when I'm out of my depth."

He nodded. "Okay. You're a control freak. I can work with that."

"I haven't hired you."

"No," he said, pointing out to where Hope was sitting on the deck, reading. "She did. Makes it harder for you to fire me in a fit of rage."

"I'm not going to fire you. I might use you as a coffee gopher, though."

"Good plan." He leaned forward, bracing his elbows on his knees. He laced his fingers together, drawing her attention to his hands. Long, blunt, thick fingers. Like he knew hard work. Like he might squeeze a little too hard if he didn't like the person whose hand he was shaking. "Is that all I'll be doing? Fetching you coffee?"

The blast of unexpected heat that surged through her at the perfectly innocent question was definitely dangerous. It was worsened by the fact that Liana didn't really drink coffee. She fidgeted in her seat and opted not to answer, because she wasn't sure what would come out of her mouth.

"What else could I maybe do to help you out? Maybe on the fourth of July?"

"Right. That." He wasn't wrong. She needed a barrier of sorts, and this six-foot-plus solid, steady, unflappable man would work in that regard.

"Are you thinking about not going to the concert?"

That was the million-dollar question. She opened her mouth, then closed it again.

He laughed, and it worked its way into her chest, loosening some of the tightness there.

"I don't know," she said with a sigh. "No. Not really. Of course I need to go."

"But…"

"But I can't bring myself to book a ticket."

"Ah." He shrugged. "Can I do that for you? Sounds like a gopher task."

A flippant no was on the tip of her tongue, but then she stopped herself.

He raised one eyebrow. "The look on your face right now is pretty entertaining. You really don't want my help, do you?"

"I don't know what I want."

He nodded. "I know the feeling." He exhaled and leaned in, his eyes glinting. "Look, I'm coming with you because Hope wants me to. So I might as well book the tickets for both of us. What you do with me when we get there can be decided later."

He needed to stop saying it like that. She could feel her cheeks heating up and she ducked her head to hide them. "Okay."

Hope came back inside while Dean was booking flights, and she gave Liana a searching look. *All good?*

Liana nodded in response to the silent question. Her stomach was a jumble of nerves right now, but she wasn't freaking out.

"I'm going to head back into town, then, if you've got this," Hope said to Dean. "And there's lots of food in the fridge if you run into dinner."

He slid a sideways glance at Liana before shaking his head. "I don't think we'll be that long. I'll be back at the BBQ before too long."

She let out a breath she hadn't realized she'd been holding. Good. She didn't know how much more she could take, although she understood there had to be some…briefing, or something.

It was the *or something* that was distracting her.

She knew she used sex as a coping strategy. Not frequently, and not unsafely, but like the other day when she'd hit on him because she was scared, she knew there was a solid chance here that she was turning her nerves into an overblown attraction to the cop.

That was dangerous, and not just because he'd already turned her down *before* he knew she was a hot mess.

"Email address?" Dean asked, yanking her back to the present task.

She gave it to him, and her phone dinged a moment later with a confirmation email for the flight from Toronto to Washington, D.C.

He gave her a long look, then leaned back in his chair. "What else do I need to know?"

Good Lord, where to begin? "I assume 'nothing' is not an acceptable answer."

"Probably not a helpful one, anyway."

"Mmm." She screwed up her face and thought about what happened in Savannah. He'd find out eventually, and if he knew now, it would be better. "My ex is hyper-critical of me."

He lifted one eyebrow. "And?"

"We had a run in at my last show. About my next album. He showed up unexpectedly and…And then…I don't know. Something happened. I'm afraid it might happen again in front of Track and that terrifies me."

"What happened?"

The words caught in her throat and she shook her head.

His eyes softened.

Damn it. She didn't want his sympathy. "I freaked out. It was…weird." The words were hard to say.

He just nodded. "Can you describe it?"

Did she have to? "I don't want to make a bigger deal about it than it is."

"I'm sure you won't."

"Maybe it was a small panic attack? Something like that. I couldn't think about anything other than escaping, which is crazy, because my tour is…fine."

He nodded. "Has anything like this happened before?"

"Not on tour."

"But at other times?"

"Once or twice." She was understating it, but she didn't want to dig into the uncomfortable memories that had only really resurfaced in the last few days. Overwhelming freak-outs around the breakup. Not being able to breathe at the first award show she had to attend where she knew Track would be there, too.

His frown deepened when she didn't elaborate.

"It's just that it's really not that big a deal. Most of the time I'm totally fine. You asked me what I needed you to do. Honestly? I just need someone to stand between me and the noise on the fourth. I don't need—" She thought of Hope and her family. "The rest of the time, it would be pretty light bodyguard duties."

"I can do that. And anything you tell me is strictly between us. I won't even tell Hope. You can trust me—and you don't need to take my word on that. I'll do my best to prove it to you as we go forward."

He was so earnest. And all she could think was, yeah, I trust you, you're obviously a nice guy…but I don't need this. She swallowed hard around that thought. Because she did need him—at least for one day. "I don't know how it's worked with other clients, but I'm looking for a very limited level of protection."

"Against Track." He said that like it was reasonable, like she wasn't crazy to fear such a beloved personality, and unexpected hope sparked in her chest.

"I guess…although I don't even know what that would look like. He's…"

"You need someone to run interference with your ex, and everyone who orbits around him, oblivious to how much of a jackass he is because he looks good in a Stetson and can pack arenas."

Nailed it almost in one. "Exactly. Except he wears a baseball hat."

He made a face. "How modern."

That made her laugh, and with the warm, rolling

chuckle, more of the tension she'd been holding tight inside her fell away.

"We've got a day and a half before we need to leave for Washington. Let's use them wisely. Teach me everything I need to know about managing bro-country's biggest star. And what I'll find on tour, other things that might be stressing you out…we've got this, Liana. It's going to be fine."

A day and a half of that spark of hope. She'd take it, even if she wasn't sure it would be enough. "I still reserve the right to fire you."

He shrugged, his eyes calm, deep pools of understanding as he looked right at her. "We'll fight over that when the time comes."

——

AS SOON AS she'd agreed to give him a chance, he pulled out a small notebook and started asking her detailed, focused questions that quickly proved he had a better-than-decent understanding of large event security and managing VIP personalities. He asked her about her band —her lead guitarist, Jackie Billings, West Jackson on drums, and her bass player, Andrew Yoast—which was just the start of an easy warm-up conversation. The guy had pretty slick interviewing skills.

"Take me through a typical performance day," he asked.

"We're often on the road for the first half of the morning. Depends how far apart the shows are. I try to write every day, just a little bit. Lyric ideas, maybe pulling one or more of my band members in for a bit of work. But the time on the bus is really our down time, other than catching up on social media."

"And when you get to a concert venue?"

"Almost always there are local radio station winners, and sometimes an in-person media event. But I'm more likely to do the call-ahead interview from the bus, talk to the morning show in the town where we're headed."

"Ever have anyone demand too much of your time? Get too close?"

"Not really. The tour manager and roadies are pretty good about that. There's always on-site security, too."

"I'll want to connect with them at each stop."

She frowned. Was that really necessary? But she didn't question him out loud. Hope wanted her to play along.

He tapped his notebook. "Look, I know you don't really need a bodyguard." He was a mind-reader. "But you're stressed about something, and maybe having me run interference on some of that stuff—or even just fetching you coffee—can help with that. So I'm going to go through the motions, just in case it makes a difference."

"Fair enough."

"And when it comes to Track…"

She made a face.

"At some point, I'll want to know more specifics about how he gets under your skin." He looked at her carefully, examining her reaction as he spoke. "It doesn't need to be today."

"I'm not going to like talking about that at any point. Might as well rip the band-aid off now."

"Sure. Your call. And you can stop, change the subject, whatever."

"Part of it is about the music I play. That's what probably freaked me out the other night. I switched up the playlist and added a song he'd tried to get taken off my last record. And we argued, which isn't new…"

When she didn't continue, he said softly, "I think that's the thing about triggers. They're often weird and unexpected."

She scrunched up her face. "Yeah. Unexpected. It was that."

"What song did you argue about?" He looked down at the notepad, and she was grateful for the bit of privacy as she talked.

"It's called 'Cravings'. It's a darker, earthier song than my earlier stuff."

His pen paused for a minute, then he kept chicken scratching away.

She hesitated. "What I'm about to tell you can never leave this room."

He jerked his head up, frowning at her. "Of course."

The instant trust she felt for this man was probably misplaced. She didn't know him. The last man she'd trusted had turned out to be a bully of the worst sort.

"Let's come back to that," he said when her silence stretched on. He turned over a page in his notebook. "I was just asking so I'd have some context should it happen again."

She shook her head. She could do this. "There's a song called 'Forget Me Not' on my second album. I hate it. It's a stupid, insipid, gross song about a woman waiting for a philandering man, and I regret that it's on my album." The truth burst out of her, leaving her shaking.

Hindsight was a fucking bitch.

Dean just nodded, slowly, his gaze sure and steady. "Philandering man?"

The memory turned her stomach as she nodded. "Yeah. We were still together then, but I'd started…questioning him. About our relationship, and what he did when we were apart. He pushed it onto the album. Used the producers to wear me down, and threatened not to publish the album at all if there weren't enough singles on it, he said. They bought the rights to that song in an auction, they told me at the time, but I've since learned that the other people supposedly interested had been approached by the songwriter, not the other way around." The manipulation and deceit still enraged her.

"Can you think of other instances where he's tried to control your music like that?"

She barked out a laugh. "How much time do we have?"

A muscle twitched in his cheek. "As much time as you need."

It was cathartic, detailing the steady and subtle derision she'd faced over the last eight years. She got mad, too, because saying out loud all the ways Track had used other people to control her framed it in a new way for herself.

A real way.

Her eyes got hot, scratchy. "So yeah. All of that. And then he drops the bomb that they're covering 'Forget Me Not', and I just lost it. That's the sum of it, I guess."

He let the silence between them stretch a little long, then double-clicked his pen on the table. "Okay. Tell me more about being on the road."

She licked her lips, a quick swipe. Back in control. Back to safe ground. "I don't talk a lot later in the day of a show. Sometimes I need to do a second interview, and that's fine, but I prefer to keep them short. Save my voice for the concert."

"Anyone give you grief about that?"

"Not really."

He nodded. "So Savannah was your last show, right? And we'll hook up with the tour again in Washington. Tell me what I need to know about the remaining dates."

She got up and gestured for him to follow her. She pulled her iPad out of her purse in the living room and sat down on the couch. He sat next to her with enough space for her to notice that he wasn't close, but not so far away that she couldn't show him the tour dates.

"We'll take the buses for these…six dates, until Tulsa. There's a break in Nashville in there. And then we'll fly north and have a few days off before Bozeman, an outdoor festival outside Idaho Falls, Salt Lake City." She shifted closer. "And then another break before we hit the west coast. So three legs of a bus tour. Some nights we'll get hotels, but other nights we'll sleep on the bus."

He twisted, his arm brushing hers as he looked at her. His eyes were hazel, brown flecked with green and gold, and shadowed at the moment with concern. "What are the sleeping arrangements?"

"I share a bus with my band. I've got a bedroom at the back, they sleep on enclosed bunks. There are four bunks and I only have three band members, so once we clear all the instruments out of the fourth pod, you can have that."

"How will your band react to me joining the tour?"

"They're super chill, it'll be fine."

"Well, that's something." A muscle relaxed in his cheek, but worry lingered in his eyes. He was so serious, and it suited him. Like he'd been born to be a cop and a bodyguard, at the ready to fight the good fight.

"Thank you for asking," she said softly.

"Just doing my job." He clenched his jaw, then nodded. "Okay. So what would your preference be in between those legs of the tour? Do you want to fly home to Nashville? Stay in the same time zone? Get away from the tour?"

She usually went home. Or, when a dark, unseen panic gripped her, ran away to her best friend's house. "No preference," she lied.

He clearly didn't buy it for a second. "Really?"

"I'd rather not stay with the tour, I guess."

His eyes danced a little as he gave her an amused look. "Was that so hard?"

"What?"

"Saying what you want."

Had he already forgotten that she'd locked him out of the house when she didn't want to talk to him? "I promise you I don't have any problem saying what I want."

"How about admitting how you really feel?"

"Now that's a lot harder," she said, an unexpected laugh following the admission.

"So you can play the diva, but you do it in a carefully constructed way?" He turned a bit more, his knee lifting onto the couch between them. She kept noticing how he took up a lot of space. Broad shoulders, stretching the confines of a dark red plaid cotton shirt. Long arms that burst beyond his personal space, often bent at right angles. Long, muscular legs.

If she'd met him in any other context, her first instinct would be to flirt with him. And even now, there was that urge inside her to use her soft, feminine ways to play off his big, brute strength, make him feel manly and distract him from his question. Because she really didn't want to admit to him that, yeah, a lot of her persona was carefully constructed. Right down to when she played the diva card.

Instead of dropping her hand and running it along the golden hair that dusted his thick, corded forearm, revealed where his shirt sleeve was rolled up, she shoved her fingers into her hair instead. "I don't know that I've thought about it exactly like that. That's an interesting observation."

He gave her a bland look that screamed, *nice try.* "Is it?"

"You're tough."

"That's my job."

"Awfully sure of yourself for a newbie."

"Really not that different from my old job."

"So why'd you leave it?"

"Now who's asking the tough questions?" One corner of his mouth lifted up. "But I guess that's fair. I'm asking a lot of you. Trust is a two-way street."

"I don't trust anyone. No offense."

"None taken." He gave her a curious look. "Not even Hope?"

She paused, then shook her head. It made her an awful friend, but it was the truth.

His gaze turned thoughtful as he set his feet wider on the floor. She hadn't realized how controlled he was until he started moving restlessly. He shifted next to her, finally leaning forward and lacing his fingers again as he braced his forearms on his knees.

"It's not—"

"I'm not judging," he quietly interrupted. His jaw flexed as he looked down at the floor. "My mom died of cancer when I was twelve. My youngest brother was two, just a baby really, and he needed her. It's not her fault, you know? Of course not. But trust…it's more of an abstract notion for me. The last time I trusted anything or anyone, I was just a kid."

She didn't know what to say. *I'm sorry* felt weak and empty, but it was all she had.

He shook his head. "I'm just saying, I get it. I'm a bit of a fatalist."

"We can form a club."

He grunted and the corner of his mouth turned up.

"There might be some drama about me having a body-guard on tour…" she took a deep breath. "With Track. If he notices you, he's not going to take it well."

"If he notices me?" Dean's eyebrows hit the sky. "He's definitely going to notice me if he gets anywhere close to you."

"Yeah. That's not going to go well."

"If that's the case, it's because he's an asshole."

She liked that Dean instinctively distrusted Track. That was a refreshing change.

By the end of the afternoon, Liana knew two things for certain about Dean Foster: he didn't give two shits that she was a celebrity, and he took his job seriously—even if he'd never done it before.

Somehow it made her feel better that he wasn't doing this because of who she was. If anything, he was doing it in spite of that fact.

When he finally left, heading back into town for the Canada Day fireworks with Hope, Liana pulled out her second phone, her secret one that didn't contain any iden-tifying information.

It was what she used to read dirty stories and partici-pate on social media sites as a random, made-up person. What she used to Google "panic attack symptoms" when she was sitting in the Savannah airport. And now, apparently, she was using it to creep on a handsome ex-cop who was strangely committed to being her bodyguard.

A bunch of hits in local Bruce County newspapers about his former role with the Ontario Provincial Police. References to his family. Four brothers and a military colonel father.

She clicked through to the second article about his police work and her breath stopped hard in her chest.

Liana didn't know a lot about the tragic death of Hope's fiancé's first wife, but Dean did. He'd been there that day, and featured heavily in the coverage.

Difficult call made by law enforcement officers…exemplary service in an ambush…

And she'd been so dismissive of his experience. What a foolish, thoughtless… she gritted her teeth. Well, sometimes that's how she was.

Damn it. When was she ever going to learn?

Her hands shaking, she clicked out of the browser window and slid the burner phone back into her purse.

Enough of that. She pinched her fingers together, then raised her arms over her head, forcing herself to be Zen. Or at least…fake being Zen. Then she pulled out her other phone—her Liana phone, that if hacked would have zero trace of porn or stalking or anything else that could be used against her—and logged in to her Instagram account.

It had been nearly twenty-four hours since she'd posted anything to social media. If she didn't put up something soon, rumours would start that she was in rehab.

She propped her feet up on the railing, framing them nicely against the setting sun, and snapped a picture. **Kicked off my boots after a lovely evening tour**, she lied in the caption. Then she looked out at the lovely back lawn that stretched down to a forest behind Hope's house.

If she walked down to the trees and back, it wouldn't be quite so much of a lie.

She stood up and went inside. Hope had rubber boots sitting on a mat beside the back door. Not a lie at all anymore.

The walk took all of ten minutes, and when she got back to the deck, she published the original picture and went inside.

____

CHAPTER SIX

"WHAT THE HELL IS AN EVENING TOUR?" Dean muttered, mostly to himself, but since he was surrounded by brothers and best friends, all of whom were as nosy as church ladies, it didn't take long for him to get an answer. Three of them, actually, all conflicting.

"Going out to piss in the dark at a bonfire," his younger brother Matt suggested.

Rafe shook his head. "Nah. It's…umm… you know, one of those boat cruises. Like with a fancy dinner."

Tom Minelli chose that moment to show up and hand out new beers for everyone. "Who's having a fancy dinner?"

Rafe pointed at Dean. "He is. Some kind of evening tour on a boat."

Dean rolled his eyes and handed Tom the phone. "What does this mean to you?"

Tom whistled. "It means Liana Hansen has nice legs. Look at those—"

Dean yanked the phone back. "Not the legs, you idiot. She said, 'Kicked off my boots after a lovely evening tour.'

I left her at Hope's house a couple of hours ago and she doesn't have a car."

"So? She's famous. It's probably staged to look like something."

Dean frowned. "Maybe."

He didn't like that idea at all.

Maybe he'd ask her in the morning.

"Can I see?" Olivia asked, handing their nine-month-old daughter to her husband.

Dean passed the phone over to her, confident she'd focus on the real point of the photo.

His confidence was misplaced.

"Wow, she really does have nice legs," Olivia said, but as Dean lunged for his phone again, she was up and away—her arm outstretched as she scrolled down the page. "Okay, I think it means like…taking a walk. There's a couple of responses with a hashtag about southern style and southern girl."

Mollified, he held out his hand, nicely this time, and she slid his phone back into his grasp. He didn't miss her wink.

"What?"

She grinned. "You're awfully concerned with Liana Hansen."

"She's my new client. My first client. I'd like to get this right."

"Creeping on her Instagram is part of the professional obligation?"

"It's not creeping. I'm more interested in what other people are saying about her than…" Her legs. Except he hadn't made it down to the comments, had he?

He'd lock that down better tomorrow.

Olivia just patted him on the shoulder. "Can you give

Rafe a ride home after the fireworks? I'm pretty sure they're going to terrify Sophie, so I'm going to jet now."

"Sure. Of course."

She gave him a friendly smile that didn't say anything like, *ha, caught you peeving on your client* or *really? You haven't noticed she's drop dead gorgeous?*

Because of course he had.

And it was immaterial to the case.

It wouldn't be the first time that Dean had to work around inconvenient attraction. He'd worked with attractive fellow officers, interviewed attractive suspects…no big deal.

Except he couldn't stop hearing that breathy *hello* in his head.

It wasn't just that he'd noticed she was attractive. That he could put in a box.

But she was so…raw. Vulnerable. And yet strong, still, and he'd found himself wanting to soothe her in ways that went way beyond the professional.

He knew this was a saviour complex rearing its ugly head. He rarely stumbled into it. He wasn't that nice of a guy. But any time there was a power imbalance, it was a risk. And Liana Hansen trigged all the major points for him.

He could see, clear as day, that her ex was an asshole.

And Dean wanted to be the anti-asshole for her. Stand between them, as she said. Hell, that's what being a body-guard was—she was casting him as the white knight herself, and he didn't have the rules that he'd been bound by in uniform.

Temptation curled and coiled in his gut, dark and hot and unexpected.

She'd already offered herself once.

But he couldn't save her and creep on her legs at the same time. No matter how nice they looked against the sunset.

——

THE BONFIRE WAS down to coals by the time Sean showed up, reminding Dean he hadn't had a chance to talk to Dani.

Fuck it. He needed to tell Sean he was worried, and then leave it alone. He was going to be gone for a while, anyway. Give his kid brother a chance to figure shit out on his own.

He got up and grabbed a Coke from the cooler, because he had to work in the morning and drive home sooner than later. "Hey man," he said, raising his voice. "You want a beer?"

Sean gave him a wary look that Dean totally deserved for mothering him earlier. "Grab me a Coke instead."

Dean tried and failed not to show his surprise to that, but he grabbed another pop and made his way around the fire, joining his brother on a wide, flat log. "Here."

"Thanks."

"You have a good day?"

Sean nodded absently. "Listen, I'm sorry about this morning."

"It's fine. I'm a nosy motherfucker sometimes."

"Truth."

They sat together in silence for a few minutes, then Sean groaned and looked sidewise.

Dean didn't like that look. "What?"

"I've been tapped to go on tour."

Oh. "When?" he asked, his heart thumping hard against his ribs. "Where?"

"Leave in January most likely. Tour would be…Turkey."

The pause told Dean it wasn't really Turkey. His brother was an officer, and an ambitious, career-oriented one. If he wasn't a professional athlete as well, he would have joined the regular forces like Zander had.

And because his career was flexible, Sean had maxed out on courses and his career progression was exemplary. So "…Turkey" meant he'd been tapped to join a training mission. Northern Iraq.

As hot as shit got.

It would be everything that Sean wanted. And as a fellow army reservist, Dean understood the desire to serve. But it was one thing to make that call for yourself, to know you'd put your life on the line for your country.

It was an entirely different thing for your baby brother to do it, even if he was twenty-seven and two-hundred-pounds of stubborn muscle wrapped around a whip-smart mind.

He forced a neutral, supportive tone into his voice. "Wow. When does work up start?"

"I'm packing up and heading to Petawawa in a few days." Where he'd spend the next five months training with the special forces team there before shipping out. Dean could fill in the blanks.

"Damn, bud. That's an awesome opportunity."

"Thanks."

"You tell anyone else yet?"

"Matt was with me when I got the call."

"That little shit. I tried to find out what was going on and he didn't spill."

"I told him I wanted to tell you guys myself. Telling Jake next."

"And the Colonel?"

Sean didn't answer. Instead he turned his face toward the dying embers of the fire.

Dean winced. "He'll be proud."

"He'll tell me I could've done this sooner if I wasn't racing, too."

Ha. "That means the same thing."

"Yeah." Sean didn't look or sound convinced.

Dean didn't really have time to manage his brother's mercurial mood right now, but even as he had that thought, guilt sliced through him. His father...even Jake and Matt...none of them really got that Sean was sensitive. He certainly didn't look it. But his tough-guy routine was a cover for a fragile kid who lost his mom before he really had a chance to know her.

If Dean ever felt alone in this world, it was nothing compared to what Sean lived every single day.

"Then don't tell him," he finally said. "Just head to Pet and let him think it's for regular training right now."

"He probably won't even notice I'm gone."

Shit. Dean wanted to tell his kid brother that he was wrong, but he wasn't sure about that. "I'll miss you."

"Nah. I hear you're maybe going on tour with that hot country singer."

Dean swallowed a growl and turned it into an acknowledging grunt instead. "Doesn't mean I won't worry about you. I can multitask."

"Ah, shut up. I'll be fine. Nail a groupie for me."

"Jesus."

"That's what she'll say." Sean laughed and ducked to the side as Dean punched his arm, then wrapped his arm around his brother's head and pulled him close for a rough hug.

"Stay safe, kid. Okay?"

"Yeah."

Fuck. Iraq. Dean had known it was coming, but he wasn't ready. Not by a long shot.

CHAPTER SEVEN

LIANA WAS HORRIFIED when Dean showed up at seven the next morning with enough grease to kill the entire Howard-Creswell household.

She couldn't control her expression as he carried in the takeout bags.

"From the diner in town," he said with a far-too-awake bounce in his voice for so early in the day.

"Stop laughing at me," she muttered at Hope, whose entire body was shaking next to her.

Dean overheard and flashed a quick grin. "You should see the look on your face."

"I can feel it." She cleared her throat and edged closer. "What sort of evil temptations have you brought with you?"

"Frank's breakfast sandwiches. I don't know where he gets these English muffins, but they're soft and big, and he makes the sausage patties himself—"

She groaned and went to the stairs, calling for the kids to come and save her from the junk food.

"Bodyguard misstep number one?" he asked when she

came back. He looked like he didn't quite care if it was a celebrity no-no to love a greasy egg sandwich.

She shrugged and shook her head. So what if they smelled amazing? So what if she'd already had a kale smoothie and had been about to do an hour of yoga, and now that sounded totally horrid? "Nope. Totally fine. Might even have one myself." Part of one. A quarter. Without the cheese or the bread. And she'd do an extra hour of yoga.

"You're being strangely agreeable this morning."

She laughed. "Was this a test? See how much of a diva I would be about the scent of grease?"

He snorted. "No. But that would be a good one. I'm going to have Zander put that in the contracts going forward. Because me and big breakfasts are inseparable."

"Good to know."

"What did you have for breakfast?"

"A smoothie."

"Delicious," he deadpanned, and she snorted. He bumped her arm with his, gently, and winked at her as he moved further into the kitchen.

It turned out that Maya only liked cheese and bread today, so Liana shared an egg and ham and tomato sandwich with the littlest Howard—she got the egg and ham and tomato, and Maya saved her by eating the English muffin, which did in fact look extra-soft and extra-big.

Extra-delicious, she was sure. But she had snug t-shirts and hip-hugging jeans to fit into. Bloating was not her friend while on tour.

Once everyone was well fed, Ryan and Hope took the kids down to the lake, leaving Dean and Liana alone to get more serious about bodyguard orientation.

He'd come prepared with more than just breakfast. He

jogged back to his SUV and returned with a black utilitarian looking messenger bag, out of which he pulled a folder of papers, a slim tablet, and the little notebook from the day before. It looked like many more pages had notes scribbled on them.

"Did you sleep at all last night?" she asked, watching him set everything out in front of her—all neatly squared off, too.

"A few hours." He snapped open the folder and crisply handed her the top two sheets. "Signed non-disclosure agreements from Zander and myself. Hope's picking up our fees, but we want you to understand that we're serious about being on your side. Nothing you tell us will ever leave the vault."

She ran her eyes over the neat rows of black ink. Smart. And she hadn't even considered… "Thank you."

"Not a problem."

Mercy, he was suddenly all business. She kind of missed the winking smile from breakfast.

"And we've worked up a couple of possible cover stories for why you're returning to the tour with a bodyguard."

"Cover stories."

He nodded.

"You worked them up?"

He set the tablet down and frowned at her. "Are you okay?"

"Yep."

"Maybe you should have had more breakfast."

"When did you guys do this?"

"This morning at the diner, while Frank was making the sandwiches."

"Oh."

"Nobody else was there."

No, she imagined not. "Everyone else was sleeping," she said dryly.

He laughed. "Not in Pine Harbour."

She took in all the work that he'd done, then looked back up at him. "Okay, I'm impressed."

He leaned against the table, his arms and broad chest flexing against another light cotton button-down shirt, this one a solid dark blue. He caught her gaze and held it. "We're not playing here, Liana."

"I see that." She nodded up at him. "Tell me what our options are for introducing you."

He waved the tablet. "We could invent a threat. Pretty easy to do, but the downside would be someone from the label wanting to get the police involved. Could also be easily exposed, although we'd go to significant efforts to cover our tracks."

She wrinkled her nose. "I don't know how I feel about that. It could be seen as a ploy for sympathy if it ever came out."

"Yeah, we agree. Next option is we fly through New York on the way to Washington. Our contacts tell us that trips to New York and Los Angeles are often times when celebrities secure the services of security agencies. Usually short-term contracts, but it could be explained away if you're going to maybe consider buying property in one of those two cities? To maintain this story, I'd recommend we visit those cities again in those down days between tour legs."

She leaned back in her chair, looking at the man across from her with new appreciation. "That's very clever."

He grinned. "Thank you. That one was my idea."

"Only problem is that I have no reason to buy real

estate in New York. Maybe Los Angeles, although it's not my favourite city."

"And it's not an easy flight to make on the way to Washington, either." He stood up and paced back a few steps. "Which brings us to option three. A variation on the truth."

Had he stepped back so she wouldn't freeze him with her chilly response? Because no. No, no, no. "That's a terrible idea."

"It wasn't mine," he said, his brows knitting together. "But Zander made some convincing arguments. And I'm not sure he's wrong. Obviously, you don't name Track as the source of your anxiety. Shift it to paparazzi, performance anxiety, a minor medical diagnosis, something else. Anything else, really. Something benign enough to not be a real threat, but understandable to the average person as anxiety-inducing for someone under a lot of stress."

"To the average person, maybe." She stood up, too, even though it didn't give her any advantage for going toe-to-toe with Dean. Not that he was pushing her into a fight, but her skin prickled defensively anyway. "But Track will see right through that, because he *knows*. And I've got an album waiting for his approval."

"Then maybe he's going to see through whatever we do anyway. And this way, you're not lying to him. The truth is always a good place to be."

"I might be declaring war."

"I know a thing or two about winning wars, too." What was with this guy's eyes? Once he locked his gaze on hers, he had her trapped in a sea of promised understanding.

But what if he couldn't deliver?

What if this blew up in her face?

"I need to think about it," she whispered.

He nodded, and his eyes got even softer. "I know. We can move on."

— —

THEY WORKED STRAIGHT THROUGH LUNCH, Liana entertaining him with thorough, maybe even exaggerated biographies of her band and the tour crew. They covered drugs, alcohol, and all other vices she thought he ought to know about. The list was surprisingly short.

He asked if she wanted him to be aware of all her comings and goings.

"Is that really necessary?"

"That would depend on the cover story."

Which brought them full circle back to the explanation for Dean's appearance on the tour. After discussing the pros and cons of each option, she reluctantly agreed that the third one made the most sense, although the light in her eyes dimmed as she gave in, and he hated that it was necessary.

By the time Ryan and Hope returned with the kids, Dean was feeling good about all the ground they'd covered, and he wanted to leave her with a little emotional reserve left in the tank. He'd booked flights for the next day that required leaving in the middle of the night, and he wanted her to have some down time, too. Bonding with Hope.

But when that bonding turned out to be a run, he changed his mind. "Can I join you?"

"Do you..." She looked him up and down. "We're pretty fast."

He laughed. They were both fit women, but Foster men chewed miles for fun. "Yeah. I run. I've got stuff in my truck."

Forty-five minutes later, he was eating that laugh—right along with Liana's dust.

It wasn't that she was faster than him, exactly. It was that she was relentless. The woman didn't flag, at all. Dean would pick up the speed and get alongside her, but there was an ebb and flow to his comfort with running, even after twenty-five years of racing his brothers. He would have sworn everyone had that point in a run that bugged them. Early on, while everything was getting warmed up. Or later, maybe a stitch in the side or a twinge in the shin. Even needing a bit of water because it was suddenly hot as balls.

Nope, not Liana. Her tight little body just bounced ahead of him, steady as a metronome. Tick, tick, tick, tick. Step, step, step, step. Bounce, bounce, bounce, bounce.

When he stumbled because his eyes had gotten tangled up in the general vicinity of her ass, he thought about crying uncle, but he gritted his teeth and stuck it out. If for no other reason than he'd needed this private warning about how good she looked in Lycra, he was glad he'd come out with them.

Now he needed them to turn around and head back to the house.

Any second, ladies.

Tick, tick, tick.

As if they weren't completely drenched in sweat, Hope casually glanced at her watch. "Turn around?" she asked Liana.

"Sure," his client said, hardly out of breath at all. "Keep it nice and quick today."

He managed to rearrange his facial features into something neutral by the time they'd spun around and sped past him back down the trail that snaked behind Hope's house.

Nice and quick.

So maybe by the end of this gig he'd be able to kick his brother Sean's ass in a race, just in time to send the little shit off to Iraq.

He pulled up to Liana and she flashed him the first completely carefree smile he'd seen from her. "Someone's found his stride."

"I was thinking of my brother. If you run like this often, by the time I get back from your tour I'll be able to kick his ass. And he races semi-professionally."

"Does he?" She raised her eyebrows. "What kind of races?"

"Marathons, Ironman, ultra-endurance. He's not the fastest guy—he's built like me, so we're carrying a lot of weight on us. But he can do twenty, fifty, even trains up to a hundred kilometres. Just keeps going as others drop off."

"Awesome." She puffed a breath at a loose strand of hair that had fallen out of her ponytail. "I've never tried anything longer than a marathon."

He was distantly aware of the fact that they'd sped up a bit, and Hope had fallen back, but he didn't care that he was running faster than his usual nine-minute-mile. He'd hit his stride, finally. "Neither have I. Honestly, a half-marathon is really my comfort zone."

"How many fulls have you done?"

"Three." And hated each of them.

"Well, that's why!" She laughed, and he wanted to

groan, because how did she have any spare oxygen for laughing? "The first five sucked for me."

"And you kept doing them." He couldn't keep the disbelief from his voice.

"Of course. I had a goal."

Right. Of course. He nodded. "I do get it, intellectually. I see that same fire in my brother. But I can't get that focused in my training. I prefer to be the cop on the motorcycle ensuring the route is safe."

"It's not for everyone." She leapt over a thick exposed root, her legs flashing in a splash of sunlight that poured in through a break in the leafy canopy.

"It's not that running's bad. I mean, I like it."

"I meant the hard training."

"I like that, too." Although he preferred running for the competitive push. He was more of a hit-the-gym guy for training hard.

"Yeah?" She gave him a look he didn't decipher until it was too late. "Then race you back to the house."

And like a shot, she was off. Hope pulled up to him and together they watched her sprint like she hadn't already been going for more than an hour.

"Better catch her," Hope said as their feet churned.

"Not sure I can," he said, not giving a crap that his voice was full of awe.

CHAPTER EIGHT

DEAN PICKED her up the next morning at three a.m.—dark o'clock, according to him.

He said it like a joke, but also like he knew what an early call time was and she obviously didn't.

Ha. Joke was on him. She'd done more morning talk shows than almost anyone in Nashville. She worked hard for every inch of success she gained. Plus first-thing flights weren't an uncommon thing, either.

And she knew how to do that, not just without whining, but in something that approached style. She was waiting for him with her bags packed, dressed and ready to go. Her hair was braided into a thick rope that curled around her neck and over her shoulder. The odds weren't high that she'd have her picture taken, but just in case, she liked to dress in such a way that she still looked halfway decent at the end of a long trip. This morning that meant a black t-shirt which she wore over black leggings. On her feet were black slip-on flats.

She had traveling down to a science, a fact Dean commented on as she slid into his SUV.

"Don't be so surprised," she muttered.

Instead of responding, he pointed to a travel mug in the centre console.

"Coffee?"

He smirked.

She lifted the mug and took a tentative sniff. Jasmine tea. She smiled despite herself. "You're full of surprises."

He just laughed. "I took a wild guess you might be one of those people who prefer green tea."

"Bag in or out?" she asked just to be difficult.

He punished her by waiting until he'd steered them onto the highway before responding.

"Out," he finally answered. "But there's another tea bag in the console if it's not strong enough, *princess*."

She gave him a genuine smile. "Awesome. Thank you."

"You're welcome."

He drove quickly and confidently, and before long they were leaving the dense tree line of the peninsula behind, his headlights showing her more farm country and small towns as they sped toward the city.

She sipped her tea, then closed her eyes. Repeated that a few times. But she was too keyed up to rest, and the car was oddly quiet.

He glanced over at her, as if he was thinking the same thing. Before she could suggest turning on the radio, he beat her to the punch. "What kind of music do you listen to?"

She laughed. "Really?"

He shrugged. "Maybe you don't like country all the time."

"Born and raised in Tennessee. It's in my blood."

He turned on the radio and found a station, but it was

on a commercial, so he turned it down again. "Ever lived anywhere else?"

"Not for any length of time. I've traveled all over the world, though."

"Favourite place?"

"Nashville."

He laughed. "Outside of your job."

"No such thing."

"Ah."

She gave him a weird look. "What are you doing?"

"We have a five hour drive to the airport. I'm making conversation."

"Oh."

He laughed. "For a celebrity, your social skills are a bit rusty."

"My social skills are just fine."

"Nobody pushes you to really talk, do they?"

"Are you nominating yourself to be my therapist, too?"

"Do you have one of those?"

"Hell no."

He didn't say anything, just gave an appraising nod and turned his attention back to the road.

"Do you think I need one?"

"Far be it from me to say," he said, and she wasn't sure if he was being sarcastic or not.

"Is that a northern equivalent of Bless Your Heart?"

He laughed. "That's how you southern girls say fuck you, right?"

She fluttered her eyelashes and lifted her shoulders delicately. "Perhaps. It can mean a lot of things."

This time his nod was slower, more appreciative, and it took him longer to glance back to the road. "Ah. I see it now."

"What?"

"This is how you charm people."

"You think I'm charming?"

"I think you're something." He turned up the volume again, finding a reasonable level where conversation would still be possible—just no longer necessary.

"And that's how you charm people, isn't it?"

His eyebrows lifted, but he kept his eyes straight ahead. She turned in her seat and studied his profile.

"It is. This no-nonsense persona...this is your shtick."

"I don't have a shtick."

She blew a raspberry. "Everyone does. There's your real self, deep down inside, that only you know. Then there's your side that you show to your friends and family. Everyone else? Unless you're completely gullible, you show everyone else a persona. Limited, carefully constructed...what you want them to see. And I doubt that a cop is gullible. Ergo...this is your persona."

He glanced at her quickly, then back to the road. "So you're a cynic as well as a fatalist."

"And you're very good at changing the subject."

He shrugged. "Okay. I accept your hypothesis. We all have masks we wear. Tell me about yours?"

She snorted and leaned forward, turning up the radio another notch. "Maybe another time," she muttered as Kenny Chesney started singing.

— —

LIANA HAD this little habit Dean had already noticed—she

made a conscious effort to relax her facial muscles. They were nearly at the airport now, and her eyes were closed, but she wasn't asleep.

She was way too tense to be asleep—everywhere except her face. She held her body stiffly, but every few minutes she lifted and then relaxed her facial muscles.

Eyebrows up, relax.

A delicate yawn that looked like a cover for stretching her cheeks, relax.

She even rolled her chin, and once when he was pretty sure her eyes were going to stay closed for a bit, he tried to mimic it.

Made himself laugh in the process.

God, she was so high-maintenance. What the hell was he getting himself into?

He navigated off the feeder highway onto the major expressway, cutting quickly across traffic to get to the exit he wanted. At least he had his car at the airport. When this whole thing was over, he was just a flight away from regaining his freedom.

Gunning the engine to overtake another car that was taking its sweet-ass time merging, he got them into the exit for the airport and followed the signs to the terminal they wanted.

"Nearly there," he said quietly, in case she was actually resting.

"Pretty sure your maniac driving gave that away," she said under her breath.

Definitely not resting.

Once he'd found a spot close to the exit stairwell in long-term parking, he gave her his full attention. "Want to go over any of it again?"

She shook her head. "I'm good."

She wasn't good. She was pale and the muscles around her mouth and eyes were suddenly tense. But she was also strong, and he wouldn't undermine that by questioning her. "Hey." He reached across and set his hand on her shoulder. "You're not doing this alone."

"I should, though. I should be able to."

"Says who?"

She shrugged, and in that moment, she looked so small, and yet still so fierce, he wanted her to see what he saw.

He reached past her and flipped down the sunshade on her side. He pointed at the small mirror there. "Look at her."

She smirked. "Dang, she looks tired."

No, she looked beautiful, but that was beside the point. "What else do you see?"

"I don't know."

"I see a survivor. A star. Someone who works hard and keeps going, no matter what."

"I ran away."

"Hardly. Did you miss any shows?"

Worry rippled across her face. "I might have."

"You know what I think? You went to Hope because you knew she'd let you lie low, and then she'd pick you up and kick your ass back onto the road."

She laughed and turned toward him. "Is that what you think?"

"Am I wrong?" He held her gaze, not wanting her to duck again.

Her eyes got wide, but she didn't look away. A flicker of something started, way deep, then it got stronger.

"There you go," he murmured. "Look at you, tough girl."

"Thank you."

"Any time."

— —

THE FLIGHT WAS OVER TOO QUICKLY, and they found a driver waiting for them at Dulles Airport. Dean gave the guy a friendly nod, handing over their bags, but he opened her door himself, keeping her blocked from possible onlookers as she buckled up. Only when the driver was ready to go did Dean hurry around to the other side and slide in beside her.

They didn't talk at all on the way to the hotel.

She texted Jackie. **We've landed. Heading to the hotel. Where are you guys?**

It didn't take long for her guitarist to pick up on the deliberate slip. **We?**

Doctor's orders. A security specialist who has training in anxiety management.

She watched the dots start and stop on her screen as Jackie considered her response. Finally, she sent back, **Anything I need to know about him? What's the story?**

Suddenly Liana was grateful that they'd gone with Zander's idea. **No cover story. I've developed perfor-mance anxiety and it's manageable, but I need support. Dean is that support.**

The truth. It might just set her free.

His name is Dean?

Liana glanced over at her bodyguard, who was

watching the jam-packed Washington traffic with a frown. **Yes. He's very nice.**

I bet.

Stop it.

You want me to tell the others not to stare at the sexy bodyguard?

He's not… Stop it. Dean glanced over at her furiously typing fingers, then back out the window again. She tried and failed not to blush as she fired off a second rebuttal message. **Really, he's nice. He's Canadian. Very polite. And nobody is allowed to think he's sexy.**

Jackie's last response came in as they pulled up to the hotel. **Got it. Nice and off-limits. Heads up, Track is in the lobby.**

Liana groaned and slinked lower in her seat as Dean got out of the car and went around to open her door. **Where are you?**

Also in the lobby, waiting for you. Holy shit, is that him?

These were exactly the kind of text messages she'd rather not have on her phone. She turned it off and grabbed her sunglasses instead. Time to armour up.

Head down, she stepped out of the car and into the shadow of Dean's body. "Track is in the lobby," she said quietly. "Jackie just gave me the heads up."

"Noted." He swung both of their bags into his right hand and guided her past the doorman with his left firmly planted in the middle of her back.

It turned out quite a number of the performers for the next day's concert were in the lobby. There had been a problem with the block of rooms booked for them, but due to parking restrictions, the tour buses had dropped everyone off and left, and now couldn't get back to pick them up because they'd gotten stuck behind the concert prep area.

So for a minute, Liana just stood there watching Track order everyone around a little too loudly. He barked at his crew, his band…even other people's staff, which was rude and off-side.

By the time he looked up and saw her, he was good and steaming. Normally that would have her ready to run for the hills, because she hated the inevitable conflict. And yeah, she didn't love it right now, but Dean was right there beside her.

And it turned out, Dean was like a literal speed bump for Track.

Her ex glared at her, then swung his gaze to the man beside her and just stopped. He stared at Dean, and she didn't dare look sideways to find out, but she was pretty sure that Dean was glaring right back.

Nice guy, her ass. He wore nice as a uniform, but she felt him turn rock solid. *Try me*, his muscles all screamed.

That was the moment she knew this would work. When Track stumbled and Dean didn't even sway.

"Everyone, this is Dean Foster." She lifted her sunglasses and deliberately didn't look at Track, who didn't need any more explanation than that. Instead she sought out West and Andrew, giving them a small smile. "You guys stuck waiting for a room?"

They both smiled back. She had a good band.

Her tour manager, Brad, stepped forward, a worried look on his face. "We weren't expecting anyone else. We're going to have trouble getting another hotel room. Everything is sold out due to the Fourth of July. As it is, our block of rooms won't be ready for another hour."

Dean held out his hand. "No worries, man. I'd never

want to inconvenience anyone. I took care of that yesterday and booked a room for myself. They had a cancellation, so I lucked out."

Brad grinned, relief flooding his face.

Liana stifled a smile of her own as Dean turned and looked down at her. "I'm gonna go check in, you want to come with me?"

She nodded, then gestured for her band to follow. "We can raid your mini fridge while we're waiting."

He gave her one of those lazy winks that she still couldn't work out. Did he even know he was doing it? They were super casual, and he did it when he was…not like he had his guard down, but when he was pleased.

Maybe he thought that had gone well, too.

Her relief lasted for exactly two hours and twelve minutes, until they were shuttled over to the Capitol Building for their sound check on the outdoor stage. Their tour buses were parked nearby, so they'd have somewhere to stay between the sound check and the live dress rehearsal show that night, but Track managed to put himself directly in her path once she was done.

Dean was behind her, but this time they didn't have the upper hand of advance warning.

Track had clearly been thinking. Stewing. He stepped in front of her, not quite blocking her path, but if she kept going, they'd be walking side-by-side, and Dean would get pushed back a few steps.

She skidded to a stop instead, and felt Dean right against her back. "Hey, Track," she said.

He nodded at her. His face was set in a hard to read expression. "I hear you disappeared after Savannah."

The country music grapevine was damn efficient. She

winced inside, but kept her face blank. "We were on break."

He snorted. "You going to have a problem on stage tonight? I'd be happy to have my set run long."

She was only doing three songs. Other than the fact that it was a dress rehearsal for a nationally televised performance—and even that shouldn't stress her out—it was the easiest gig possible and they both knew it. "What a sweet offer, but I'm fine."

He rocked back on his heels.

She just smiled coolly and waited for his next volley.

It didn't come. His lips tightened for a moment, then he nodded. "Have a good one, then."

She returned the slow head bob as he turned and walked away.

"Breathe," Dean said quietly behind her.

Her chest hurt as she exhaled. He squeezed her shoulder, a quick, warm touch that grounded her. "Come on." She led him through the maze of curtained-off spaces, a makeshift backstage in the centre of the nation's capital that spilled out into a tight line of tour buses. They weren't the only performers in the show, not by a long shot, and there were a couple of hundred people milling around the space between the stage and the Capitol Building.

Nobody paid them any attention as she led Dean to her tour bus.

"This is our home away from home," she said as the door swung open for them. "And this is Dwayne, our house mother."

The bus driver laughed as Dean climbed aboard. They shook hands. "A little bird told me we were getting another body on board. Welcome."

"Thanks, Dwayne."

She gave Dean a little smile for using the driver's name, and he flashed her one of those winks she was starting to *want*. Danger, she told herself. No crushing on the bodyguard.

She gave him a quick and dirty tour before showing him his bunk. Then she excused herself to lie down in her room, because she found herself wanting another wink more than she should.

Six more weeks. She could do anything for six weeks. Especially now she had that big, no-nonsense man in plaid on her side.

But no more wanting his touch and his looks. She needed to be more disciplined about how she responded to basic human kindness from him. Just because it was rare on her end didn't mean she could read anything more into it on his end.

CHAPTER NINE

DEAN WATCHED Liana disappear into her bedroom, then turned to face his inquisitors when the door clicked shut.

Her band members all had different looks on their faces. Jackie was the softest, which surprised him, but she'd had the benefit of a heads-up from Liana, at least in text form.

Andrew and West—whose names he kept switching in his head, that needed to stop—were harder to get a read on. So he didn't even try, he just gestured to an empty chair. "Can I sit?"

West nodded. "Sure."

Dean pulled out the chair, but it jerked to a stop when Andrew's foot looped behind the leg. The bass player crossed his arms. "You'll need to answer some questions first."

"Sure." Dean glanced down at the chair, and the tension slipped away as Andrew pulled his foot back. He sat down and spread his hands wide. "What do you want to know?"

"Liana hired you?"

He nodded. Close enough to the truth.

Jackie cleared her throat, and West turned pink. Dean slid her a quick look before returning his even gaze to the two younger men. And they were younger. Both in their twenties. Both probably quite emotionally attached to Liana, either having crushed on her or thought of her as their sister.

And in walked this guy they don't know, and he's got his hands on their boss, who probably doesn't share a lot with them…

They were protecting her and they had no idea what the threat was. That was noble. Dean could get behind that. Jackie knew more, clearly. He gave her a respectful nod, and she returned it.

"I'm not looking to get in anyone's way, and nobody on this bus has anything to worry about. I'm not spying on anyone, you know?" He gestured toward Liana's room. "I've got her back when she's out in the bigger world. That's all."

"Jackie says you're Canadian."

"I am."

"You like beer?"

He grinned. "I do. Not when I'm on duty, but yeah, I'm sure there's a time or two when we'll get a chance to drink to your boss."

"You on duty now?"

"Fraid so." He laughed at the legitimately disappointed look on West's face.

Andrew cackled at his band mate. "None of us drink much. Poor West isn't quite enough of a loser to do it on his own."

Dean knew that Jackie was sober. Liana hadn't told him that Andrew didn't drink, and he made a mental note to find out more about that. "I do play cards, though, if anyone wanted to take my money."

West groaned again, this time with an edge of excitement in his voice. "Shit. She told you."

"She did."

"She warn you that we're good?"

"Yep."

"Then put your money where your mouth is. Twenty dollar buy-in."

He got out his wallet as Jackie called for Dwayne to join them, and just like that, the inquisition was over before it really got rolling.

He won enough hands to earn respect, and lost more because he wasn't stupid.

— —

THE DRESS REHEARSAL went off without a hitch, and they went back to the hotel for the night. Liana insisted Dean didn't need to walk her to her room, and he insisted he did, but when they got there, she found herself not wanting to say goodnight just yet.

"Would you like to come in and debrief?"

He hesitated just long enough for her to worry that maybe it had sounded like an invitation for more than she'd intended, but then he nodded.

"You looked confident tonight," he started, settling into the chair at the far end of the room. "It feel okay, being on stage?"

She nodded as she sat on the bed and unzipped her

boots. Wiggling her toes, she set them next to her suitcase which had appeared thanks to the magic of her crew. She grabbed her purse and pulled out her phone, holding up a finger to pause Dean's next question. "Sorry, I just gotta send a quick thank you note to the roadies."

HEY GUYS!

A big thanks to whoever delivered my suitcase to my room. Much appreciated.

L

SHE TYPED IT OUT ONE-HANDED, hit send, then dropped her other hand with a flourish, indicating for Dean to continue.

He laughed. "You tried to warn me how chaotic it is, but there's nothing like seeing you in action—at the concert, with your band, even multi-tasking like that—to remind me that there's a lot of moving parts to the machine."

"Mm-hmm." She yawned.

"I'll let you get to bed."

"No, it's okay. I want to debrief a bit. I'm just worn out, even though I had a rest. Hey, speaking of that, I heard you playing poker with the band."

His eyes warmed. "Thanks for that tip."

"You're welcome. That went well?"

"Yeah. They're a good group."

"They really are."

He kicked his legs out in front him and crossed them at the ankles. "I liked that last song you played tonight, by the way. 'River Bed Lullaby'? I've heard it before, but wow, in person it was something else."

Oh, she loved that song to pieces. It thrilled her that he'd chosen that one to compliment her on, even if it was probably a random pick. "That's my biggest hit to date. It was my first single." She sighed and he gave her a curious look. What the hell…she'd already shared a lot with him already. "I was just thinking, as I often do…I wonder if I'd have been given a chance to record it if I'd been with Track when I wrote it." He gave her a horrified look and she laughed without humour. "Yeah. That's the depth to which I fear he's controlled and limited my career. Nice, eh?"

Dean's face tightened as he waited for her to continue. It was a sad truth she never said out loud to anyone, and she was surprised she was sharing it now. But in some ways, the fact that he knew little about the industry made it easier.

"Anyway, all of that fuels some pretty ugly negative self-talk in my head when I try something new." She let out a rough exhale and closed her eyes for a second. *Get it together*. "Remember I was telling you about 'Cravings'? It's just one of those songs I can't give up on, even though it didn't get to be a single. It's totally different from 'River Bed Lullaby,' but in my heart it feels the same."

"That's what you wish all of your songs were like. From the heart?"

"Every songwriter thinks that. And it's not necessarily autobiographical in anyway. Just…songs that I *feel*, you know?"

"I don't know if I've heard 'Cravings.'"

"Probably not." Only people who'd bought the entire album would have. Track had even stymied an inquiry to have it in a movie soundtrack. She scowled at that memory.

"I'll listen to it tonight."

"I can give you the album…" She moved to get up and fetch a CD from the ever-present box of swag in the corner of her room, but he held up his hand.

"I own it." He winked when she failed to stifle her surprise. "I bought all your stuff after Hope hired us. I just haven't had a chance to listen to everything yet. Been kind of busy."

"Well, enjoy. It's what I want my next album to sound more like."

"Awesome."

"Maybe."

"What's not to like?"

She laughed. "That's…a whole big thing to explain. But long story short, the label approves my song selections."

"The label."

"Yeah."

"Track."

"Yeah."

"So every day you're on tour, every day that passes by, brings you one day closer to having that fight."

Her mouth fell open. Yes, yes it did. "Huh."

He gave her a small smile, as if to say, *how about that?* How about that indeed?

"I hadn't thought about it like that."

"Just something to consider. Naming the fears changes the power dynamic."

"You sure you're not a stealth therapist?"

He laughed. "No, just a guy who's been around a lot of fear."

"I'm sorry."

"I'm not. That's life." His voice got darker, rougher. "I don't know if you want to talk about the conversation with Track today?"

Oh. She shifted uncomfortably, heat swelling across the top of her chest, spilling down her arms. "Yeah, he wasn't so bad this afternoon."

"Whoa…" Dean stood up and moved toward her, dropping into a squat right in front of her. "No, he was awful today."

"He didn't really say anything bad."

"That's his game. He picks his words carefully to sound reasonable." He peered closer, really examining her, and she started to blush. "That's better. I was worried there for a second. You went pale."

"He makes me second-guess myself," she whispered.

"You didn't show that. But I should have stepped in."

"Not yet." She shook her head. No, they couldn't do that too soon. "I need to get through tomorrow. I can't escalate anything with him."

"Then I need to do a better job of not letting him near you in the first place. What's the schedule for tomorrow?"

She closed her eyes and pictured it. "I'm meeting some radio winners for photos and a meet-and-greet here at the hotel, then…nothing until the concert."

"Keep your eyes closed." His voice was closer, lower. Warmer. He squeezed her shoulder, then moved away for a second. The chair scrapped against the carpet, and then he was sitting in front of her, his knees brushing her shins. "Tell me what a good day tomorrow would look like."

She laughed gently. "I don't know."

"Try. It's called visualization. It can be a powerful tool."

"I'm tired." She blinked her eyes open. That took more effort than she liked.

"Okay." He was right in front of her, his face steady and calm.

She frowned. "I'm not avoiding the exercise."

"I didn't say anything." But he didn't move out of the way, either. His legs bracketed hers on either side, not close, but they were there. If she turned, she'd bump into him. "I just want to help you have a good day tomorrow."

She looked at him. Most of the time he was either behind her or across a room. There was something different about him when he was up close like this. She couldn't put her finger on it, but it was there, hovering beneath the surface. She'd get it sooner or later. "Why did you take me on as a client?"

His eyebrows lifted at the deliberate change of subject, but he rolled with it. "Because Hope hired us."

She told herself she didn't feel disappointment at that. That was the right answer. He was debriefing the day and prepping her for tomorrow because that was his job, nothing more.

If she felt anything, it was fatigue. Her nap on the bus before the show hadn't fully made up for the fact that she woke up five hours before she wanted to.

"Today was a good day," she said softly. "Thank you. For the company and the moral support."

They stood at the same time, her sliding off the bed and him pushing his chair back. Their knees brushed, and he settled his hands on her upper arms as she straightened up.

Somehow she found herself in the circle of Dean's arms, closer than ever before, and that was when she saw it.

Behind the cool, hard planes of his face, beneath the granite jaw and the hazel eyes, there was a shadow in his gaze. Deep, dark concern. She worried him, to the point where when she wobbled, he held on long after she found her footing.

"I'm fine," she whispered. She meant it in more ways than literally in that moment. It was mostly true.

"Think about it tonight," he said roughly. "When you're lying in bed. Close your eyes and think about what you want tomorrow to be."

"It'll be what it'll be." She gave a little laugh. "I thought we were the Fatalists Forever club."

"I'm not talking about imagining something warm and fuzzy. Remember, I know how to wage war. If you visualize how the battle will go down, you can control it."

"I don't want to do battle, Dean. I just want to sing."

"That's what you've got me for." He ran his hands down the outside of her arms, then he leaned in, just a bit. As if he might kiss her forehead.

He froze, then pulled back with a jerk.

Her breath caught in her throat as he looked at her, a storm brewing in his eyes. Not the same worry as before. Something not quite as kind. Not mean, either, just—

He cleared his throat, snapping her out of her thought spiral. He dropped his hands and took a long, confident stride away from her. "Good night, Liana."

"Night," she whispered, turning with him.

"Text me when you wake up."

"I will." She pressed her lips together to keep from saying anything else and watched him leave her room.

Beneath that solid, quiet exterior lay a lot more than she'd given him credit for. Dean was suddenly quite complicated, and she didn't know what to do about that.

What had she expected? Dudley Do-Right?

She sat down heavily. Well, yeah, sort of. He'd been

like a Ken Doll/Superman hybrid for days. He was the living embodiment of a safe Good Guy.

Was he attracted to her after all?

If he was…how did she feel about that?

He wanted to fix her.

And she was a hot mess—but not so screwed up that she couldn't see how leaning on him too much would be a recipe for disaster. She didn't need saving.

For nearly a decade, she'd been saving herself just fine.

Well, mostly fine. Surviving kind of fine.

She didn't want to think of all the ways that she didn't have her shit together.

After she washed off her makeup and went through her nighttime routine, when she crawled into bed and closed her eyes, she tried to just go to sleep.

Tried not to think about Dean and the way his hazel eyes turned dark when he was close enough. Told herself it wasn't whatever she'd imagined. It was just…he wanted to fix her.

He didn't want her.

He just wanted her to be less broken. She was a job to him.

Visualize how the battle will go down.

She pictured waking up in the morning. Going through the day, carefully avoiding Track. She made mental notes about the possible points of intersection in their schedules and imagined Dean neatly moving her down another hallway, ducking her into a secret nook, pressing her against the wall…

Her eyes flew open.

No.

She tried again, her heart thumping in her chest. Avoiding Track all day, having a great performance. She could hear the crowd applauding, feel the rush of patriotic pride. Tears pricked the back of her eyelids as she smiled.

Yes. She wanted that. Wanted tomorrow to be a good day with no conflict, so once she was finished the concert, she could stand with her bandmates and watch the fireworks burst high above the Washington Monument.

A warm, bubbling excitement started low in her belly. This could work. She let the visualization bloom to a full, three-dimensional movie in her head. The warm night. The roar of the crowd. The celebration.

Turning in the safe circle of Dean's arms. Tipping her face up to see him wink at her.

This time she didn't open her eyes. And when he lowered his head to hers, she imagined what it would be like to kiss him.

Yes. She wanted that, too.

She was screwed.

CHAPTER TEN

DEAN WOKE up before dawn and hit the gym.

After four brutal arm sets, he still didn't feel better about the night before.

What the hell had he been thinking, getting that close to her? She didn't need him to kiss her damn forehead or anything else. She needed him to watch her back.

When his biceps burned so much he thought he couldn't lift any more, he dropped to the ground and made himself do another ten push-ups.

Then he stalked back to his room and took a cold shower, leaving his phone on the counter where he could see it if Liana woke up.

She didn't message until he was out of the shower, drying off. And just the simple pop up of her name on his screen made his dick pulse.

He was going to hell.

She's vulnerable. Don't be an asshole.

This wasn't like him. He was a serial, casual monogamist. He didn't date needy women, and he didn't get involved in anything messy. He found someone who liked him and appreciated the physical release they could find together a few times a month.

It had been nearly a year since his last relationship ended, although he'd had a nice weekend in the fall with an ex-girlfriend who needed a plus-one for an event.

It had been too long since he'd gotten laid, and Liana was gorgeous.

And smart. And funny.

And off-limits.

A client.

High-profile.

Drama city.

Wounded and fragile.

He could make a list of all the reasons she was wrong for him. He just had, and now the words scrawled through his head in technicolour.

All of them lies, because they weren't why he couldn't have her.

He couldn't have her because he would hurt her.

His junk didn't seem to care.

He'd have to find a way to show her that he wasn't to be trusted as a man. Tricky when he wanted her to trust him on every other level. Even—maybe especially—as a friend.

He liked her too damn much to let his attraction muddy the waters. And she needed him to be someone she could depend on, not someone she needed to worry about.

At least she didn't seem to be worrying yet. Her text message was breezy and had two smiley faces attached to it. **Have you had breakfast? Just ordered room service. Jackie and the boys are here.**

He sent back a quick **be right there** message and got dressed.

But when he arrived in her room, she wasn't as breezy in person as her text had suggested. She was short with West and snappy about the breakfast options. And in the next breath, she was apologetic and sweet, even flirty. But it was confusing for her band—Dean got the impression this was out of character behaviour—and he was pretty sure it was his fault.

When they finished eating and everyone scattered back to their rooms, he stayed behind.

Liana moved around her room, restlessly packing up.

Not looking at him.

Damn. He cleared his throat, getting her attention. "I should apologize for yesterday."

Surprise rippled across her face as her cheeks turned pink. "No reason for that. Last night was fine. I did the visualizing thing."

"Good."

They'd moved towards each other as they spoke, and now she was right in front of him. *Take a step back*, he told himself, but he couldn't move.

"It's just a performance day, that's all."

"That's all?"

"Of course," she said, her voice shifting, lightening as she gave him a small smile.

"Your band usually that skittish around you?"

"You think you can read us all that well?"

"Reading people is my job."

She gave him a small smile. "Right."

"I don't want things to get complicated between us."

"Nothing complicated about flirting."

"You say potato, I say—"

"I know, *potato*," she said in an exaggerated Canadian accent. "Point taken. We have different ways of dealing. Just ignore me if you don't like my flirting, okay?"

"I didn't say I didn't like it." Jesus, why did he say that? *Because it was the truth.*

She looked at him, silence pounding between them, then she stepped back. "Well, I don't mean anything by it, it's no big deal." She mock-sighed and pressed her hand to her chest. "And here I had such high hopes for a torrid love affair with someone that says *potato*. But I assure you, the offer has definitely expired."

"Noted." He gave her a rueful half-grin. "Torrid?"

"I'd have shocked all of your polite Canadian sensibilities."

God, he wanted to set her straight. There was nothing polite about what he wanted to do with her. To her. "Dodged a bullet, clearly."

She laughed under her breath as someone rapped twice on her door—Andrew—and then they weren't alone anymore.

Saved by the band.

The morning sped by a whirlwind of activity. She did her own makeup, but a woman from the crew came and did her hair, transforming her naturally glossy waves into something straight out of a music video, big bouncy curls that matched her dark eyes and perfect pink lipstick.

She was suddenly a star again, in a way she hadn't been for the dress rehearsal the night before, even though she'd done the hair and makeup thing for that, too. But that had been on the tour bus right before she went on stage.

This was performance blurring with real life as he

trailed her on her way down to a room on the ground floor of the hotel.

Part of the wall had been covered in plastic vinyl sheeting with her name scrawled on it over and over again, and it was this backdrop that she stood in front of for nearly two hours, spending a minute or two with a hundred and three fans, each one wanting a photo and a hug and private word.

For each of them, she gave them her full attention and her brightest smile.

When the last fan stepped up to see her, eyes full of tears, Liana started crying too. Dean passed over a tissue box and she dabbed the corners of her eyes like the pro that she was. "Honey, what's this all about?" she asked the radio listener.

"I almost didn't make it," the woman whispered through hiccups. "My credit card didn't work in the parking lot and I didn't have any cash on me, so my husband is circling the block right now."

"Oh, bless you. Well, I'm thrilled you made it. Are you coming to the show tonight?"

The fan nodded.

"I can't wait to sing for you. What's your favourite song?"

"River Bed Lullaby."

"And what's your name?"

"Ashley."

"Well, Ashley, I'm singing that song tonight, and I'm going to sing it for you. Okay? Now dry your eyes, and we'll take a picture together. You're beautiful."

Once they'd taken not one but three pictures, because Ashley blinked in the first one and Liana was laughing in the second—although Dean was pretty sure that one would be Ashley's favourite for life—Liana walked her new best friend to the door and gave her one last hug before saying goodbye.

The second the door was closed, the mask dropped. It wasn't that she hadn't genuinely wanted to make that woman's day, Dean was certain. It was just that being that *on* didn't come naturally to her. Which made how authentic she was with her fans all the more impressive.

"Lunch?" Jackie asked. "West headed over to the venue early, he's recording something for his fan group. But Andrew's around if you want to talk about the show, or just veg."

Liana sighed. "I need to get online and do some stuff. Would you mind if I WhisperSnipped while we eat?"

"Of course not."

It was like they were speaking in code. What the hell was whisper snipping? That didn't sound healthy. Dean stepped ahead of them, making sure the hallway was clear. He'd gotten his hand on a copy of Track's schedule and the headliner was scheduled to be at a White House lunch for veterans for a few more hours, but it never hurt to be careful. Then he followed along silently as they talked about how much to share about the new album.

"Who knows what songs will end up on it." Liana rolled her head from side to side, stretching her neck. "You think I've got time to fit in some yoga?"

"Sure. We'll get out of your hair after lunch. But maybe if we talk about what we're excited about, we can shape fan interest, get them to push the label."

Liana snorted. "You know better than that."

"I'm being optimistic for the new guy," Jackie said, flashing Dean a grin.

He spread his arms wide. "I literally have no idea what

you guys are talking about. I heard lunch, yoga, songs. I'm officially a fan of all three."

Liana turned around, walking backward as she talked. "I should ask you, too. How do you feel about being on a WhisperSnip?"

"No clue. I'm half-afraid to ask what it even is."

"It's a live video feed that goes out to all your social media sites. I try to do one a week or so. Fans tune in, ask questions, react to whatever we're talking about. It's good market research."

He pointed ahead of them. "Watch where you're walking, there's our turn up ahead."

She didn't miss a beat as she spun around the corner and pushed the button for the elevator. "I just do it from my phone. I've got this little tripod I set up. You can sit behind it if you want."

He didn't care. He shrugged. "Up to you."

She smiled as she stepped into the elevator. "You're cute. Let's get you a fan group."

"What?" More people joined them, pushing him closer to her. No, he didn't need a fan group. And what happened to their agreement not to flirt?

On her other side, Jackie nodded. "I agree with Liana, you'll go over well. But we can play that by ear."

The car jerked up to the second floor, and more people got on. He braced his hand on the wall of the elevator, shifting a bit so Liana was protected in the corner.

She grinned up at him. "You'll get a name."

He was still stumbling over the fact she'd called him cute. "I have a name."

"No, not *you*. The fans will call themselves something. Like Dean's Dealers."

"That sounds vaguely criminal."

Jackie snorted.

Liana's smile got even bigger. "Jackie's group calls themselves the Jack o' Lanterns."

"No." He chuckled under his breath, because that was kind of funny. But for Jackie. Not for him. "This wasn't in the contract."

Her eyes twinkled. "There's a lot we didn't discuss."

"I'm getting that message loud and clear."

"You really don't have to be visible at all."

"I walk four feet behind you everywhere you go. I'm going to have my picture taken."

"There's something more intimate about the videos, though." Her voice had dropped as they talked, and now she was murmuring barely above a whisper, and he was leaning right over her.

Which meant that when she said intimate, and his brain was still rolling around the fact that she thought he was cute, he became way too aware of how close they were.

And when he stiffened, so did she.

Ding.

"This is our floor," Jackie said, patting him on the shoulder.

Saved by the bell.

Andrew was pacing in front of Liana's room, and when they piled in, he grabbed the room service menu. Liana told him she wanted a salad, but when she started to list all the substitutions she wanted, he tossed it her way and told her she was in charge of doing the ordering. The bubbling, happy chaos was the perfect shield for Dean to fade into the background and give himself a shake.

"What do you want?" Liana asked, waving the menu in his direction.

That was the million dollar question, wasn't it? He stuck with the safe answer. "A hamburger. Cheese, no onions, extra mustard."

"Fries?"

"What kind of question is that?"

"A healthy one."

"Yes, fries."

"Your heart attack."

"I worked out for an hour this morning. I can handle some deep fried potatoes."

"You should have told me. We could have worked out together."

"It was dark when I got up."

She wrinkled her nose. "Okay, thanks for not waking me up."

"You can thank me by not judging the fries."

"We should be WhisperSnipping this conversation," Jackie said, curling up on the bed next to Liana.

Right in the middle of Dean's line of sight. And then she winked at him.

Grown men don't blush. If he kept telling himself that, maybe he could fight off the painful awareness that the guitarist saw right through him.

Instead of looking away, he leaned back and returned Jackie's inspection instead. She was his age, maybe, late thirties, early forties. Fit and attractive in an intense kind of way. Her blonde hair was streaked with grey, but she had an interesting combination of youthful vitality and jaded cynicism that would normally be right up his alley.

And it was—as a friend. He'd immediately liked Jackie, and hoped he stayed on her good side. But he wasn't attracted to her.

Not the way he wanted Liana.

And the comparison, right in front of him, was like a bomb going off in his head.

Jackie would normally be exactly his type, because she promised no strings, no expectations, no demands. A friendly affair would be right up her alley, he'd bet. He could profile her in a heartbeat. Divorced, self-sufficient, comfortable with her body. A woman who enjoys sex.

But Liana…

Jesus, he needed to stop this.

First of all, everything he thought about the singer was probably wrong. She was going through a shit time, that didn't make her needy. And if she was needy, he wasn't the man to take care of her.

But he wanted to.

Except he knew he'd let her down—so he needed to remember she wasn't his type for a reason. He wasn't good enough for someone like Liana. Not whole enough. Not nearly capable enough of the feelings that women like her deserved.

He thought of Jake and Dani. Of how Rafe looked at Olivia. The way Zander and Faith couldn't stop touching each other in the sweetest ways. How Ryan had stumbled out of his grief and found Hope—and how the other man would now do absolutely anything for the woman he loved.

Dean wasn't that guy. It wasn't in him to be that self-less with a woman, because he knew it would always come to an end.

He wasn't dumb enough not to see it. He was emotion-ally stunted at twelve years old.

Liana didn't need that bullshit piled on top of every-thing else.

He kept telling himself that fact through lunch and

Liana's WhisperSnip broadcast. At one point the video feed caught his arm, when he reached past her phone for some napkins, and Jackie and Andrew snickered over the fan guesses as to who the arm belonged to.

"They like your arm," Jackie said before sticking out her tongue.

"And now they want to know who Jackie is talking to."

Liana rolled her eyes at her phone and gave her unseen fans a teasing smile. "Let me have some secrets, okay?"

Dean told himself that next time she did this, he'd get the app and watch it for himself.

So he could understand how it worked. Not so he'd get that smile pointed in his direction.

Fuck, he was such a liar.

Four days he'd known her. Four days he'd had this job, and he was already fucking it up.

That thought propelled him out of his chair and into the hallway—where he nearly ran into Track Gantley, who'd been about to knock on Liana's door.

Dean closed said door behind him and stood in front of it, arms crossed. "She's doing a live video for her fans right now."

The other man stepped back and they sized each other up.

Dean had a few inches on him, but he had a few inches on almost everyone. That fact didn't normally make him quite as happy as it did right now.

"I need to talk to her."

"Now's not a good time."

"You sure about that?"

"Yep."

"She's overreacting. This performance anxiety isn't

new. You should know that. She's always struggled. I don't know what she's told you—"

"She's told me she sings better when her time before the show is protected. That's my job, and it's literally the only thing I care about." That second part was a lie. Dean cared a hell of a lot about this asshole saying Liana was overreacting, but that wasn't his role.

"Look, you can't coddle her on this." Track turned on what everyone else probably saw as charm. "Man to man, I gotta warn you that she's gonna—"

"Stop." Dean needed to tread carefully here. He could tell from the look in the other man's eyes that he genuinely believed the horseshit he was spewing. And Dean couldn't —wouldn't—expose Liana's awareness of Track's manipulative efforts. Especially not when they might be subconscious. He forced a friendly, understanding tone into his voice, just like if he was talking to a suspect. "Look, I hear you. But I've got rules I gotta follow, you know? And the quiet time before the show seems to be helping her. But I can tell her you wanted to see her."

"Nah, don't bother." Track flashed him an extra-white smile and headed down the hall.

Dean couldn't help but notice that his cowboy boots seemed extra tall today.

— —

AFTER LUNCH, they headed to the National Mall in the shuttle bus. Today the elaborate stage was draped in even more red, white, and blue than the day before. While Liana did a quick sound check, Dean took some once-in-a-life-time photos of the Washington Monument perfectly framed at the other end of the giant green lawn, quickly filling with people.

Even though Liana had done a show the night before, and gotten amped up, there was still something different about her today. Nervous energy that he hadn't seen before poured out of her as she spent time with the other performers in the VIP tent backstage.

She glad-handed her way through the crowd, barely looking at him but always having a quick smile when she did. And he did his job, having her back and making sure that Track was always somewhere else.

The sun was low in the sky when they were ushered into the wings of the outdoor stage. Dean stepped out of the way as Liana posed for a backstage picture with the host, but she tethered him back into her orbit with a single glance as soon as she was done.

Don't go far, her body language whispered.

Like that was even an option.

It was dangerous how much he wanted to be right next to her. How much he wanted to simply stand behind her, have his hands on her shoulders and feel her heat against his front. Dangerous how he could still smell her hair from where he almost kissed her forehead the night before.

He wasn't going anywhere, even though, in theory, he knew better.

Something had flipped inside him yesterday and now he felt constantly close to crossing a professional line. If she'd said anything other than, "I'm going to bed," he probably would have kissed her.

He'd lock it down again. If he hadn't spent the entire day half a step behind what they were doing, because they spoke in half-sentences and used a dense vocabulary for which he didn't have a dictionary, maybe the simmering awareness inside him wouldn't have exploded into such restless, wild wanting.

If he hadn't had free rein to watch her warm up, get ready, transform, all with the pervy hunger of a voyeur... maybe he'd have already switched it off.

But somewhere between watching her big hair get even better and catching her blow herself a red-lipsticked kiss in the mirror before hustling to the wings, he'd filed away this Liana alongside the others: the quiet loner, the runner, the kind and generous star. And now the larger than life performer, in a tight black t-shirt, even tighter jeans, and killer heels...there was no point pretending he wouldn't dream of this Liana tonight.

Which meant he was doing a shitty job, and Fosters didn't punch below their weight. The Colonel would cuff him for mooning over his protectee, even if all he was protecting her from were raw feelings.

And Liana, a perfectionist to the point of harming herself, deserved nothing less than his best.

He wouldn't put his selfish desires above what was best for her.

Right now, what she needed was for him to get his eyes off her ass and back where they belonged—scanning her surroundings and keeping her in a safe, secure bubble, away from the toxic reach of her ex.

They got the five-minute heads-up from the stage manager, and the band slid to one side, knowing the performers on stage would be filing past them in a minute. Liana reached her hands out and wiggled her fingers. He'd watched them do this yesterday, but today West didn't reach past him. Today Dean was right in the way, and on one side West took his hand and on the other, Liana closed the circle.

What was Dean going to say? *Nope, not my thing?* For the next six weeks, he was her shadow. Her things were his things.

So that meant her hand in his hand. Cool, slim fingers, squeezing tight. An extra pulse as she whispered *amen* in that slight, melodic twang of hers. Like it had three syllables. *Ah-ma-en.*

His blood felt like sludge as they broke apart, making his limbs heavy and his chest hurt. It was a day for painful revelations, clearly. He wanted to want her. Resented that his brain thought it best to shut down this feeling when it was unlike anything he'd ever felt before.

She was radiant, all the energy pulling tight inside her like the start of a nuclear reaction, and as soon as she hit the stage, she turned on that power and blew him away.

He watched her set from the shadows. The night before he'd circled around to the front, watching the crowd, watching her face, but tonight he stayed in one spot. Most of the time she was in profile. He hadn't realized how often she looked up at the sky.

Singing to the heavens. Like an offering, a plea. Except for when she started River Bed Lullaby, and she looked into the crowd, as if she was actually looking for that listener from earlier, and she softly said the woman's name. "This one's for Ashley, and everyone else who needs a little extra hope tonight."

He couldn't get over the power of her voice. Of her.

The way he was drawn to her talent, her spark, her vulnerable softness...he didn't want Liana in the way he usually wanted women. This felt different because it was different. It wasn't like seeking like, it wasn't the casual happenstance of mutual chemistry.

They weren't even in the same solar system. She was a star, a goddess in more ways than one, and he was a regular Joe.

It was just a crush.

Damn. For the first time since Dean was a teenager, he had an honest to God *crush*. The kind where everything the other person did was magically special, where he got flustered and embarrassed over nothing more than the fear that someone could look at him and see all these feelings, these big, *special* feelings.

He was fourteen again, and full of ridiculous hope.

This couldn't end well, but just for tonight, he couldn't turn it off, either.

CHAPTER ELEVEN

THEY LEFT Washington in the middle of the night to avoid traffic snarls and were in Raleigh, North Carolina by breakfast.

In the end, the night before had gone just fine, much to Liana's surprise. She'd pasted on a smile and made her way through the VIP tent after the concert. Dean stood between her and Track, who'd clearly decided to give them a wide berth. And then it was over.

Somehow the lack of confrontation hadn't brought the relief she'd expected.

She actually never slept that well when the bus was on the highway, so once they arrived, she hung her do-not-disturb sign on her door and slept for a few more hours.

When she woke the second time, everyone was gone.

Except for Dean.

She found him sitting on the couch in bus's small living room, reading a worn paperback.

"Good morning," he said, closing the book and tucking it into the little lip where the couch met the window.

She glanced at the clock on the wall. "For another forty-five minutes."

"Doesn't matter."

"Where is everyone?" She glanced around. Even their driver was gone.

"Dwayne and West went on a supply run to Walmart with some of the crew. Not sure where Andrew and Jackie are."

Liana had a pretty good idea, but their secret wasn't hers to share. It wasn't even hers to know, but she'd caught enough hints to have a pretty good guess they were somewhere inside the arena.

Alone.

Like she was with Dean.

Suddenly the bus was stuffy even though the air conditioning was running.

"Ah." She leaned against the wall and tucked her hands into the pockets of her cut-off jean shorts.

He looked at her, which made sense, because they were talking, but they were alone and she was aware of her bare legs and the way her t-shirt pulled across her breasts, which suddenly felt heavy and hot.

She worked out. Paid a lot of money to people to keep her skin bare, her hair shiny. She knew how to dress for cameras and red carpets.

But Liana never, ever felt sexy.

Not deep down. Not in the powerful, *hell ya he wants me* kind of way. Because real men didn't want her most of the time. They passed her over as too high-maintenance or aloof. Too busy. Not doting or domestic enough. Too much, not enough, never quite right for the kind of guy she wanted.

She'd found it easier to date other celebrities. Actors, musicians. The occasional industry professional.

And in order for a man to see her naked…there were pretty significant mental hoops she had to jump through to be in the right place for *that* to happen.

Right now, with Dean looking at her legs?

Liana was suddenly aware that he *liked* her. He thought she was *hot*.

She liked that so, so much.

She licked her lips and wiggled her hands deeper into the pockets of her jean shorts. Her t-shirt pulled tighter around her curves and his eyes followed the welcoming path she created for his gaze. And then she jerked his attention back to her face by opening her mouth. "So… you're just reading."

He was good. He didn't miss a beat. "Yeah."

"I might go do the same." She pointed behind her to her bedroom.

He nodded.

She didn't move. Heat sizzled beneath her skin.

He didn't disappoint. With a lazy, wide sweep of his arm, he gestured to the compact couch. "You could sit out here."

Yes, her boobs begged. She crossed her arms over her chest. It didn't pay to be too obvious.

"Or we could go for a walk?"

"No." She smiled, a slow, sweet curl of her mouth that matched the way he was looking at her. "Reading sounds lovely."

She went and got her book, and a light cotton hoodie because she was pretty sure her nipples were going to slice through her bra and t-shirt any second.

When she returned, he'd grabbed one of the chairs and

propped his feet up on that, leaving lots of room on the couch for her. She grabbed a sparkling water for herself and offered him one before settling in next to him. She pressed her back against the arm of the couch so she was facing him and bent her knees to set her bare feet on the seat between them. Her book rested on her thighs, so she could sort of read and mostly watch him.

She was hopeless.

But he was really good-looking, which seemed like a reasonable defense, especially when his brow furrowed and he chewed on the corner of his lip as he read.

She forced her attention back to her own book, and the black-ops mission underway on the pages. She loved thrillers for the over-the-top action and macho heroes, but today the quiet man in front of her was way more interesting.

"How'd you sleep last night?" she asked, interrupting the silence.

He made a humming noise and kept reading for a second or two more, like he was finishing a paragraph. Then he marked his spot with his finger and looked sideways at her. "Yeah. Okay, actually. The bunk is quite spacious."

She laughed.

"Better than an army cot."

"Okay, I'll give you that."

"You don't like sleeping on the bus, eh?"

That was an opening for her to tell him that she never slept well. About the disquiet, the worry she always felt but that had gotten much worse this tour.

But then he'd know that, and worry about it, and then he might figure out how she coped...so...no. That was staying in the vault.

Besides, the bus rule was that once people started to go to sleep, you did the damn same, because a band that didn't get enough sleep didn't perform well.

Hence her morning nap.

"No," she finally said. "Not that well. I never do."

"That was a lot of thinking for such a short answer."

She took a deep breath and held it.

He laughed gently.

"I'm being a dork," she finally admitted in a rush of words.

"I told you that you didn't have any social skills," he teased, low and warm, and she blushed as she let her book drop to the ground.

He'd turned, just a bit, and his hand grazed her knee as he lifted his arm and stretched it across the back of the couch.

His hand was *right there*. She could lean forward and press her lips to those long, strong fingers.

Her leg slid off the couch and she shifted.

Now she wouldn't even need to lean forward.

Instead she turned the other way, swinging around so they sat side by side, thigh against thigh. "Share your footrest," she whispered.

He dropped his far leg and looped his foot under the leg of the chair, pulling it closer. "Nope," he whispered back. "This isn't going to work. My legs are longer than yours."

"Mmm." She shifted again, abandoning the shared footrest idea. Her hand brushed his thigh as she turned to face him, this time with her legs curled beneath her.

"Liana…" Yes, she liked her name rolling off his tongue. Even if it was accompanied by a wary narrowing of his eyes.

"Yes?"

His phone vibrated between them. He paused, then leaned away from her and dug it out. He glanced at the screen. "This is my brother. He wouldn't call if it wasn't important."

She waved her hand. "Yeah, of course. I'll go read in my room."

"Stay." He touched her shoulder before standing up. "I'll step outside."

— —

DEAN HIT the answer button as he levered the bus door open. "Sean. What's up?"

"Hey."

That was all. One syllable, followed by a stretch of silence, and Dean knew. He swore silently and kicked his foot against the ground. "You got news?"

"Yeah. I got the call. I'm going sooner than later."

"No work up?"

"It'll be fine. There's a need for a…" The phone crackled and for a second, Dean thought maybe his brother was already headed overseas, that he was calling from a foreign airport and the pain in his chest felt like a heart attack. "Sorry, shitty signal. I'm on the lake. Anyway, I'm going up to Pet on Monday, and then I'm heading over sometime in the next few weeks. Lots of stuff in flux. Just wanted to tell you."

"Okay. Thanks." Fuck, he wasn't ready for this. He hadn't felt like this when Jake had gone on his tour. But this was Sean. Mr. Mercurial. The baby.

"How's the hot singer?" Sean changed the subject.

Smoking hot and really complicated. "She's nice. I like her band."

"Are there groupies all over the place?"

Dean laughed. Sean was still a pile of hormones. The eleven years between them sometimes felt like a lifetime, although when it came to Liana, his hormones worked just fine. "No."

"Shame."

He threw his brother a fictional bone. "Well, who knows. Tonight is the first real concert. I'll report back."

"I'll hold you to that!"

Dean snorted. "Hey. I'm proud of you. You know that, right?"

A hesitant pause. "Yeah."

That worried Dean more than he wanted to admit. *Sean's going to be just fine* warred pretty hard in his head with *get on a plane and go see for your fucking self.* "Talk to you later."

"Peace out, bro."

He stood there for a minute, hands on his hips, head down, before turning back to the bus. When he did, Liana was standing in the open doorway.

"Everything okay?" she asked, pushing a loose strand of hair off her face. Gentle frown lines creased her brow.

"Yeah."

"You look worried."

"My youngest brother's leaving for overseas sooner than later. Last minute call up."

"With the military?"

He nodded and slowly walked toward her. She stepped up the stairs, making room for him to follow her out of the mid-day heat. He closed the bus door behind them, but he didn't sit down inside. He was suddenly restless. "Hey, you want to go check out the workout room inside the arena?"

"Sure." She shot a quick look at the clock on the microwave. "I have a meet-and-greet in an hour and a half, but I've got time for a workout first. Let me grab my bag."

He should address the thing that almost happened between them before Sean called, but that hadn't gone well the day before, and right now he really wanted to just lift heavy stuff and not think about anything for an hour or two.

— —

ONE OF THE earliest lessons Liana learned in Nashville was that sometimes opportunities slipped through your fingers. A great song gets picked up by a bigger performer, even though you heard it first and were in talks with the songwriter. You miss a call to perform at the Grand Ole Opry at the last minute. Schedules don't line up with a producer you've been drooling over.

Or on a personal level, your super hot bodyguard gets a phone call at an inopportune time and comes back distracted by something that has nothing to do with you.

It was important not to dwell in the regret of the missed opportunity, and instead plan ahead. Be ready for the next lightning strike, because that's often what it was —dumb luck at the right time.

Too bad the infinite patience she'd cultivated for her professional persona was missing right now.

She jabbed the button on her treadmill to jack up the speed. Maybe if her muscles burned enough she'd stop ogling the muscles in Dean's back as he did free weights on the far side of the gym they had all to themselves.

She watched him push himself through more arm exercises than she'd thought humanly possible—a fifth set? Really?

But when she got off the treadmill and his gaze caught hers in the mirror on the wall, it was dark and unexpectedly intense—not the calm, level-headed man she'd come to know at all.

"What's wrong?" She grabbed a spray bottle and spritzed the treadmill handles, but kept her attention on him.

He did the same with his weights, but he didn't answer her.

What's on your mind, mister?

Then he slung his bag across his body and met her in the middle of the room.

"I'm sorry, I shouldn't have asked." She didn't mean it. She wanted to know. Maybe because she was nosy—she was intensely curious about most people's stories, and Dean intrigued her more than anyone else. Maybe because she wanted to know *his* secrets more specifically.

"You can ask," he said quietly. The subtle lines of his face seemed deeper than before. "I just can't answer. I'm not really sure. Family stuff is the short answer."

"Ah. Well, I know all about big feelings that I don't understand." She gave him a rueful smile and tipped her head toward the door. "I've got a meet and greet. I need to shower."

"I'll do the same and wait for you on the other side." He didn't move. His gaze didn't drop from her face, and as she stood there, his expression softened. "I didn't mean for you to see that I was upset."

"That's…fine." She frowned. "Of course it's fine. And if you ever want to talk, I'm a pretty good listener."

"That probably wouldn't be appropriate."

She propped her hands on her hips. "Why not?"

"Because I'm working for you. I'm supposed to be professional."

"You are." A laugh burst out of her. "But you're human, too. Right?"

His jaw flexed and her laughter grew.

"Oh, Dean." She patted him on the chest. That flexed, too. The soft cotton clung to his muscles, and she tried not to think about the sweat-slicked skin beneath the fabric. Now was not the time to hit on him. Robots didn't respond well to inappropriate advances, she'd learned, even though a big part of her wanted to keep trying. "Okay. Shower time."

She was still giggling as she stepped under the hot water in the change room. Still smiling when she towelled off and carefully applied her moisturizer.

And when she met him in the hallway, Dean still looked tense. She didn't comment on it again. It wasn't her place.

Not yet.

CHAPTER TWELVE

THE RALEIGH SHOW was Dean's first chance to see what a regular concert was like, and it was everything Liana had warned him about: chaotic, epic, and exhausting.

When Liana pulled into herself, doing her quiet thing before the show, he left her in her dressing room and did a quick loop around backstage while the opening act was playing.

Then he settled into a seat where the tour manager promised him he wouldn't be in the way and just enjoyed Liana on stage again.

Tonight she did a broader range of songs than she had in Washington, and they were all good, but when it came to the last song of the night, "Cravings", he realized she'd saved the best for last.

It was different than the rest of her set, just as she'd told him, although he could hear the same soul in it as in "River Bed Lullaby."

But this song was…well, it was sexy as hell.

Her voice purred as she moved across the stage. Slinked, really, and the crowd ate it up.

This was the song Track hadn't wanted her to put on her album. Dean couldn't understand why not. It was fantastic.

GIVE me a chance to
   Show you what I like
   I'll pour you a drink
   Of the sweetest wine

HE MAY HAVE ONLY KNOWN her for five days, but his gut told him that while it was damn sexy, it wasn't an overly personal song for her. She may have co-written it, but it wasn't a confessional.

She wasn't revealing anything about her relationship with Track in it, and as hot as it was, it wasn't anything that crossed any lines.

It's the kind of song he'd expect to hear racing up the charts, not that he was a music expert.

It was a damn shame she felt her career being stifled if this was the kind of music she really wanted to make. And the crowd ate it up.

Dean did, too.

As the arena turned black, she hustled off stage, but didn't come as far as where he stood. He'd been prepped on this—the concert wasn't really over. They'd do an encore set of a three-song medley.

And it rocked, but he was still thinking about "Cravings".

— —

IT WAS LATE when they got on the bus and drove to Charlotte. But it wasn't that long of a drive, so everyone stayed up, playing cards and working on music, until they arrived at their hotel for the night.

They were all staying in the same hallway, a domino sequence of rooms. Dean was closest to the side exit out to the parking lot, and as he was brushing his teeth, he heard that door click open, then close again. A sixth sense had him move to the window just in time to see Liana jog down the concrete path. He swore under his breath and did the world's fastest change into his own running clothes. Sean would be proud, it was nearly a triathlon transition-worthy time. Shorts, shoes, and he was pulling on his shirt as he hit the summer heat outside.

What was she thinking going running at this time by herself?

Even as he thought that, he could feel his sister-in-law reaching across time and space to smack him in the head. Time of day didn't matter. As a cop he knew that. As a man, though…

And it was his job to go with her.

He tried to pretend it was entirely a professional concern.

But when he caught sight of her a block ahead, thankfully going a bit slower than his max speed, he eased up and followed from enough of a distance that he couldn't say he wasn't watching her selfishly.

She went out about two clicks, running down the main road lined with hotels and fast food restaurants. It was brightly lit and easy for him to keep an eye on her, and when she checked her watch and slowed down, he was close enough to a stand of trees that he could duck into the shadows.

But he didn't. He slowed down himself and stood under a street light instead, arms crossed.

She saw him immediately when she turned around.

She didn't stop.

"You're following me now?" she asked as she sped past him, going faster now.

"I thought we had an understanding that I would accompany you out in public."

"There is nobody out at this time of night, and I didn't know that I wanted to run until I was already in my room."

"You have my number."

"I didn't want to wake you up."

"You didn't."

"How did you…" She trailed off and took a deep breath instead. "I went right past your room."

"You'd make a terrible spy."

"I wasn't sneaking out, obviously. I just didn't think it mattered."

"It didn't. But I was up, so I came with you."

She shot him a quick grin. "Couldn't catch me?"

Sure. He'd rather she think that than realize he was just watching her run because he loved the way she moved. "You're fast. You do this middle of the night running routine a lot?"

"Sometimes."

"Tell me next time, okay?"

She nodded.

"You had a great show tonight," he said. "Really impressive."

"Thank you." She stared straight ahead. "It felt good."

Polite, but not expansive. What was he expecting from the middle of the night? He let her finish the run in silence. When she stretched against the side of the hotel, he mirrored her, then followed her to her room.

She stopped before going inside. "My apologies for the moment of stress that caused."

He shook his head. "No stress. But I'm glad I went after you."

She gave him a curious look, then smiled. "Me too."

He grinned and stepped back. "Now get some rest?"

"Definitely."

And he did sleep, like a baby. Except with totally grown-up dreams.

CHAPTER THIRTEEN

CHARLOTTE WAS a repeat of the incredible performance in Raleigh. Dean was starting to get the hang of the tour, and he had the best seat in the house.

When the lights came down after the encore, she bounded off the stage with the band. They handed over their instruments as they moved deeper backstage, then she flung her arms around Jackie's neck, then squeezed West hard and planted a wet, sloppy kiss on Andrew's cheek.

But the whole time her eyes were on him.

He gave her a slow, proud grin. "Good show," he said as they headed through the crowd backstage.

"Thanks," she breathed.

He cleared a path all the way to her dressing room, and when she opened the door she hesitated. He felt the invitation loud and clear.

He could look around and slip inside if nobody was watching. But he was quickly learning that he didn't have a lot of will-power when it came to the temptation of Liana Hansen. "I'll stand guard."

She nodded in understanding, her eyes dancing. She totally had his number—yeah, he wanted her. No, he wasn't going to do anything about that just yet. At least she was amused by his moral dilemma.

But she didn't step inside right away. Instead she leaned against the door, stretching in front of him the same way she had earlier in the tour bus.

Vixen.

She smiled slowly. "There's an after party."

"You deserve a celebration." A crowd of people pushed past behind him, and he moved a little closer. He didn't miss how her eyes lit up at the increased proximity.

Danger.

"You'll be right here?" Her voice had dropped to a whisper and it tugged at his gut.

"Right here."

"Good." Another smile, this one breathy and softer. Less deliberately seductive. Hotter than ever.

He was so screwed.

— —

THEY DIDN'T HAVE an after party every night, but it was only a four-hour drive to Knoxville, and with the mountains in between, their drivers preferred to make the drive in the daytime.

So they could linger after the show, and this particular arena had a very hospitable staff.

Fine by her. She felt like letting a little loose.

Liana changed, then they joined the local opening act

and her band crew, plus a bunch of VIP fans and local business people at the after party.

The arena staff had laid on a pretty nice spread of food in the second largest green room, which had great couches and a couple of nooks that suited conversation well.

She poured herself a Jack and Coke on ice, and offered the same to Dean.

"No whiskey in mine."

"You sure? You're off-duty. Or I don't have to."

"You totally should. And that's why I don't," Dean murmured, smiling down at her. He lifted his glass. "Cheers."

They moved deeper into the room. People smiled and took pictures with her, but conversations faded when she hung around too long, so she kept moving until they reached an empty couch. Then she sat, grateful for a moment of quiet, but even as she released a sigh she'd been holding in, her old familiar friend, doubt, made its regular appearance.

Was anyone watching her? Thinking *look how lonely Liana is, because she pushes everyone away, and really, that's her own fault, but how sad. If only she was more giving, more loving, more forgiving—*

She took a big sip of the cold drink and waved her free hand at Dean, who was standing beside her looking ten feet tall. Fuck it. She could talk to her damn bodyguard without starting a rumour. Maybe. Hopefully.

She took another drink. "Sit down."

He gave her an amused look as he moved around to the front of the couch and settled on the edge. "Yes, ma'am."

She laughed. "I told you not to call me that," she teased, knowing he'd done it on purpose.

"If I wanted to make a good impression," he said with a completely straight face. "Maybe I'm over that now."

"Or maybe you think you've made a good enough impression for the day already."

He glanced at his watch. "Technically that was yesterday. And really mostly the day before. I didn't do much today other than watch you tear up the stage."

"Nice side step."

He glanced around the terrace and spread his legs a little wider, like he was deliberately taking up real estate in front of the couch. She sank back into the cushions, grateful for the privacy he afforded her.

She should go be social, but she really just wanted to sit and have a drink and watch the room. And he was giving her that. It didn't really matter if it was deliberate or accidental, she appreciated it either way.

West was holding court on another couch nearby. The fact that he usually paid for more than his fair share of the beer made him popular with the crew, and he knew how to work a crowd to get the extroverts telling jokes and keep the introverts feeling comfortable just hanging out.

A sharp contrast to the way Track used to hold court when they went on tour together. She'd seen a glimpse of that again in Washington. He'd dominated the conversation near the bar in the VIP tent, a little too loud and a little too forceful. She'd recognized the story he told, about a concert where everything went wrong, and she'd winced, because some of the crew involved in that show were in the tent at the time.

He was so tone-deaf sometimes, but it never seemed to splash back on him. He was made of Teflon. It was like people were so drawn to his charisma that they didn't realize they were being served up a pile of narcissistic crap once they were pulled into his orbit.

What she saw as oily others saw as slick and impressive. Ugh.

"I need another drink," she said, finishing the last sip of the one in her hand.

Dean pressed a hand to her forearm. "Whoa. You okay? You look mad."

She shook her head. "Just remembered something that happened yesterday."

"What?"

She shrugged her shoulders. "Nothing."

He looked at her warily for a second before nodding. "You want me to get that drink for you?"

"Would you?"

He laughed and shook his head at her gently. "You understand so far this has been the easiest job in the world, right?"

She frowned. She didn't like the reminder that he worked for her. "I'll get my own drink."

"Hey." One quiet, firm word and she jerked her eyes up to meet his gaze. "There's nowhere else I'd rather be. No one else I'd rather fetch a drink for, or sit beside at a party."

"Don't spoil me now." A reluctant smile spread across her face as they shared a look, then he nodded, his neat, white teeth set against his lower lip, his eyes half-lidded as he set his hands wide across the worn denim hugging his thighs and pushed himself up to stand.

She watched him cross to the bar, his long legs eating up the space like it was nothing. She tried to picture him naked. Another drink was probably a terrible idea. She bit her lip and giggled to herself. But that butt…seriously.

And those legs. Tight muscles, long limbs, maybe a light dusting of hair in all the right places.

Not a good place to go.

She jerked her head away from where Dean was laughing with someone at the bar. She scanned the party again, trying to distract herself.

For someone so calm, he sure stirred up a decent amount of chaos inside her.

When her eyes found him again, he was striding back, and right on cue, something tugged hard deep in her belly.

He handed her a new plastic cup, cool from the ice. She took a sip. "Perfect."

"Cheers." He tipped his cup against hers, then quickly swallowed some of his Coke before rejoining her on the couch. "You doing okay?"

"Yep."

"I hope this comes across as a compliment, but you seem like a totally different person than a few days ago."

She laughed. "Thank you. Yes, I'm feeling pretty good."

"Good."

"Are you going to check in every day to make sure I'm not freaking out inside?"

"Yep."

She dropped her gaze to her drink and smiled to herself. "Good."

"But you're tough. I think you were right. You don't need me here." He nudged her gently with his side, his thigh sliding against hers, and she wanted to lean into his warmth.

"Maybe I like having someone around who knows that I'm secretly crazy."

"You're hardly that. Secretly badass."

"Oooh, now you're just sweet-talking me."

He chuckled under his breath. She glanced sideways at him at the same time as he twisted to look at her, his eyebrows pulling heavy over his eyes.

"What?"

"You really are secretly badass. You're all southern charm on the outside, but you're a fighter."

She blushed. Delicately, she hoped, but she was on her third drink. It was entirely possible that she should cut herself off before she said something foolish. She cleared her throat and tried to shift the subject a bit. "Maybe? I learned that from Hope. She's…well, you know. She doesn't take any shit. She doesn't wallow. We met like… three weeks after I'd broken up with Track. And I was still stunned. Didn't know how it would affect my career. Couldn't see a future without him, even though I'd been the one to end it. I was afraid. I thought I was heartbroken. I was so innocent. But Hope is way more cynical than me. I'm the romantic. She's the realist. And she said, quite rightly, that I was really mourning the loss of a dream, not the actual man. Because—well, obviously not actually the man. So she took one look at me and said, 'let's get you the fuck over him.'"

Dean barked a laugh, and she joined him.

"Right? Can you even imagine her saying that?"

"Actually, yes. I just couldn't imagine you repeating it."

She gave him a ladylike mini curtsey before continuing. "So we did all the things that women do after a break up. Ice cream. Late night wine chatter about how small his…hands are. Extra gym visits. Ritual burning of his belongings."

Dean was nodding along, amused at her rant, until the last one. He blinked at her. "That's not a real thing."

"He's never been able to find his favourite tour t-shirt for a reason." She made a poof gesture with her hand, her fingers splaying wide. "Ashes on the wind."

"You really burned his shit? I'm pretty sure nobody has burned any of my belongings."

She had some thoughts as to why that might be, but they were best kept in her head. She just gave a noncommittal shrug in response.

"What?"

"Oh, no. Nothing."

He laughed. "Sure."

"You tell me, then. What?"

"It's just that I'm friends with most of my exes."

Ha. Likely story. She tried not to roll her eyes.

"You don't believe me?"

Clearly she'd failed. She took another drink. "Sure."

"What?"

"Well, if you're still friends with them…maybe they were more friends with benefits than girlfriends. I mean, it's hard to still be friends with someone that you loved once they stop loving you."

He hesitated long enough for her to realize she'd just made a big assumption.

"They weren't that serious?"

He shrugged. "Not really."

She was hardly one to judge. Her only really serious relationship had been with someone that maybe she hadn't wanted to spend a lot of time naked with. She won the prize for messed-up, that was for sure. "Ignore me, then."

"But you're probably right. On the other hand, I'm not ashes on the wind anywhere, so there's that."

"Good point. To not getting entangled in anything

messy." She held up her already empty glass. "Oops. Need another drink."

She pushed off the couch before he could offer to get it for her, or suggest she'd had enough.

She suddenly wanted Dean to watch her walk across the room the way she'd just ate him up with her eyes. She'd changed out of her performance clothes, but put on a very similar outfit—a dark red silky blouse instead of her t-shirt, but another pair of her four-hundred-dollar jeans that made her ass look fantastic.

The ass that Dean was staring at right now as she poured herself a drink, hip cocked to the side.

He didn't even hide it when she turned around, dragging his gaze lazily back up her body. Whew, boy. She needed to either do something about that or shut it down. Probably.

It was getting to be that time of night. She stopped where Jackie was standing against the wall, nursing a Diet Coke. "You heading back to the bus soon?"

Her friend shrugged. "Soon, maybe. You want a chaperone?"

"Stop it."

"If you aren't riding him like a bronco by the end of tour, I call dibs."

Liana's mouth twitched, because there was no way her guitarist wanted Dean right now. "You want him? He's all yours."

Jackie groaned. "You know."

"Just a guess." She glanced around for Andrew, who was nowhere in sight. "He's cute and serious. Exactly your type. And you've both been extra-professional. That was the giveaway."

"It's just a fling." Jackie cleared her throat. "He went back to the bus a few minutes ago."

"We'll be a little while still, if you…"

"Nope. We're not doing this. This is not summer camp and I don't need a cover. Wipe your mind of whatever you're thinking. This is not a group project."

Liana laughed and threw her arms around her friend. "Okay."

"Now go tell that polite Canadian boy that Southern girls like oral."

"I think all girls like oral," Liana muttered, her face turning red as she turned her back on Dean for a minute. Give the man another chance to ogle her ass while she pulled herself back together.

"Who likes oral?" West asked, draping his arm around her neck.

Where had he come from?

She groaned. "Go away. We're having girl talk and you're making me uncomfortable."

He kissed her cheek. "I'm hurt. Normally I'm invited to all girl talks."

"Those are fake. We have them just to throw you off our scent."

"Wow. Stay up late enough and it all comes out." He mock sniffed and patted her on the butt before sauntering off to get more beer.

This time when she turned around, Dean was definitely not looking at her ass. He'd sprawled back on the couch and was staring at a nothing point somewhere just past her shoulder.

Interesting.

She threw herself back on the couch next to him, close enough to resume their private conversation, although the way he wasn't quite looking at her, she feared that was over anyway.

"Is that a thing, you and West?" he asked abruptly.

"No."

"Just a musician thing, the touching?"

"Are you *jealous*?" The question was out of her mouth before she could stop herself. Damn third drink.

He gave her a slow, careful look. "No."

That annoyed her. Alcohol stripped away the protective layers that pretended she didn't want to be special enough, to be worthy of a possessive feeling or two, even from—maybe if only from—a hot stranger. She wrinkled her nose and took another sip of her Jack and Coke.

"I wouldn't use that word…" He said, trailing off. No, of course he wouldn't, and she shouldn't have said it in the first place. Way inappropriate. But there was this pulsing chemistry between them, and he wasn't a liar, so if he was aware of it… His eyes told her all that and a little more, something dangerous and exciting, as he leaned in. "I didn't like it, though."

"Okay." Liana swallowed hard. "I told him to go away."

"I saw that. I didn't like it for how I reacted, too. You can do whatever you want."

She almost snapped a bitter *thanks* for the all-clear, but she thought better of it. "You're really good about that. Like…extra good."

"About what?"

"You're very careful not to judge me."

"I think you're just more aware of it because you face it every day from all corners."

"You're really looking to dodge this compliment, aren't you?"

"Basic human courtesy shouldn't garner a compliment."

"It's rare enough in my world that it does."

"That's fucked up."

"Mmm." But it was her reality.

She turned her attention back to the room. Her tour manager, who was married, had cozied up with a fan.

Not your problem, not your business. Get involved and he'll brand you a busybody. God, no, she wasn't going to say anything. But it was time to go. Infidelity was such a trigger for her.

She downed the rest of her drink and stood, waving at Jackie, who nodded but didn't leave her spot on the wall.

Dean followed her out of the green room and she headed down the empty corridor. A security guard leaned against the wall next to the exit, reading something on his phone. Did she want to go back to the bus and go to bed?

Not yet.

She grabbed Dean's hand and pulled him down a side hallway.

CHAPTER FOURTEEN

EITHER LIANA HAD BEEN to this arena before or she had an intuition for where to find a private room, but Dean couldn't ask her because as soon as they were inside that private room, her mouth was on his and talking time was over.

She tasted like sweetness and secret need, and he couldn't resist either. She'd fisted the front of his shirt and hauled him down to her level for the first hungry volley, but when his back thumped against the wall, he spread his legs, equalling out their height difference.

It was cute she thought she'd be in control for more than the first kiss.

"I couldn't help myself," she whispered as he tried to hold her still. She turned her head and nipped at his palm. The scrape of her teeth against his skin was hardly a deterrent—it sent a heads-up alert to his balls.

No heads-up. No sex. Just some kisses.

But jeez, she tasted good. And while he wanted to haul her hard against him and take her mouth, her neck, strip her out of that blouse and make her scream with his tongue on her nipples…if she wanted to be the one to kiss him, he could deal with that. Maybe.

"I know the feeling."

"Oh thank God. I wasn't sure." He didn't miss the relief in her voice. He didn't like that doubt. He wanted to know more about where it came from—whatever bullshit mindfuck bit of history he didn't know about yet.

He would, though. He'd find out every awful echo in her head and erase them for her.

"You needed this to know how much I wanted you?" He dragged a ragged breath into his lungs. "Let there be no doubt on that score. I want you so much it hurts."

She pressed closer, running her hands over his body.

"Take it. Take what you want." He groaned as she pressed her mouth to his neck, then set her teeth gently into his jaw, shooting an electric current right down his spine.

"I love the scrape of your stubble at the end of the night," she whispered against his cheek as she rose onto her toes, rubbing her breasts against his chest. "It's exactly as I imagined it."

"Tell me more about that."

"Uh uh. Secrets." She was closer to his mouth again. The barest of kisses at the corner of his lips. A little laugh. "But you're hot. And I've definitely been thinking about that. About you."

"Good."

"Very." She sucked his lower lip into her mouth, then nipped again.

Had she figured out how much he liked that? It was getting hard not to grind against her. His dick raged against his fly and he wanted her pressed against him there. Her hand, her leg, her belly…he didn't care. Just some part of her sweetness rubbing against his cock before he started begging. "Kiss me," he ground out.

"Okay."

So simple. So sweet.

So completely filthy. She slid her hands down his chest, over his abs which were flexing with a mind of their own as she tugged up his shirt. And she stroked him there, lazy and hot with her clever little hands as she pressed her mouth against his, open and wet.

Stroke. Lick. Sigh. Liana kissed liked she sang, husky and low and sweet, and maybe he'd been wrong to think "Cravings" wasn't about her innermost desires. Her kisses were pure sin.

He liked it so damn much it hurt.

She tweaked all of his buttons. Kind. Feisty. A little dirty. They could have so much fun if they weren't trapped on a tour bus. Nashville. They'd have a few days in Nashville.

They could wait until then.

Five more days.

"We should—"

She cut him off with her tongue in his mouth and he gave up, losing himself in the heady rush of sliding together. He'd been clenching his hands at his sides to keep from taking over, but when she pulled his arms around her in invitation, he let himself go, following her lead.

Her waist was warm and soft beneath her blouse, nipping in above the swell of her tight hips. Her body felt even better than it looked, and when he got his hands on her bottom and pulled her hard between his spread legs, he found she fit against his perfectly, too.

Score one for sexy heels. And walls to lean against. Not

to mention two bodies that seemed to know what to do like magnets.

And still she kissed him with hints and teases, the softest, sexiest brushes of her tongue and lips. Her breath danced between them as she teased their top lips together, swirling heat and need around them as she rocked against him.

Her shirt slid up a few inches and on his next rough inhale, their bellies rubbed against each other.

Hot, warm, skin.

Fuck.

He groaned something incomprehensible as he spun them around and lifted her up, holding her hard against the wall as he plastered himself against her.

Need shifted hard inside him, roaring a demand for more of her, all of her. His erection throbbed between her thighs and his thought processes had dropped to simple, primal grunts. Make her moan. Hear her moan. Make her come. See her come.

He'd give her what she wanted, but he'd take something, too. Greedily steal her pleasure as his own, because there was a time and a place for him to get off and it wasn't now or here.

This was all about Liana. He could feel her shaking under his touch, and as he snaked his hands up her shirt, her breathy little gasps told him she was close. He found her breasts, full and heavy, and his brain scrambled. God, she felt good. His balls pulled tight, like he might actually —nope. He was a grown man. He could get her off without losing it.

Probably.

Her bra was made of that barely-there stretchy kind of fabric that meant he could feel every pebbly bump of her nipple right through it, but that wasn't good enough. He wrenched it out of the way on both sides, freeing her tight little peaks to rub against the silky fabric of her blouse.

He couldn't figure out how to get that off in the semi-dark of the room, so he lowered his head and sucked one nipple right through the fabric. Then the other. At some point they'd slid down the wall and he'd put her down—because if he ground his cock against her once more, it would be over.

And the only way this was ending was with her screaming her orgasm into his mouth, her hot little pussy clenching around his fingers.

He'd have paid anything for a bed, but having her lean back against the wall as he yanked open her jeans and sucked on her tits, leaning over her like a man in prayer, worked too.

Under her jeans she had a matching pair of barely-there micro fibre panties that posed zero barriers to him as he brushed over her curls and between her soaking wet folds.

She cried out when he circled his fingertips back up to her clit with some of that slippery moisture. It didn't take long to orient himself to the basic geography of her body. Even blind like this he knew she was beautiful. Sensitive. Sexy as hell.

"Next time I do this with my tongue."

"I'm going to hold you to that," she whispered.

"That's the idea. You'll twist your fingers into my hair and take what you want."

"Ooh...." She bit her lip and he watched her face twist tighter as he stroked her. Back and forth. Back and forth. Circle and rub.

It was gorgeous. But still not quite what he wanted.

With his free hand, he shoved her jeans down a little lower and palmed her ass, tilting her body out from the wall even more.

He shifted his hand and tentatively circled her opening. "Is this okay?"

"God, yes."

One finger slid inside. His thumb found her clit.

She clenched around him as he stroked out, then in and again, discovering the most secret part of her body. Another finger, and his thumb circled and rubbed. Closer, closer.

A little whine broke past the weak barricade of her bitten lip and he covered her mouth with his. *Give it to me,* he said with his tongue. He wanted her noises and her climax, and he wanted them all to himself.

When she burst, it was like those fireworks the night before. Bigger and brighter than he expected. She came with her entire body, gushing against his hand and it was beautiful, so he told her that, over and over again.

He took his time buttoning her back up. He didn't want to give up her soft, smooth skin, didn't want to wash her scent off his hands, but this had been a stolen moment and it needed to come to an end.

She was clearly on the same regrettable wavelength. "We should get back to the bus."

He kissed her softly before nodding. "Sweet dreams tonight."

"The sweetest."

"Try not to blush too hard when I send you dirty text messages tomorrow."

"Oh." She glanced away to the side, then back up at him, her eyelashes fluttering nervously. "So…about that."

"Dirty texts a no go?"

"No, they're okay. But I'll give you a different number."

"You've got a secret phone?"

She laughed. "Is that totally paranoid?"

"No." It was smart as hell. "I'm turned on all over again."

Another small laugh, and she started to tell him the number.

"Wait," he said, digging out his phone and handing it over. "Just type it in. I'll never remember it in the state I'm in."

"Can I help you with that…state?"

He shook his head, no, and dropped his mouth to the bare stretch of her neck as she created a new contact for herself in his address book. "Tonight was all about you."

"Really?"

"Call me old-fashioned."

"I'll call you a masochist, because there's never a time I'll voluntarily go without an orgasm."

He grunted at the unexpected pleasure that little admission gave him. For all her worry about being a good girl, doing the right thing…for all the ways that Track had messed with her head, she still had the autonomy to say, "I want my pleasure". Good for her.

Plus, hot as fucking anything. He kissed her hard and fast, then tugged her hair as he pressed his forehead against hers. "Every single time. You use me and abuse me until you come as often as you want. Got it?"

She beamed at him. Jesus. He wanted to carry her away from this tour as fast and as far as he could go, but she had people relying on her. So he'd do second best and build a wall around her. Let her ride the roller coaster a little more easy because he'd be able to give her this.

"Dirty Liana is in your phone as Sweet Tits."

"You nicknamed yourself Sweet Tits."

"Can you think of something better?"

"It's perfect." Another kiss, then it really was past time to be getting back.

He cracked the door open and shot a quick look down the hallway, listening as much as he was watching. Nobody. He took her hand and squeezed her fingers as they headed back to the main corridor. That, too, was empty, save for the guard who'd put his phone away. Dean waited until the guy did a slow turn around to look out the door, and he tugged Liana into the open, as if they'd just come out of the after party.

Dropping her hand was surprisingly hard, but the lazy, satisfied smile she shot him made up for it.

Before he could dwell any longer on what they'd just done, his phone vibrated with a text message. He pulled it out as they walked past the security guard. *Matt.* It was the middle of the night. Matt was either drunk-dialling or something had happened.

"I need to check my messages," he said quietly as they crossed the parking lot. "Maybe make a phone call."

"Everything okay?"

"I'm sure. It's one of my brothers. Odds are good he's just out partying."

She tilted her head to the side. "The one who's going overseas?"

"No, Matt, the next oldest. I'm sure it's nothing."

Behind them, the arena door creaked open and a wave of people spilled out. They weren't alone anymore.

He glanced back down at her. She was looking at the ground now, and he wanted to lift her chin and kiss her mouth, soft and sweet. So he lowered his voice instead and made his words warm, just for her. "No, go on in. Get a head start on those sweet dreams. I'll be there in a minute."

After she disappeared onto the bus, he turned his attention to his phone.

Quick question, Matt's text started. **How long are you away? Any chance I could use your place next weekend?**

Dean scowled. Despite the late hour, he stabbed his thumb at the screen and dialled his brother, who answered right away, his voice bright and beer-happy against a background of bar sounds. "Dean!"

"No, you can't use my place. You have a perfectly good apartment."

"My landlord doesn't want me throwing any more parties."

"And you thought I would?"

"Well, I wasn't going to tell you about the party. I was hoping you'd just text back a happy-go-lucky *yes*."

"Sorry to disappoint," Dean said, rolling his eyes.

"No kidding." Matt didn't sound upset. "So how's it going? Hook up with any groupies yet?"

"I already told Sean there weren't any groupies."

"Yeah, but we don't want to believe you."

"Is he out with you tonight?"

"He is."

Dean looked down at the dusty parking lot and scuffed the toe of his boot against a small pocket of dirt. "He in a good mood?"

Matt laughed and his voice shifted, like he'd moved his voice away from the phone receiver a bit. "Dean wants to know if you've told the Colonel about your tour." He moved the phone back to his mouth. "That would be not yet. So yeah, he's in a good mood. He's got a hot babe in his lap."

A feminine protest came through the phone line no problem and Dean shook his head.

Matt didn't seem deterred. "What? You're totally hot. And a babe. And—" He broke off, laughing. "Okay, I gotta go. No parties at your house, I promise. And we want a groupie report soon!"

"No groupies. Not that kind of tour."

"Bang the hot singer, then."

The right response to that was *Go home, Matt, you're clearly drunk,* or *Stop thinking with your dick, asshole.* Stuttering silence was a dead giveaway.

Dean was already cursing himself when Matt started howling. "Oh Jesus. You did. You fucking dog. Yes. Man, I'm so proud—"

He hung up the phone. He couldn't have that conversation with his brother.

Because that was *not* what it was.

Even if it was a hook-up—which the thought of made his stomach flip uncomfortably—he'd never crow about it. He didn't do that. Ever.

His brothers needed to have their heads knocked together.

But the conversation still made him uneasy in a new and worrisome way, because he also didn't ever get involved with a woman without some clear parameters.

And if one thing was super fucking clear, it was that with Liana, he had zero boundaries. Like being in her orbit stripped him bare of all defences. Before they did any more kissing, they needed to talk.

CHAPTER FIFTEEN

THEY BARELY GOT another second alone together for nearly forty-eight hours.

They drove all day to get to the show in Knoxville. The entire trip, Liana was aware of Dean's presence in a brand-new, super intense kind of way.

As soon as they arrived, she had a sound check, then a meet and greet.

Her cheeks hurt from smiling by the time Dean swung open the door to her dressing room. No sooner had she stepped inside than the wardrobe assistant followed her in with her clothes for the night, and behind her came the make-up artist to retouch her face.

She made a face at Dean in the mirror over their heads as they bustled around, and he held her gaze, his mouth curving into an amused grin.

He hadn't shaved. A few more days and he'd have a full-on beard.

She liked that. She should tell him how much, before he went and did something foolish like shaved it off.

He lifted one eyebrow. *What are you thinking about?*

Her cheeks flamed. "Hey, can I have the room for a minute?" The crew members looked up, surprised. "Just like five minutes. Three. Feeling kind of stressed out with the bustling."

It was a total diva move that normally she'd apologize for, but as soon as they were out of the room, Dean had her backed up against the counter, his mouth on hers, and she didn't care.

"Stressed out?" he asked against her lips.

"Just needed a kiss," she murmured back.

"Good thing I'm here, then." Both of his arms were around her now. She was well and truly trapped, and the next brush of his mouth was a rolling wave that caught her and pulled her out to sea.

He lifted her effortlessly so she was sitting on the counter and nudged his way between her legs. Yes, oh definitely that. She squeezed her legs around his hips and tried to slide their bodies together just so, but he pressed her back against the mirror.

"Just a kiss, princess. No time for anything more."

"Spoilsport," she said breathlessly, giggling until he took her mouth again, hard and rough, stealing the laugh and her breath. He sent her spinning into the riptide again.

Slick, wet heat. A crazy kaleidoscope of sensations twirled inside her as he explored and caressed her with his tongue, his lips, his hands. He kissed her with his entire body, his embrace commanding and addictive.

Drowning had never been so tempting before.

A quick knock at the door killed that thought quick.

Dean slid her off the counter, helping her find the floor with her feet before he stepped away.

Her heart pounded in her chest.

"Thank you," she whispered. It wasn't the right thing to say, exactly, but he'd turned her brain to mush.

He tugged on a lock of her hair, tucking it behind her ear as he bent over her. He kissed her cheek. "Our secret, princess. No worries."

"That was fun." She grinned up at him.

He winked as he walked backward toward the door to let them back in.

She tried and failed not to look at the substantial erection pressing against the front of his jeans.

And that was all they got for the rest of the evening.

Andrew didn't have the greatest night. A problem with his in-ear monitor, and then he'd snapped at Jackie, which was probably the stupidest choice he could have made for more than one reason.

And then she'd had to intervene when he'd gone ballistic on the sound engineer after the show. It was a shame, really, because she'd had an *incredible* show, and she attributed at least a bit of that to the breathless excitement that rioted through her every time she thought of Dean's kiss.

She'd wanted to show him just how appreciative she was, but that would have to wait, because as soon as Andrew calmed down, they were back on the bus to get to Louisville by the next morning because her next show was a daytime slot at an outdoor festival.

— —

DEAN KNEW MANAGING a grumpy band wasn't how

Liana wanted to unwind after another spectacular concert. Jackie was pissed because of something Andrew had said to her during the show, so she stomped off her to her bunk as soon as Dwayne pulled onto the highway.

West pulled out his tablet and sat right in the middle of the living room, taking up a lot of real estate on the couch at the same time as he propped his legs on a chair.

Liana looked exasperated with him, and Andrew, who was slouched over the table, spinning a coin over and over again.

Clearly she wasn't the oldest of four brothers.

Dean kicked the chair out from under West's feet.

"Hey!" the drummer protested.

Rule one of a grumpy house full of boys: everyone suffered the same consequence. As soon as Dean had realized that trick, the Foster home had way less bickering.

"Get the cards," Dean said. "We'll play a few hands."

Rule two of a grumpy house full of boys: give them something to fiddle with while they sort out their shit.

The tablet, the coin…those were fine, and they'd eventually get there on their own, but Liana was tired and Dean didn't have time for this shit. Getting them doing the *same* thing increased the likelihood of whatever was simmering between the surface with those two actually boiling over—and then getting dealt with properly.

Rule three of a grumpy house full of boys: big brother leads by example. He pulled out his wallet and tossed a twenty on the table. "Who's in?"

Andrew didn't move.

Neither did West, but he made the classic mistake of sniping from a distance. "Andrew won't get in the game. He'll just sit there be pissed that someone else wins."

"Fuck off." Andrew's voice was quiet, but filled with

enough anger that Dean did a slow glance up at Liana. He didn't know these guys that well. He needed her to be the arbiter of when enough was enough.

She was still in her stage makeup, heavy dark eyeshadow and a too-smooth face, so it was hard to read the subtle signs in her face, but the not-so-subtle tightness around her mouth was enough to broadcast to all three men that she wasn't happy. Silence stretched as she looked back and forth between Andrew and West, then finally settled her attention on Dean. Her eyes were filled with questions, but her lips softened as she exhaled. "I'm in. Let me just get changed while you set up the table."

"You gonna let Liana take the new guy's money?" West goaded, and Andrew stood up so fast, Dean got between them.

No fists were flying tonight.

"Put your money on the table and get the chips." He pointed a finger at Andrew, then glanced back over his shoulder at West. "If you want to say anything, you can do it when it's your turn to bid. Or between deals. Got it?"

"I don't got nothing to say."

"Is that because you're—" West cut himself off when Dean turned, giving him a warning look.

"Table. Cards. Chips. Money." When neither man moved fast enough, he used his NCO voice. "Now!"

That did the trick.

By the time Liana returned, her face scrubbed clean, her hair up in a loose, swinging ponytail that made him want to tug on it something fierce, the table was set for four people to play some poker.

Dean only paid enough attention to the game to win every third hand. The rest of the time, he watched West poke at Andrew. Andrew's anger build. Liana get pushed closer and closer to the breaking point, until West sneered one too many times and she slammed her cards onto the table.

"What the hell is *your* problem?" she asked, staring at her drummer in disbelief.

It was Andrew who answered instead. "He doesn't know when to stop."

"You know what? I don't care. You turned a little thing into a big fucking deal tonight," she stormed, gesturing sharply at Andrew. "And you—" she snarled at West. "He's absolutely right. You don't know when to stop. And I don't know why. Have we just hit that point in a tour where we're in each other's faces too much? Is this some sort of delayed fallout from my anxiety last week? I don't get it. And I want you both to stop. Right now."

To their credit, they both looked sorry. Too bad they also looked sullenly, stubbornly insistent that it was the other guy's fault.

Dean decided it was time to pull the pin. "What happened earlier today?"

West's face turned ruddy and Andrew's eyes flared wide.

Ha. Oldest brother, twenty-year veteran NCO. They never stood a chance. He raised his eyebrows and looked at Liana, who blinked at him in surprise. He restrained himself from smirking. Something serious still needed to be sorted out.

He didn't have a clue what it was—just that something must have happened between West and Andrew, and if pushed enough, they'd come out with it.

"He overreacted—" West said.

Andrew sputtered right back, cutting off his bandmate.

"And he keeps rubbing my face in the fact that he's making more money than me!"

"What on Earth are you talking about?" Liana glared at Andrew. "I assure you that y'all are paid the exact same. And if I could, I'd dock you both a good amount for ruining my evening."

"Not for being in the band." Andrew slinked low in his chair. Dean could practically see the younger man's inner toddler pout. Oh boy. "He's been building his solo stuff on iTunes. And now he's rubbing my face in it."

If speech bubbles were a thing in real life, Dean would bet money he'd see a black squiggle over Liana's head right now.

"So you let that spill onto the stage?" Her eyes flashed with bright, righteous anger. "If you aren't happy with where you're at in your career, you have a bus full of people who have shown over and over again they're happy to talk business. We'll support you, but not if you're a jerk about it. There is no room on my stage for jealousy. Pull a stunt like that again and I'll fire you without a second thought. Do you understand me?"

"Yes." Andrew sat up a little straighter. If Dean was his platoon 2IC, he'd have rapped him over the knuckles for not being ramrod straight, but this was no longer his scene to direct.

He got to sit back and enjoy watching Liana tear a strip off two idiots.

It was pretty damn hot. He cleared his throat, and Andrew gave him a wide-eyed look. Dean raised his eyebrows.

Andrew flinched. "And I'm sorry."

Liana rolled her eyes. "Maybe start with that next time."

"There won't be a next time."

"I'm sure that's not true," she said softly. "We all let our emotions get the better of us from time to time."

"I'm sorry, too," West said, but he wasn't looking at Liana. He held out his hand toward Andrew. "I was being a dick."

They shook, then Liana slapped her hand on top of their clasped fingers. "One more hand before bed?"

"Nah," Andrew said, shoving back from the table. "I'm out, if that's okay."

"Sure thing. Hey…tomorrow we'll kill it, right?"

He held out his fist for Liana to bump against. "Kill it dead, boss."

"That's better." She wiggled her index finger and he ducked his head so she could kiss his cheek. "Love you, stupid."

He laughed and tugged on her ponytail.

Dean felt a totally irrational stab of jealousy. Second time in two days. Danger.

West started to deal another hand, but then he took a second look at the stack of chips in front of Andrew's chair and grabbed the four twenties from the centre of the table. "Hey, you…" he swore under his breath. "This might be why you don't have more money, you idiot. You walked away from the table with the highest stack."

"Oh."

Liana met Dean's gaze across the table as Andrew doubled back, and they both burst into laughter.

"I think it's bedtime for everyone," she said.

Dean started packing up the poker set. "Yeah."

West shook his head and clapped Andrew on the shoulder as they both headed to their bunks.

Liana took her time moving around the common space.

Long enough for West and Andrew to both get tucked in, their bunk partitions closed.

The living room was open to Dwayne in the driver's seat, but he was playing music, and suddenly, they were pretty close to alone again.

Not really alone, and after what happened the other night, he knew there was a world of difference.

I want to touch you, he thought as he they stood a few feet apart. It physically hurt, how much he wanted her. His palms itched and his chest felt tight.

"How did you know Andrew's problem was with West?" she asked quietly, her eyes drifting sideways to the couch.

He sat in the middle of it, carefully scoping the line of sight from the driver's seat and the bunks. The corner of couch was probably pretty private. He gestured toward it with his hand, and she took the hint, settling herself right in the corner so he could slide in next to her.

"Because West parked his ass right in the centre of the storm. I can't tell you how many times Jake did something to Matt, then sat innocently at the kitchen table while Matt raged around and took it out on Sean. It took me a long time to realize it was Jake being an asshole."

She frowned. "Your brothers?"

"Yeah."

"Why...you mean after your mother died? Did it all fall to you?"

"Not all of it." Just ninety-five percent. "My father's not...maternal."

She rolled her head to the side, resting it against the wall as she gave him a sympathetic look. "I'm sorry. That's hard."

He shrugged. It was in the past now.

"But you guys are close?"

"Yeah." He grinned. "Even though they're jackasses, my brothers are my best friends. And Jake's not an ass anymore. He outgrew that as a teenager. He's an old soul. Matt and Sean, though…they're still young bucks."

She laughed quietly. "Like Andrew and West."

"Very much so."

"And you're the one they go to with everything." She licked her lips, the pink tip drawing his attention to where he wanted his own mouth to be. "The phone calls."

"The what?"

She grinned, and he pulled his eyes up to meet hers. "From your brothers. You've been gone a few days and at least two of them have called you."

"Yeah." He dropped his gaze back to her mouth. "I guess."

She giggled and slid her leg against his body. "Distracted by something?"

"Maybe."

— —

LIANA LICKED HER LIPS AGAIN. "Is this a good idea?"

She'd never get enough of looking at his face. The hard planes of his jaw, his cheekbones, his brow. The expressive little muscles that turned a smirk into a question, a stern frown into a private laugh. The light in his eyes and the softness of his lips. *Obviously it's a genius idea. Why question it?*

Because he was a better man than she was used to. And

before she got in too deep, she wanted to make sure they were on the same page.

"Depends what this is, maybe." His hand settled on her calf. He squeezed gently. "I work for you."

"You work for Hope."

"That's a technicality."

"But what would happen if I tried to fire you? Because I would. For another kiss…"

All she got in reply to that was a grin. Did he think she was kidding? She so wasn't kidding.

So she moved closer to make her point.

"You don't need to fire me." Another squeeze on her leg, this time higher. Her knee was on top of his thigh now. If anyone came out of their bunks, this wouldn't be able to be explained as anything other than an intimate moment.

They should shelve this conversation for another day. Another time.

Instead, she reached out and touched his chest. Against her fingertips, his heart thumped slow and steady, and her stomach did a delicious roll over.

"I've done the romantic fantasy thing. Left it in ashes and haven't looked back," she whispered. "I'm not going to try and complicate this, I mean. I'm not a delicate flower anymore."

"Oh, I know. You're tough as nails, Liana."

She closed her eyes. Oh, she liked the way he said her name way too much.

His lips against hers were so light she almost thought for a second that she'd imagined it.

Her eyes flew open, and he was right there. She was just out of sight of Dwayne. He covered his lips with his index finger.

Shhhhh.

She nodded.

"You're the most beautiful woman I've ever laid eyes on," he said quietly, his gaze serious as he looked at her. "You sing like a whiskey-tinged angel. And you're a smart fucking business person. And I spend nearly every minute of the day thinking about how much I want to kiss you. That you're trying hard to be sensible about it just makes that hotter, I promise."

She swayed against him, wanting to wrap her arms around his neck and pull their mouths together again. But the blind spot in the corner of the couch wasn't big enough for that, and the chances of getting caught were too high. Instead she patted him on the chest and smiled as he shifted away from her.

But he didn't go far. He caught her wrist as he slide over, and he held her hand between them long enough for the warmth of his body to dance through her fingers and up her arm, filling her with a bright, light heat.

Like maybe holding hands was even better than kissing.

Then he looked at her mouth and the heat twisted inside her, the flames licking higher. Okay, maybe not. But damn…both were pretty incredible.

Sensible.

Sure. They could pretend that they would be sensible about this.

CHAPTER SIXTEEN

DEAN THOUGHT he'd like the outdoor festival, but like the concert in Washington, it was jam-packed full of other performers, and unlike Washington, they were all arriving and leaving at different times. Liana almost got hit by a tour bus tearing out of the parking lot, and even before they got backstage, he was on edge.

Their crew had gone ahead, setting up in the prep area just behind the mainstage. There wasn't a green room or dressing area, so Brad radioed to one of her roadies and they got the heads up when it was time to head to the stage—which all sounded good in theory, but it meant that Liana was majorly stressed by the time she was five minutes out from performing.

Dean wanted to pull her aside and give her a hug. Wrap her in his arms and shut out the noise. Well, he couldn't hug and kiss her, but he could physically block it out. He hooked his fingers gently around her upper arm and turned her around, tucking her into the shadow behind a stack of speakers. With him standing in front of her, she was essentially alone for at least the moment.

"Close your eyes," he said quietly.

"Visualize my success?" she asked, her lips turning up slightly at the corners. He tried not to think about other, more effective ways of making her smile. Sigh. Moan.

"Exactly." The word was rougher than his first instruction, and she blinked up at him.

"Close them."

"But that sounded like you might be thinking about something dirty."

"Shush."

"Tell me later?"

"Definitely. Now think about that crowd. They're totally into your song. You own them." He pictured himself as he watched her, and his voice got lower, rougher, more raw. "You hold them in thrall. You're a queen."

She inhaled, more deeply this time, and held it for a second. A slow exhale followed, and then again, in and out, twice more. When she fluttered her eyes open, she was smiling with her entire face.

She wiggled to a beat that only she could hear and he stepped back.

"Good to go."

"Uh huh." She looked him up and down. "In thrall?"

She was going to use that against him later. He couldn't wait. He tucked his thumbs into the pockets of his jeans and winked at her. "Definitely."

That got him a secret smile and a whispered thanks as she slipped by.

— —

LIANA GRABBED her water bottle from where she'd set it on the speaker and gave Jackie an *all's good* thumbs up. It wasn't, really. After two good shows, she was suddenly wound tight again.

Plus now she had the worry about tensions flaring in other directions as well.

Jackie might still be mad at Andrew—with good reason—but she'd leave it off stage.

Could Liana do the same?

Fucking anxiety.

She tried to breathe as West led the prayer. In and out. Then the boys were gone, onstage and ready for her.

Jackie gave her a quick nod as they still stood in the shadow of the side stage, then played the familiar start to 'River Bed Lullaby' before walking on stage. This was most impressive in an arena, where the spotlight would follow her all the way across to the far side, then split into two, the second light tracking back to pick up Liana as she walked into view.

But even though it was mid-afternoon and they didn't have the theatric lighting effects, she still felt the crowd shift to her as she prowled into view.

Come to me, she thought as she growled out the aching lyrics.

They usually did this song at the mid-point of the show, but for an outdoor festival, the setlist was different—they didn't have a captive audience, and most of these people weren't necessarily there to see her. They started with a powerhouse ballad and then they'd build from there, doing all the party anthems in her catalogue before ending with Cravings.

But first, she had to do a little flirting.

"Hello, Louisville!" she said into the mic as she ran to the front of the stage and leaned out into the crowd, waving at the fans who held up signs with her name on them. "You are looking beautiful this afternoon, I gotta say. Yes, you. Stunning."

She grinned, then pressed her hand to her chest. "Anyone feeling a little sad right now? Anyone here need to escape, maybe? Yes? You?" She blew a kiss to those who'd hollered *yes*. "I know. Me too. But there's joy to be found in music, right?"

That was West's cue, and the rest of the set went perfectly by the book.

Until she glanced into the crowd during "Cravings" and found a man sneering at her. Her head immediately tried to minimize it—because this happened, especially at big, multi-performer concerts. He was here to see a good ol' country boy, and she wasn't that.

It was fine. And if it was a dark arena, she'd never have seen him.

But the mocking look on his face, like he was laughing at her, reminded her too much of Track.

She stumbled over the lyrics, then tore her gaze away from the stranger in the crowd because fuck him, but the damage was done.

This wasn't as bad as Savannah, but as the song ended, she knew her reprieve from doubt was over.

— —

THEY WERE STAYING in a hotel that night because St. Louis wasn't a far drive. After the shaky performance, she needed a good night's sleep.

Part of her was desperate to get alone with Dean, too. But another part wasn't so sure that was a good idea. Of course that part fell mute when, after they checked in, everyone else ended up in the other wing.

She was breathlessly aware of Dean following her down the quiet hotel hallway to her room. All alone, and in three, two, one second, she'd have a chance to invite him into her room.

"Thank you for today," she said quietly as she slid her keycard into the door. She didn't look at him.

"Of course."

She pushed the door open and stepped into the dark of her room. Dean reached past her at the same moment she stretched for the light switch, and their fingers brushed.

"Let me get that," he said quietly and she moved further into the room as it lit up.

The door shut behind them.

She started to undo the buttons on her blouse. She had a black tank top underneath. It wasn't indecent...but it was direct in a way she suddenly couldn't find the words to say.

"Liana..." Yes, she liked her name rolling off his tongue. Even when it was accompanied by a wary—but definitely interested, thank goodness—narrowing of his eyes as she turned around.

"Yes, Dean?"

He grinned at her. "What are you doing?"

"Getting a bit more comfortable. No reason not to, right? We're all alone."

"So we are."

She tipped her head to the side as she dropped her blouse on her bed. "First time for that."

"We were alone the other night." When he'd almost kissed her.

"I was tired and emotional then." *And you're a good guy.*

"And now?"

"Now I'm…" She shrugged. "Okay, still tired and emotional."

"I should let you get some rest."

See? Good guy. Phffft. "Ah." Well, he wasn't wrong on that count. "In a minute."

She prowled closer to him. He was so tall and broad. She wanted to pet him all over. That would be an excellent distraction.

"That's a dangerous way to look at me," he said quietly.

"Are you saying I'm not safe with you?" she asked breathlessly, fluttering her hands against her chest. That would be a fun game to play.

He gave her a lazy, dirty grin that said he knew exactly what she meant. Oh, God, that look was a panty-melter for sure. "Definitely don't assume you're safe with me."

Ha. So not completely a good guy. That was just fine by her. She leaned in, close enough to breathe in the scent of him. She caught the hint of a sharp, masculine body wash, but mostly he smelled like a warm, sexy man. She wanted him with a burning intensity that shocked her to the core. "You want to take advantage of me, Dean?"

"No comment. I think you should go to bed."

"Yes…bed." She reached for his hand and he laced his fingers through hers. "Tuck me in?"

He groaned as she moved them closer to the bed, but

stopped her before they got all the way there. Spoilsport. She moved closer and pressed her hands against his chest. He was warm and hard and strong all over.

He circled her wrist with his fingers, then tugged her hand off his body. But he didn't let go. "I want you like crazy, Liana. You know that."

"But…"

He gave her a pained look and tugged her a little closer.

Not close enough.

Not by a long shot.

"I don't want to hurt you," he murmured, brushing his other hand against her cheek. Just a glance. Just a tease.

She shivered. "Don't overthink this. Maybe it's just a really good way to spend the next six weeks. Or ten minutes. I don't expect anything."

He shook his head, and when he looked at her again, his eyes were softer. Green flecks glinted at her as he searched her face, first with his gaze, then again with his fingers. He touched her jaw, her cheekbone, and down to the edge of her mouth.

She parted her flushed lips and resisted the urge to lick them.

His fingers drifted down her neck, over her throat, making her swallow hard, and around to the shadow at the nape, where he tangled his hand gently in her hair.

"Here's the thing, princess. You had a rough day today."

"I'm a big girl," she protested.

"No doubt. But I don't want you burning my t-shirt, either. I want to kiss you again, but I don't want to hurt you."

He had no idea how close he was to treading on sensitive ground, but now wasn't the time for that. He wanted her and she *oh so much* wanted him. Her messed-up head and stupid ex didn't get to be a part of this moment. She could push past that and just take what she wanted without it getting complicated.

"You want to kiss me." She grinned. "Let's focus on that."

"Is that all you heard?" He groaned again, this time weaker, and she laughed as he wrapped his arms around her. "You were amazing today, you know? Even though you wobbled a bit. You were still brave and strong. And for that, you get a goodnight kiss. But that's it. I'm heading to my room in a few minutes to have a very cold shower."

"That's no fun," she said softly. Warmly, though, too, because that didn't sound like a bad idea, actually.

She had six weeks to wear down his defences. Six weeks of teasing him into kisses in dark corners.

It was a refreshing change to not feel pressured into anything more, and she wouldn't dwell on how much she wanted *more more more* with Dean.

His lips brushed hers, his breath warm against her mouth. "Good night, princess."

"Good night..." she started to say, trailing off as he teased her lips slightly apart with the tip of his tongue before easing back to scan her face one last time. If he was looking for permission, he had it in spades.

The full, warm press of his mouth against hers, more firmly this time, was enough to make her head spin. His hands were hot everywhere he touched, and she was ready to crawl out of her skin with need when he cupped her face and held her still.

Anticipation burst into delicious, disorienting pulls of

his lips, commanding slides of his tongue against skin, just a lick at first, a question against her bottom lip.

May I?

She parted for him, because of course he could. He groaned as he slowly slid inside her, and she could feel him holding back. Trying to be on his best behaviour even as he gave her a kiss so dirty it made her head spin.

She curled her fingers into the soft fabric of his shirt and urged him closer. More, she wanted more—well, she wanted everything, truthfully. She wanted that shirt on the floor and the big, brawny weight of him pressing her back against the bed. She wanted to feel his mouth everywhere on her body, then hear those groans deepen as she returned the favour.

His hands cupped her cheeks as he eased away, but he didn't get far before his mouth crashed against hers again, this kiss hungrier than the last.

And when he finally stepped back—fully away from her, with enough space between them that kissing again by accident would take fancy choreography—he was breathing heavily and he looked as affected as she felt.

She touched her fingertips to her lips and smiled. "Wow."

"I'm still your bodyguard. I can't get distracted from that."

"Of course not." But her smile was wider now. She couldn't wait to distract him.

"Sleep tight."

"I will."

He walked backwards to the door, eyes on her until the last second, and when he finally let himself out, she sagged back against the bed with a groan.

Oh. My. God.

She wanted to do that again and again and again. "Next time I'm getting under that shirt of his," she promised herself out loud, then laughed gently as she closed her eyes, warmth blooming through her chest.

CHAPTER SEVENTEEN

ST. LOUIS WAS good to Liana, a rocking afternoon performance that put a sparkle in her eyes Dean very much liked. When they piled back on the buses for Memphis, where they'd stay for two nights, everyone was in good spirits.

Even Mr. Cold Shower. Jesus, it had been hard to walk away from her the night before. But now they'd have two nights at the same hotel, and Dean had every intention of taking advantage of the privacy. And he didn't need to wait that long to get her worked up.

They were on the bus, eating a late dinner and West was telling them about his new EP album that he was getting ready to publish to iTunes himself.

Dean listened with one ear as he scrolled through his contact list, looking for Sweet Tits.

He got half hard just thinking about how good her breasts had felt in his hands. On his mouth, through the silk of her top. How had he kept his hands off them the night before? He deserved a medal for that.

He found her secret identity and hit new message.

Remember that time in St Louis when I should have licked you until you screamed before the show?

Liana was sitting at the table, working on her laptop. His cock thickened further when she glanced down at her bag. She'd heard the notification.

He flipped over to his email. A lot of messages back and forth, planning a going away party for Sean. He fired off a quick response that he expected to be back in the third week of August, but he'd try to fly home for the party.

No sooner had he hit send, and up popped Liana's response. A question that made his balls ache. **In the... Dressing room?**

God, yes. This was way more fun than talking about publishing music direct to listeners, no offense West. **No, that was Memphis.**

She smothered a laugh.

St Louis was your bedroom on the bus. Actually it was right after your set. Right after Cravings. I followed you back to the bus and told you I wanted all of your sweet wine.

Her eyes went really wide and she stood up. After stretching and giving a big yawn, she tucked her computer —and her burner phone—into her bag. "I'm going to take a power nap."

"We'll be in Memphis in forty-five minutes," Dwayne called out.

"I'm going to do a WhsiperSnip broadcast from the hotel," she explained probably unnecessarily. "So…a rest would be good."

Dean stared at the text message he was writing on his phone. **Rest, good. Yes. You're not getting much sleep tonight.** He waited until her door closed, then he hit send.

Her response came back immediately. **You're dangerous.**

Are you complaining? And by bedroom on the bus, I meant hotel room.

Not complaining. She added a smiley face that made him grin. Was sexting supposed to also make you laugh?

Are you touching yourself?

Should I?

Yes.

Okay. Yes.

I'm going to kick everyone off the bus.

I've stopped.

No, don't stop. I'll pretend to talk to West about his music.

It's really interesting.

Really interesting is what you're doing with your fingers. Tell me.

Can't.

Yes you can.

Fingers busy.

Killing me.

Mmmmmmm.

This was crazy. Reckless. Insane. It also felt completely, utterly right.

"Did we lose you, Dean?"

He did a slow, cool slide of a glance up to meet Jackie's too-innocent face. "Some of the industry stuff goes over my head. I was emailing with my brother."

"Ah." She turned back to West, and Dean clicked back to Liana's latest message. **You should go to your bunk.**

Too obvious. Jackie's watching.

That'll kill the mood.

Nothing kills my mood for you.

Awww.
You don't sound busy.
I want to wait for you.
Killing me in a different way now.
Soon. Forty-five minutes.

— —

THE PROBLEM with a lie is that you inevitably get caught in it.

While Liana had been sexting with Dean, Andrew had tweeted that she would be doing a live WhisperSnip broadcast from her hotel at nine o'clock, and there were now three hundred people expecting her to show up and be funny and sexy and sweet—the last thing she wanted to do right now for anyone other than Dean.

She wanted to be Sweet Tits and get ravished by her bodyguard, but apparently that was the kind of fantasies she couldn't allow herself if she didn't come up with a better cover story.

"Okay," she said weakly as they climbed off the bus.

Dwayne gave her a sympathetic smile. Little did the driver know that it wasn't fatigue talking—she was just being selfish.

"You want to join in the fun?" She teased him.

He surprised her by saying yes, which is how literally everyone from the bus ended up in her room fifteen minutes later.

In the same span of time, Dean sent her five dirty text messages, and one sweet one. **You take such good care of your band. That's hotter than almost anything else.**

Almost anything?

You touching yourself in the back of the bus still wins.

Mostly sweet, anyway.

She tucked her burner phone away in her bag and set up her regular phone on the tripod after signing in to her WhisperSnip account. As soon as her face appeared in the live streaming video, hearts started dancing up the screen.

"Awww, thanks for the love, everyone!" She blew a kiss to the screen.

Usually she prepped for these things, because usually they were planned. Not a freaking lie so she could be alone with dirty text messages.

"Let's do a Q&A tonight," she ad libbed. "I've got the usual crew here, plus Dwayne our driver is making a guest appearance. Those of you who regularly watch these broadcasts will remember him from our first recording on the tour, when I showed you the bus. Say hi, Dwayne!"

She swivelled her phone around and Dwayne waved.

Andrew started laughing from where he was watching on his own phone, volume turned off. "Oh, lots of comments now. They saw Dean."

"Uh oh." She made a face as she spun the camera back to herself. "Oops. That's the guy with the arm from the last video. Ignore him." She looked over at Dean and shrugged apologetically. *Sorry,* she mouthed.

He gave her a slow wink. *It's okay.*

"Okay, what do you guys want to know..." She perused the list popping up. "New music? Yeah, we're working on some stuff on the road. Just rough ideas right now, but I've got a new album in the pipeline. I'm excited."

"Maybe when we're in Nashville..." Andrew trailed off

when she shot him a warning look. "Never mind."

She stuck her tongue out at him. Nobody liked a grumpy star. *Keep it light.* Easier said than done when she just wanted to be done this and kick everyone out of her room. "Ignore him. Andrew's not authorized to leak spoilers."

A chorus of exclamation marks and *SPOILERS??* sailed up the screen in front of her. She suppressed a grin.

Bonus pay for Andrew.

"Okay, how about we do this. We'll go around the room and everyone will say what song they want to hear more of the same of on the next album." She winked at the camera. "And then we'll ask you guys, okay?"

Thumbs up from like a hundred viewers. Awesome.

She started with Dwayne, who stumbled and mumbled and probably expanded his fan base by dozens for being so cute and real. He finally said he liked her first album, and "River Bed Lullaby" was his favourite.

West said "Tailgate Girl" from her third album, the first single, which was a gimme to the fans who'd loved that party anthem. Bonus pay for West.

Jackie wanted to say "Cravings", Liana could tell, but she bit her tongue and agreed with Dwayne that a return to Liana's roots with River Bed Lullaby would be awesome. Off camera, Liana winked at her guitarist, because that wasn't far off-base from what they'd delivered to the label.

Andrew tossed in an agreement with West, he wanted more anthems. Of course he did—they were more fun for the band to play.

She was about to swing the camera back to herself when Dean cleared his throat. Every head in the room swivelled his way.

Andrew looked at his phone. "Everyone wants to know what Arm Guy has to say."

Arm Guy, she mouthed, wiggling her eye brows. He now had an official nickname.

Dean jerked his head, indicating he wanted the camera turned his way.

She bit her lower lip and did as requested. What was he doing?

"Hey," he said, looking straight at her phone. She'd watch this later, from the recorded video feed. She'd watch it a million times because he had the most adorable look on his face, like he couldn't quite believe he was doing this. "So first things first. Not Arm Guy. Come up with a different name for me."

From across the room, Andrew hooted. "Too late. They're already calling themselves Arm Guy's Army."

Dean gave his rapidly growing fan base a stern look that made Liana's nipples whimper. "Guys. No. Not cool. I'm more than my arms."

"CountryGirl52 says Complete Package would also work," West added.

Liana agreed, but she needed to get this broadcast back under control. She laughed. "Enough! Tell us what song you want to hear more like on the next album." *Arm Guy*, she added silently.

"'Cravings'," he said easily. "I hadn't heard it before the tour started, and now it's my favourite song. I'm surprised it wasn't a single."

Heat rushed up her torso, flooding her face.

"Lots of hearts for that idea…Fan4Life just shared a link to a fan video for those that haven't made it to a concert yet," Andrew reported.

She pressed her lips together and spun the camera

around to face her again. All those hearts and comments racing up from the bottom of the screen... She couldn't process, and she told them as much. "I love you guys so much for all the support, thank you! Okay, this seems like a good place to stop tonight. So...I guess go watch that video. Kisses for Fan4Life for sharing that. Wow. Tell me where you are and we'll get you a backstage pass for the nearest concert, deal?"

She flashed the camera a thumbs up, blew them a kiss, and ended the broadcast.

Dean looked around the silent room, then back at her. "Did I say the wrong thing?"

Andrew and West jumped up. Dwayne followed suit.

Jackie was slower. She looked back and forth between Dean and Liana, frowning. "I almost said the same thing."

"I know you did. It's fine," Liana said, patting her friend's shoulder. "I need to talk to Dean alone, though."

They all filed out, and as soon as the door clicked shut, Dean started to apologize.

She held up her hand. "No. Don't. Give me a second."

She needed to compose herself first. She was dangerously close to saying something she might regret.

"Here's the thing," she said when she turned around after pacing across her room and making sure the drapes were fully closed. "I second-guess myself all the time. The inside of my head is like a worry bomb went off. And then someone sprinkled doubt dust all over the rubble. So I play everything safe."

"If I—"

She shook her head. "Let me finish. That was...that was honest. It was the thing that Jackie wanted to say, you heard her admit as much. And it got the response I was secretly hoping for from fans. And I know you heard Jackie and me talking about that—"

"Whoa. Slow down." He got right in front of her and gently pulled her worrying hands apart, quieting them with a gentle press of his own. "I just answered the question. Nothing else."

She beamed at him, unable to hide her true reaction any longer. "But it was exactly the right thing to say. I mean, terrifying, depending on how Track reacts to it. But it was perfect."

He did a double-take. "Perfect?"

"Yes. And terrifying."

"I didn't miss that part. That part was more obvious from the way your band ran out of here like you were going to chew my head off."

"Right. That. I might have given them that impression so I could get you naked and thank you appropriately."

He stared at her like she was insane.

Which she possibly was, but right now wasn't the best time to remind her of that.

"The only other man to know all the mess inside my head looks at me like I'm trash. So if you could maybe not say no—"

He cut her off by pulling her into his arms. His mouth swept against hers, the first brush of a gale force wind, the edge of a storm. His grip stayed tight as he pulled back, his eyes glinting hard and bright as he searched her face. "You wonderful, sneaky woman."

A wave of relief crashed over her. "You like?"

"Yeah. Let's trick them more often." His hands tightened on her back. "Come here."

This time his kiss was more brusque, barely restrained hunger as he tugged up her shirt. She did the same, wanting to feel his skin against hers. Up, up, up, she pushed the fabric, revealing those tight, defined abs she'd petted the other night. His gorgeous midsection led to a broadly planed chest with just a light dusting of blond hair in the middle. Her mouth went dry at the size of him. She'd known he was strong, and tall, but half-naked, he gave Thor a run for his money.

"Look at you," he whispered.

"You stole my line."

He stroked her shoulders and down her arms, finding the waistband of her jeans. Her belly fluttered as he retraced slightly familiar ground—but still new enough it filled her with nerves.

But he'd already touched her. Already told her she was beautiful.

And the way his face was buried between her breasts told her everything she needed to know about how he felt about her. He traced the top curve of her bra with his tongue as he grinned up at her.

It was rough and dirty and perfect. She laughed. "Hi."

"Hi. Can I take this off?"

She nodded and he buried his face in her cleavage as he worked the clasp in the back. When the bra fell away, he replaced the cups with his palms, gently lifting and caressing her swollen flesh with his fingers.

"I want to touch you, too," she whispered.

"Mmmm." He rubbed his face gently against one breast, then the other. "Okay."

But he didn't move. Instead he kissed and rubbed and stroked every inch of her breasts until she was shaking, and then he circled one nipple with the tip of his tongue.

"Dean!"

"Want more?"

"Yes."

He opened his mouth and covered her peak with wet, sucking heat that flooded her already wet panties. Those had to go, they were just getting in the way.

She wrapped her arms around his head. Kind of a terrible way to push him back. Really sending mixed messages there. Except his mouth—oh—and his hands, still, and—oh—"Dean!"

"Yeah, I like it when you say my name," he said, his voice full of gravel after he let go of her with a wet pop.

She took her opportunity and dropped to her knees in front of him.

His eyes darkened and his lips parted as she reached for his fly.

"I think I might like it if you said my name, too." She licked her lips and he groaned.

"Liana…"

"Yes?" She blinked up at him innocently. Just like that. She wanted him growling for her.

"Get back up here."

"I want to see all of you first."

He leaned back on his hands and watched through hooded eyes as she smoothed her hand over the heavy erection pulsing beneath the denim. "Take him out, if you insist."

Heart pounding in her chest, she did just that, slowing unzipping and folding back the denim, then tracing her fingers over the thick ridge that popped out, pushing his black cotton boxers up into a tent.

She leaned in closer, lips parted.

Dean's hand tangled in her hair. Not stopping her, exactly. Just slowing her down. "Hey. You first."

She shook her head.

"Liana."

She ignored him and kissed the tip of him through the fabric. He smelled clean and masculine, and she wanted to bury her face right there, but she couldn't, because she was flying through the air.

"Okay, that's a mean trick," she gasped as he crawled on top of her, now that she was flat on her back on the bed.

"You weren't listening. Sometimes I just take action." He grinned down at her and flicked open the button on her jeans. She breathed roughly as he slipped his hand inside, his gaze slipping out of focus as he groaned with her. "Yeah. I've missed you."

"I've been right in front of you."

"And untouchable."

"I know." She wasn't sure how they were going to last the rest of the tour.

He dipped his head and kissed her chest, her sternum, her belly as he worked his way down her body.

Her jeans went flying, and with them went her worries as he peeled open her legs and kissed her where she was sticky and wet for him.

It helped that he kept telling her how much he liked her, and when he climbed back up her body he had a couple of condoms in his hand.

"For later," he whispered as he shucked his own jeans and settled between her legs to kiss her.

"Why later?"

He grinned. "Because I want to do this for a while."

Then he covered her mouth with his and chased her thoughts off to the same place her worries had fled.

— —

DEAN WAS TOTALLY LYING. He'd wanted to be buried balls deep in Liana since the second she'd given him the green light, but he also wanted her to be completely into it, and she had so many thoughts racing around in her head that needed to be turned off before it was truly just the two of them in the bed.

It was a strange and unfamiliar place for his head to be at, too, and that might be part of his reasoning for going slow tonight. He normally didn't care if his partner was distracted by work or anything else. As long as everyone had a good time, got to come at least once, and left happy and cool with doing it again, he called it a win.

The stakes were higher with Liana.

Way higher.

Scary high, and he was ninety percent sure he couldn't meet them. He wasn't going to fuck it up on the first night together, though.

She was the most beautiful woman he'd ever had in his arms. Her confidence on stage, with her fans, her band…it was incredible. But here? He could still taste her fear.

"Tell me what you want," he murmured against her lips.

"Everything." She pressed against him. "And that means you need to be all the way naked."

"Help me, then." He kept kissing her while she shoved his boxer briefs down his hips. His dick popped into her hand, happy as a puppy to finally be given a rub on the head.

Simple bastard.

It wasn't that easy.

Except now that they were tangled together, maybe it

was. Liana's eyes sparkled as they kissed and caressed each other.

"Grab me one of those condoms," he said quietly, not wanting to break the moment. She arched her back, brushing those gorgeous pink nipples against his chest, and he played with them lazily, his fingertips circling the pebbled flesh as she ripped the foil open.

"Here," she said.

"You do it."

She grinned. "You're really into this group effort thing."

"I just like any excuse for you to touch me." He hissed in a breath as she sheathed him, then lifted her top leg and draped it over his hip. "And I'll take any chance to touch you, too. You turn me on, Liana. God. So much."

He reached between them and slid his fingers through her wetness. She rocked her hips toward him and he met her in the middle.

His forehead pressed against hers as they found each other, her folds parting around him as he fitted himself against her and pressed inside.

Her lips parted in a wordless gasp as he stretched her out, and he groaned at how good it felt. "You're perfect," he growled. "So tight. Hot. Uhhhhh…"

Her breath hitched as she slid her arms around his neck. "Dean…"

"I've got you."

"More." She swallowed a gasp as he pulsed inside her. "Yes. That."

He pumped his hips, slow and smooth, until she was moving with him, and then he planted one hand at the top of her ass, holding them together as he rolled her onto her back.

They came together as one, their hips surging in choreography that just clicked. Her thighs climbed up his body, wrapping around his waist as he braced his arms on either side of her and pushed in, again and again.

Each time he sank into her body, he wanted to curse and growl at how good it felt. But it went beyond the physical heat and pull of her. It had a lot to do with the way she was looking up at him, at the sounds she made and the way she held on to him, like this was incredible for her, too.

Like maybe she'd never known it to feel like this before. As if all the unbelievable feelings of their bodies working together was just the start of it. He laughed a little at that, but he held her gaze as the shaky chuckle worked its way through his body, and she nodded. *Me too.*

Her hands moved restlessly over the hotel bedspread. Her fingers were wiggling, and he reached for them with one hand, then the other. They were connected nearly everywhere they possibly could be, and it still wasn't enough.

He drove deeper into her, needing to hear her scream as his need started to curl hard inside him, pulling his balls up tight to his body.

"Come on, Liana," he bit out. "Come for me."

"Kiss me," she breathed. "Kiss me and I'll come."

With a desperate grunt, he fused his mouth to hers and plunged his tongue inside her. It wasn't sweet or elegant. It was rough and dirty and so needy it would embarrass him later.

But as he filled her body and her mouth and held her down, she cried out for him, chanting his name as she spasmed around his cock and then beneath his body. Her climax started deep inside her and spiralled through her entire body, and he felt it everywhere he touched her.

The answering release burst out of him almost by surprise, and he slammed one last time into her as he came hard and fast.

His vision blacked out at the edges and his thighs seized up, and he held himself over her, telling himself there was no way in hell he could just collapse onto her.

Not cool to crush the woman who'd just blown his mind.

Not cool at all.

She didn't get that memo. She kissed his neck and tightened her grip on him, pulling him down, then pushing him to the side. He grabbed the condom as she slipped off him, and gave himself a count of ten before he forced himself to go deal with that.

He ended up taking fifteen seconds—and only six to get rid of it.

Six seconds of not holding her he'd never get back.

Fuck.

His heart was pounding a mile a minute as she settled against his chest. "That was really, really nice," she murmured. Her eyes were already closed.

He already wanted her again. He wanted her tomorrow and the next day.

This was a strange and uncomfortable feeling, how much he wanted her, because he'd made it his life mission not to want anything that he couldn't afford to lose.

Somehow when he hadn't been looking, Liana had slipped under his radar.

And he was terrified that he was going to lose her before he was ready. That he might not ever be ready for that goodbye.

CHAPTER EIGHTEEN

LIANA WOKE UP WITH A HEAVY, warm man wrapped around her.

It was still dark out. She turned her head, looking for the clock. Just a little after midnight. They hadn't been asleep long.

"You awake?"

Maybe it was just her that had drifted off. "I am."

"Good." He kissed her shoulder and pressed his erection against her bottom.

"Hello there," she whispered.

"You sore? I'll be gentle." His hand shifted from stroking the flat of her belly up to cup her breast possessively.

Warmth bloomed low inside her. Not too sore. "Gentle sounds perfect."

"Shower sex?" He kissed her neck softly. "Or I can be gentle right here, too."

Definitely not too sore. "Maybe back here for round three?"

"God. Yes. You are…" He rolled her onto her back and

kissed her hard on the mouth. When he pulled back, his eyes were glittering and bright. "You are perfect. In absolutely every way."

She rolled her eyes and pointed to the bathroom. "Go start the shower."

It turned out rounds two and three both happened in the bathroom, once on the counter and the other with her pressed up against the tiles as he took her from behind.

Neither was particularly gentle.

She couldn't stop grinning.

"Are you going to send me back to my room tonight?" he asked as they crawled back into bed.

"Not if you don't want to go," she whispered. It had been a year since she'd slept the night with anyone. If Dean was offering, she'd grab that with both hands.

"I'll be careful leaving in the morning. I'll set my alarm." His voice was extra gruff and she cupped his cheek, making him look at her.

"It's not that I wouldn't want people to know…in general."

"I know."

"I mean, you're Arm Guy. You're three accidental WhisperSnip sightings away from a cult following. I should be so lucky to date Arm Guy."

He grinned. "That name is sticking, isn't it?"

"Like glue, I'm afraid." She squeezed his corded, thick forearm. "I don't think you understand just how hot your arms are."

He flexed and she groaned. He gave her a curious look. "Arm Guy does it for you?"

"Really does. So hot." She got a shrug at that, and he lay down, stretching those magnificent arms wide across the bed. Rolling onto her stomach, she snuggled up.

"Maybe me and my arms can take you out for dinner in Nashville."

Dinner sounded like a dream. "I'd like that."

"Can you do that? Go out for dinner?"

"Yeah. I mean it's possible I might get recognized, but most of the places I go are only frequented by locals, and to them, I'm just another musician."

"Little bit of ordinary?"

She smiled. "Yep."

"Good." He kissed her head. "I'm glad you'll be going back to that when this is over. I'll worry about you."

"Angling for a longer bodyguard job?" she teased, but he bristled. Shit. "Wait, I take that back. Delete, delete, delete."

"It's fine."

"I didn't mean it like it's an employer-employee thing."

"That wasn't how I took it."

She frowned, trying to figure out what then— "Oh. You wouldn't be around for a longer job."

He didn't answer right away, and when he did, his words were slow and careful. "It's not that I'm not, necessarily, but I wasn't planning to be away from home that long. Do you think you'll need security after the tour?"

Ah. "No. Just...let's pretend that conversation didn't happen."

"I can't do that." He tightened his grip on her. "Tell me more about the album stuff. With Track. I don't like that he has that power over you."

God, her and her big mouth. "That's nothing. It's that mental game, like with running. I can do anything for an hour. Two. Three. Four. You know? As the long run training stretches out. Even when it feels impossible, I know I've done it before. And then I hang in there and lo and behold, I survive."

"I wish life was more than just surviving for you."

"Oh, of course it is. I'm blessed, Dean. You've just seen me at my worst. But I'm so, so lucky."

"You love singing." It wasn't a question. He'd seen how it transformed her, but it also terrified her, and he'd seen that, too.

She nodded. "I really do."

"You were young when you made your first album, right?"

"Eighteen." She shook her head. "Hard to believe. And that's why I'm in the position I'm in now. It pains me to think of how young I was and I was signing contracts that would dictate the next twelve years of my life."

"And now you're nearly at the end of that."

"I am."

"Is that…exciting? Scary?"

"Both. But other than choosing a different producer, a different label, reading contracts more closely… not much else will change. It's still kind of isolating, no matter how big you get. Maybe even more isolating the bigger you get."

"It's a bizarre life, in a way, right? I can already see that, although you're really grounded with the crew and your band."

"Yeah. But it makes me really value moments like this, you know? Like, I know how special this is right now with you. It's private and real. And I don't mean sex, but talking. I don't need to hedge what I'm saying at all. I get this with you, I get it with Hope…a little bit with Jackie, but even then, I'm her boss. You know? I pay her. So I have to be on and positive and I can't show her how weak I am."

"No. You're the strongest person I've ever met."

She laughed. "Your brother is literally going to war, right?"

"Bah. That's standard fare for Fosters."

"Have you ever been overseas?"

He shook his head. "Never got a chance to go on a tour. Couldn't get the time off work. Might now that I've left the police force, but there aren't that many open spots for reservist Warrant Officers. I've been promoted out of the ranks that usually get sent on tour."

She traced an imaginary circle on his shoulder, then filled it with a kiss. "I think your army talk is as foreign to me as music talk is to you."

"We'll have to teach each other."

When would they do that? Suddenly the end of the tour felt around the corner. She pushed that away. It didn't matter. They had this, they had tonight. Another circle. Another kiss. "Okay."

She curled into his side. She expected to be the one to stay awake this time, but he stroked her hair and, before she could stress about not getting enough sleep, she drifted off.

When she woke up the second time, it was dawn.

Dean was dressed, and bent over her. His lips brushed hers again. Oh.

She smiled. "A wake-up kiss?"

"A wake-up-and-go-back-to-sleep kiss. I'm sneaking out."

"Bring me coffee in a few hours?"

"Of course."

She poked her hand out from under the covers and wrapped her fingers around his hand, planted on the bed beside her. "Thank you for last night."

"Our secret," he murmured with a smile.

She touched her fingers to her lips as he quietly strode to the door, checked the peephole, and slipped into the hall.

— —

DEAN HIT THE GYM, then found a Starbucks and…

He pulled out his phone. **Embarrassing fact: I don't know what kind of coffee to get you from Starbucks.**

Skinny hazelnut latte.

He made a face and ordered it along with a black drip coffee for himself.

He wanted them to have the morning alone together, but he knew that was a pipe dream, so when he saw West and Andrew in the lobby, he lifted the coffees in the air. Hiding in plain sight, as she'd said. "Morning. Going to wake up Liana."

They were on their way out to a diner they always hit when they were in town. Two down.

But he didn't see anyone else from the tour until he got to her room—and he was glad he'd just knocked politely instead of using the key in his pocket, because when the door swung open, Jackie was on the other side.

He handed Liana her latte and held out his drip coffee to the guitarist. "It's black, but it's yours if you want it."

She shook her head. "I'm good. I'm heading down there myself shortly, I was just giving Liana the heads up."

"That's why I told you to come up to my room," Liana

said, drawing out the words as she made deliberate eye contact with him.

Uh oh. "Okay. I'm here."

"So it seems some industrious fans got to work and Arm Guy has now been identified."

"They figured out my name?"

"Name, company, that I'm your first client they're pretty sure, and the fact you have never been married."

He burst out laughing. "Seriously?"

"There are also photos."

"Of what?"

"You." That's the kind of ominous statement that usually preceded someone being shown embarrassing pictures. A nude photo shoot from way back or a grainy still of a drug deal.

Dean didn't have anything like that in his past, so he frowned. Unless there were cameras here in the hotel room last night, he didn't have anything to hide.

She handed him her phone. And sure enough, there he was.

The photos weren't embarrassing.

Walking behind Liana. Walking in front of her. Carrying her bag into the arena.

Pressing his hand against the small of her back—or at least, that's what it looked like in the photo.

He was pretty sure he hadn't actually touched her in that moment. He could feel the brush of her t-shirt whispering against his palm, but he'd held back from actually touching the firm muscles along her spine.

No, they weren't embarrassing, but they were damn revealing.

So much good that restraint had done him. The way he felt about her was written all over his face.

He slowly lifted his gaze to her face. "Liana…"

She lifted one delicate shoulder, her dark waves tumbling down her back. "I know, right? This changes things."

"I…"

"Don't worry about it. I mean, I know you don't. But don't think that *I'm* worried about it. I'm not. It might actually be fun to see people spin over this, if you can handle it."

"Fun?" He wasn't following the conversation. Maybe she hadn't seen the same thing in the photos he had.

"You're the tour hottie." She wrinkled her nose. "I'm sorry about that, of course, but it's quite a brilliant move, really."

He didn't want to be a *hottie* for anyone other than her. "And if that shifts into a rumour that you're having an affair with your bodyguard?"

"They won't get that from the pictures."

He snorted. In his peripheral vision, Jackie winced.

Liana swivelled her head back and forth between them. "Really? He's just walking behind me."

Jackie pressed her lips together and shook her head. "I dunno. I'm heading over to the arena. You got anything on the schedule today?"

Liana looked at her phone. "A radio call-in at noon. That's it."

"All right. Good luck."

Dean watched, suddenly furious with himself, as Jackie left them alone.

Liana crawled across the bed and held out her hands for him.

This was a bad idea. He still took her into his arms and let her kiss him. God, she smelled good. He breathed her in, a rough inhale followed by an even rougher exhale.

He hadn't seen this coming, because he was an amateur.

"What's wrong?"

"You need a professional security team."

She laughed gently. "You are a professional."

"You need people that understand the industry."

"You don't think they'll get the same treatment from fans and the media?"

"I have no idea what they'll get." His skin crawled with the reminder of all that he didn't understand. "I need to talk to Zander."

She frowned at him. "Okay. But you can talk to me, too."

Clearly he couldn't. "You don't think this is a big deal."

"Because it's not!"

"Time will tell, won't it?" He was getting madder now. Not at her, but just in general. He paced away from her, turning so she didn't see the look on his face.

— —

LIANA COULDN'T BELIEVE her ears. "You're overreacting."

"Maybe." But when he turned back, there was a weird tightness to his jaw, and his eyes—normally bottomless pools of calm—were dark and stormy.

"What is this really about?"

"I need to go." He took a deep breath, avoiding her

gaze. "Text me if you need to go somewhere unexpectedly. Otherwise I'll be back at the next timing on the itinerary."

She bit back her retort, because she needed to think this through before pushing him for something he clearly was having second thoughts about.

A day effing late, buddy.

Instead she just shook her head. "Okay."

He sighed.

Yeah, she'd said it in the way that clearly meant it was *not* okay, but he was being ridiculous. And it wasn't okay. But it was still his not-okay call to make. "I'll see you later?"

He just nodded and walked slowly to the door, still wound tighter than her grandma's curlers.

Men.

She grabbed her phone and called Hope. As she waited for her best friend to answer, she took a sip of the coffee he'd brought her.

Stupid men.

And that's how she opened the conversation as soon as Hope answered. "Why do men suck so much?"

"Umm…I don't know."

"Ryan isn't stupid?"

"Not generally, no."

"Damn it."

"What happened?"

Liana scowled and took a sip of her coffee. "I slept with Dean."

"Ah. Well, they can't all be great."

"No! He was—" She stopped herself. "That's not the problem. That's the backstory."

"Oh. So he was…"

Incredible. Right up until she proved to be too complicated, too public, too much. "There were some pretty innocuous pictures of us printed this morning. Just him walking beside me, but I sort of outed him as part of my entourage last night, and now it's a thing and he's pissed."

"Oh. Shoot." Hope's voice immediately went from teasing to understanding. "Yeah, that would be hard for Ryan, too. These Pine Harbour guys are private. I'm sure if you just talk about it, he'll come around to understanding that's just the industry."

"I tried that! He stormed out."

"Well, maybe it'll take him more than a New York minute to get used to the idea of sleeping with a celebrity." Hope hesitated, then softened her voice even further. "Or maybe it's not meant to be."

That hurt, right in Liana's chest. A red-hot, stabbing poker kind of hurt. Was Dean just yet another short-lived affair?

Was that all she got, forever and ever?

That's what you let him think you wanted. Well she'd lied.

To herself, to him…

Damn it. She blinked away a suspicious wetness from her eyes because no, she wasn't crying. Not over a guy she'd just kissed a few times and slept with once.

She wasn't that kind of girl anymore.

"Liana?"

"Yeah." God, her voice sounded small.

"Oh, sweetie."

Shit, now she was actually crying. "It's fine," she said through a sniffle.

"It's not. Damn it, I'll kill him."

"It's not his fault."

"You really like him."

"I do," she sobbed. "And I told him it was no big deal.

I told myself I wouldn't try to complicate this with feelings."

"Well that was stupid. Everyone has feelings."

"I just wanted it to be simple."

"Love rarely is."

"I didn't say anything about love," she snapped, and Hope laughed gently.

"I know. But liking someone…that's really just a test run, isn't it? To see if it might grow into more?"

"But we know better than to think…" She trailed off. Except Hope had found true love. And it had been rocky as hell. "What made you take a chance on Ryan?"

Hope didn't answer right away, and Liana pressed the phone closer to her ear. So hard it hurt, but she needed to hear the answer—if it was the answer she thought it might be. "Because when I looked at him, and when he looked at me, the world felt lighter. I'd been alone for so long, and he'd been through so much, but we could be a refuge for each other. Does that make sense?"

Liana nodded before remembering Hope couldn't see her. "Yeah."

"Doesn't mean it was easy."

Another useless nod. "Right."

Liana didn't know all the details, but she knew that after Hope had fallen in love with Ryan, she'd left Pine Harbour for a period of time. If you love someone, set them free… And it wasn't until she returned that they finally admitted just how much they needed each other.

But Liana didn't need Dean.

This wasn't like that.

She didn't need anyone. She shoved the tears off her face with the heel of her hand. "I gotta go."

"Don't do anything rash," Hope said. "Give him time.

These men…they're so independent, so tough, but they're bred to be fearless. And that's stupid, because we all have fears. Give him time to wrap his head around whatever's going on, and I bet he'll come back to you. He's a good guy."

He was.

And she wouldn't do anything rash.

Not yet.

CHAPTER NINETEEN

HER SHOW that night was incredible.

Raw and bittersweet, but from the tweets Dean was following, people were calling it her best set yet.

It blew his mind that there were people out there in the crowd who'd followed the tour for the entire leg. Bought tickets to show after show, some to blog about it, some because they were die-hard fans.

But those people knew her better than anyone, really, and they knew there was something different tonight.

Because he was an ass.

She hadn't looked at him since he'd left her room that morning. The band all knew she was pissed at him, and at least Jackie had figured out why, so she wasn't talking to him, either.

He'd talked to Zander after he left Liana's room and got an ass-kicking he rightly deserved. But Zander's simple instructions— "Make it right, you idiot. And learn some social media basics this afternoon, for the love of all that is holy"—were easier given than followed.

Before West had clued in that Liana was mad at Dean,

he'd been more than willing to help. So now Dean had Twitter, Instagram and Facebook apps on his phone, and followed Liana from all of those places.

He wasn't a complete moron—none of the three accounts had similar information on them, so he hopefully wouldn't be found out as Arm Guy. They were generic accounts, totally locked down, and disconnected from his personal details in every way.

He felt like a stalker, but a stalker with more social media context than he had a day before, so the creepy factor would have to stay for a bit.

From where he stood in the wings, he watched her performance and Twitter, back and forth. For the live, in-the-moment stalking, Twitter was where it was at, he'd decided. Although the Instagram pictures of her...

Jeez, she was gorgeous.

He'd had her in his arms for what felt like a nanosecond. Not nearly long enough.

And he'd let her go at the first hiccup.

Well, he hadn't let her go, exactly. He'd just stepped back.

They'd reconnect after a cooling off period. He'd done this rodeo enough times to know that a little break was often a good thing. Usually his relationships didn't burn this hot, this fast, but all the lessons he'd learned over the years still applied.

Distance and boundaries. That's what they needed. So when it ended, neither of them got hurt.

He thought about what Liana had told him about getting over Track. He'd never had a breakup like that.

But then again, nobody else had ever turned him into a creepy stalker, either. And distance...who was he kidding?

Not himself. He wasn't that obtuse. The only reason

they had distance between them right now was because he'd pissed off Liana. She had him at arm's-length because he'd bruised her trust in him. If she gave him another chance, he'd be whatever she wanted.

As the lights came down on her first of two sold-out shows in Memphis, the crowd roared, and he stepped into the shadows.

When she came off the stage, she waved down Brad, the tour manager. Dean couldn't make out what she was telling him, but once they talked, she turned to her band and had a quick conversation with them while Brad started talking rapidly into his radio headset.

The band went back on stage, and a song that Dean had only heard once before started playing. It was a party anthem she'd covered on her third album, and usually she didn't do covers in her concerts.

"Deep Ain't It All Cracked Up To Be" was a snarly, mocking call-to-arms for women not to give a fuck about what was expected of them. In life, and in relationships.

Well, damn.

— —

DAMN, but Liana felt good belting out that cover. Her legs burned from dancing in heels for the last two hours, she was sure that her t-shirt was sticky and gross by now, but under the lights and in front of thousands of people who just wanted to see her sing, she felt like the queen Dean had told her she was just the day before.

As she hit the last high note and slowly waved good

night to Memphis, she pulled all the love from the arena right to her chest and rubbed it against her skin. "Good night," she whispered into the mic, smiling as they gave her one last deafening round of applause.

Yes. Thank you. Yes. She dropped to her knees as the lights cut out, and waved off West when he came forward to help her. She was fine.

Wiped.

Completely exhausted. But totally happy with how that had gone.

She'd practically bled for them, and they'd eaten it up.

Dean's kisses had spurred her to some excellent performances. Then she'd struggled, and he'd been a rock that she'd desperately wanted, too.

But tonight?

Tonight she'd reminded herself of something incredibly important. She didn't need him. She just needed herself—open and vulnerable, as scary as that was. She needed to feel.

She didn't need a rock. A rock was great for hiding behind. But nothing spectacular happened from the shadows.

She pushed herself up and gave Jackie a high-five as a roadie stripped her of her mic and her in-ear monitor.

"You up for meeting some fans?" Brad asked as she strode off stage.

Dean was standing near the exit to the backstage hallway. She caught his gaze for a second, then nodded to her tour manager. "Yes, definitely. Just need to change."

She swept into the hallway, Dean falling into step behind her. They didn't exchange any words, and when she got to her dressing room, he took up station outside without saying anything.

Inside, she leaned back against the door and closed her eyes.

Staying strong was easier said than done. She wanted to shake him. She might not need him for anything, but she still wanted him.

She rubbed her hand against her chest. Ew. Sticky.

A shower helped. Instead of doing her hair again, she towel-dried it and did a quick braid. Light makeup, new clothes, and she was ready to meet some fans.

Dean was right where she'd left him.

"Ready?" he asked gruffly, and she nodded.

The shower had washed away some of her righteous indignation, too, so she gave him a gentle smile. "Let's do this."

It wasn't a full-on after party, but there were a bunch of VIP backstage pass holders, so the arena staff had put out snacks and Coke.

One wall was covered in step and repeat banner, her name scrawled across it, and Brad pointed her to a spot two-thirds of the way down the wall. Dean moved off to the side, watching as the fans took turns having pictures taken with her.

She tried to ignore him, and at first it was easier, but about halfway through the line, one young girl kept sneaking looks over at him, and after she reached Liana and they had a quick hug and a nice photo, she hesitated.

"What is it, sweetie?" Liana asked, already knowing the answer.

"Is that Arm Guy?"

She raised her eyebrows anyway. "It is! You want to meet him?" Ha. Take that, Dean. But she wouldn't push it too far. "No pictures, though, okay?"

"Okay," the girl whispered.

Oh, honey. No forearms were worth that level of excitement. Not even when they were attached to someone as awesome as Dean. Because even someone as awesome as Dean was fallible and human, and the forearms totally distracted girls of all ages from that reality.

She caught his attention and beckoned him over.

"This is Dean, part of my security team." She smiled sweetly as she shifted her attention to the new celebrity. "Arm Guy, this is Kaylie. She's a big fan."

To his credit, he didn't even blink. "Nice to meet you, Kaylie." He held out his hand, and when she giggled, he extended his arm and she slid in next to him for a half-hug. "You can call me Dean."

"Okay," the girl giggled.

"Do you want a picture?" he offered gruffly, and Liana's heart squeezed.

"Umm…Liana said they weren't allowed." But oh, Kaylie's eyes were begging that yes, she very much did want a photo together.

"Well, that was very nice of her," he said, sliding his gaze Liana's way for a split second. "But I think for you, we can make an exception."

"Okay. Wow. Thank you." They rearranged so Kaylie was in the middle, and took a picture of the three of them. Then Dean stepped out of the way so Liana could carry on with the photos, and Kaylie followed.

Another fan moved over to talk to Dean as the tail end of the group wrapped up with Liana, and when she was done, he was still deep in conversation with that woman and her husband, Kaylie long gone.

She smiled to herself and went to find a plate of veggies and dip.

"That was interesting," Jackie said as she came up behind her.

Liana turned and shrugged. "I don't know what you mean."

"The looks are back. So you guys had a fight for what, twelve hours?"

"It wasn't a fight exactly."

"What was it?"

She took a deep breath. "Regret, I think."

"Ah. Well, I know all about that."

Liana winced. "Still not talking to Andrew?"

"Not talking to you about it, either."

"But you came over to *me*," she laughed.

"Yeah. To talk about you and Dean. You weren't clever enough to keep it a secret."

"We thought we were."

Jackie shrugged. "He's good for you, though. Like in a not-secret way."

"Oh, no. Regret, remember? He's not like that."

She was starting to think that very few men were the forever kind of guys.

Besides, she didn't want one of those. She had a forever kind of career, and fantastic shoes. A really nice house with a big walk-in closet. She was good.

"Mm-hmm." Jackie twisted around, facing Liana as Dean excused himself and headed their way. "Sure thing. Whatever. Anyway, I'm heading back to my room to text Andrew an invitation for angry sex. That's your little gimme of sharing. In return, I expect you to talk things out with the super nice hottie who can't stop looking at you. Deal? Good. Deal."

And then she was gone, and he was in front of her.

"Hey."

"I'm ready to head back to the hotel," she said.

"Want to do a final spin around the room and say goodbye to anyone?"

Yes, yes she did. "You learn quickly."

He shrugged. "Sometimes."

He trailed behind her as she made her goodbyes, and when they stepped outside, there was a car waiting for them. He held the door, waiting for her to get settled before he went around to the other side.

They didn't talk on the way back to the hotel.

When they arrived, he followed her silently to her room. She didn't open the door. He wasn't getting an invite tonight.

He leaned his shoulder against the wall. Not going anywhere, but not expecting to come inside, either. Good. She crossed her arms in front of her body and he groaned.

"Hey," he said, holding out his hand. A formal peace offering. "I'm sorry."

"For what?"

"For overreacting."

She gave him a small smile and took his hand, shaking it solemnly. "Good."

But she wanted more, now. She wanted an opening to tell him how she felt.

They stood there, her hand in his, for a long enough beat that her heart started to ache, and then he pulled her closer. She almost resisted the tug, but that would be foolish. She wanted a hug more than anything else, and she let herself relax against his chest.

He smoothed his hand over her hair.

"You deserve way better than a guy like me," he said roughly. The rawness of his words and the matching burn in his eyes made her throat close tight.

Why on Earth would he think that? She shook her head. "That's a stupid cliche. I deserve to be happy. To not have a guy throw barriers in my path to finding my own happiness."

"Pretty sure I failed on that front today."

"Yeah, you did." She sighed. *No kisses for you tonight, mister,* she thought to herself. "But just today. And it's just a stumbling block because…"

Because we didn't see these big feelings coming.

Because we're human and scared.

Because there's a time limit here and we haven't talked about that.

"Because I want to make you happy."

Oh. That was a pretty good answer. She swallowed. "You do?"

"So much it scares me."

Even better. Good that they were scared together. "I know the feeling."

"But I really don't think—"

At the end of the hall, the elevator dinged. She pulled back and got out her room key. She didn't need to say anything for him to understand the conversation was over.

He waited a beat, then nodded. "Good night. I hope you sleep well."

She let herself into her room, once again closing him out on the other side of the door. That didn't feel right in the least, but she'd let him twist in it tonight. There was always tomorrow.

— —

DEAN SLEPT LIKE TOTAL SHIT. His eyelids felt like sandpaper when he finally gave up pretending he was going to get any more rest and wrenched himself out of bed at half past five. He threw on his shoes and zipped his phone into a pocket in his running shoes, then hit the street. Dawn was just cracking over the horizon as he headed away from the hotel. He ran until the light changed, then turned around and pushed himself harder on the way back.

He walked up the six flights to his floor to cool down, but stopped short as soon as he stepped out of the stairwell.

Liana was approaching his room from the other direction.

She stopped, too.

"Morning," he said, wiping sweat off his brow.

She started walking again, meeting him at his door.

He pushed the card into the slot. It lit up green and beeped, the sound loud in the early morning quiet of the muffled, carpeted hallway. Equally loud were his breathing and his heartbeat. He wasn't ready for this, whatever it was. "You're supposed to text me when you leave your room."

She held up her phone, an unsent text message on the screen. **I'm coming to your room.** "I didn't send it because I was afraid you might duck out if I did."

"I wouldn't do that."

"I hoped not, but…"

"What are you doing here?" He was being rude, but he was scrambling to catch up.

"I should have invited you in last night."

"No. We needed some space."

She moved deeper into his room. He stayed near the door. He needed to hop in the shower before they talked.

Liana didn't notice. She turned, her fingers twisting in the soft cotton of her t-shirt. "I dreamed about you last night," she said softly. "About your hands and your mouth. I missed you."

Jesus. His mouth went dry. "I—"

She waited.

He didn't say anything more. He couldn't.

She moved closer again. He took in her yoga pants and t-shirt. Bare face and loosely twisted hair.

"I need a shower."

"I could scrub your back."

So. Damn. Tempting. "Give me two minutes."

"If you take more than three, I'm coming in there."

He wouldn't. He threw himself under the spray when it was still cold and did the world's fastest once over with shampoo from head to toe.

When he re-entered the main room, a towel slung low around his waist, she was curled up in the chair beside the window.

She gave him a lopsided smile. "I like the towel."

He stopped a few paces from her. "Should I get dressed?"

She shook her head. "If this goes as I plan, we can go back to bed together for a few hours."

His dick pressed against the cotton terrycloth at that promise. He told himself to settle down. There was a solid chance this wouldn't go according to her plan. "Maybe I should dress anyway."

"Or maybe you should take off the towel completely." Her eyes danced as she slowly, languidly unfolded herself from the chair and reached her hand for his. "Come on."

He let her lead him to the bed. They lay side-by-side, facing each other, hands tangled in between their bodies.

"I like you." Her eyes sparkled, brave and bright. "In a too-much, too-soon kind of way. It's really scary. But I want you to know that."

He nodded slowly. "I like you, too. So much. But I've got a pretty shitty track record with relationships."

"Me, too."

He shook his head. He couldn't let her think it was the same. "No. You've been burned. This is different."

She gave him a too-knowing look. "You've always been the one to break it off."

"No." God, he was way too underdressed for this kind of admission. "That would be better some ways, maybe."

"Dean." She said his name lightly, but there was a new strength in her voice.

He made himself look her right in the eye, and hold his gaze there.

She lifted her eyebrows and gave him a gentle glare. "Fatalists forever, right? I know you don't trust relationships. That's not a big surprise to me, I promise."

"And yet when I tell you that I'm not good enough for you, you ignore me."

"Because I still want you. Flawed and likely to push me away at some point. I. Still. Want. You."

He had trouble wrapping his head around that, because his track record almost guaranteed they'd crash and burn. That he'd let them, maybe even passively engineer it, and he didn't want to do that to her. He didn't want to hurt her out of some misguided fear of commitment.

"It's okay, you know. I'm not going into this blind. I know we come from two different places. I know that you can't let yourself want too much." The softness in her voice just about killed him.

And she was so, so wrong. He tried to be equally gentle, but it was hard, because that wasn't his nature. "You don't think I want you?" He took a deep breath. "I want you so much it hurts. I want you in ways I don't understand, because you're not my type."

"Gee, thanks." She stuck her tongue out at him.

"The type I allow myself." He scrubbed his face with his hands. "Because the truth is, I like everything about you. Everything. And that scares the shit out of me."

"That's the nicest sideways compliment anyone has ever given me."

"It wasn't meant to be…let me start again."

She shook her head. "You don't need to. I get it." She paused. "You never let anyone get this close to you?"

He shook his head. It was kind of an idiotic thing for a grown man to admit to, but she deserved the truth.

"So all your relationships…"

He finally voiced what he'd danced around before. "I've waited for them to fall apart. Encouraged them to die a natural death, maybe. And you deserve a guy who will fight for you. I'm not that guy."

"Trust me, fighting tooth and nail doesn't work either." She kept looking at him, steady-like, as if he hadn't just said he wouldn't fight for her. Or maybe like she'd heard him and opted not to believe him, which took a crazy level of faith he didn't have in himself, and he told her as much.

She just shrugged. "But if you figure out what you want, you won't let it get away. You've told me about how that is in every other facet of your life. It just hasn't happened in love yet. And maybe it won't. But I'm not afraid of…" She trailed off. *Loving you.* Maybe that was the end of that sentence. Or maybe it was something simpler. Wanting you. Giving it a go. Those were more likely.

But even if it was love she was hinting around, that didn't scare him as much as he thought it would.

If you figure out what you want, you won't let it get away.

He wanted her that much. He wanted her with every cell in his body.

They lay there for a moment, and then she glanced away. "Can I tell you something else?"

His voice was hoarse when he finally remembered to answer. "Anything."

"I had a bit of revelation last night. It was an emotional show, you know, because I was strung tight from the night before and yesterday morning. And I've always run scared from those big emotions. That's what happened in Savannah, the night before I flew up to see Hope. The night before I met you." She slid her fingers through his, pressing her finger tips against the blanket beneath them. He watched as she flexed her hand, then pulled it free of his so she could rub her knuckles with her thumb.

"May I?" He touched her gently and she nodded.

He rubbed her fingers, rolling the skin gently as he massaged up and down each digit, and slowly she continued. "In Savannah, my fear got the better of me. And maybe last night wasn't fear, but it was still a lot of big emotions, and I didn't let the wave pull me under. I didn't mean to, but I feel like I crested it, instead. And it was so powerful." A tear popped out of the corner of her eye, just one, and she didn't stop talking. He watched as it rolled down her cheek and plopped onto the pillow. The whole while she kept talking in an awe-filled voice. "I've always been so scared to give up that control. To really let go. And I didn't need to be scared of it, you know? Because there's magic there, in the places we get pushed."

"Yeah." He wouldn't have put it like that. But now that

she had, damn but it made sense. "Control is a big deal for me, too. I don't know what it feels like to let go."

She re-focused on his face, her eyes soft. "Maybe I can help you with that."

"You think so?"

She walked her fingers across the bedspread until she was close enough to touch his bare chest. "I know so."

"How are you gonna do that?"

"First, I'm going to get you out of that towel. And you're not going to move a muscle until I say so."

"That wasn't what I meant."

"Too bad." She pushed him onto his back and stroked her hands down his chest. Under her touch, his muscles tensed, a faint tremor whispering that she had him. "And after tonight's show, I'm going to take you to Nashville, and show you where I come from."

"Oh yeah?"

"Yeah."

"I can't wait." And damned if that wasn't the truth.

"For Nashville?"

"For all of it."

CHAPTER TWENTY

"WHEN YOU SAID you were going to show me where you came from, a hole-in-the-wall bar was not exactly what I pictured," Dean said, sipping his beer and looking around the crowded honky tonk a block off Broadway where Liana got her first break.

She beamed at him. "Well there's no way I'm taking you two hours out of town to look at an abandoned trailer park. As far I'm concerned, this is where Liana Hansen was born."

From the number of people who'd stopped to say hi to her since they'd arrived, it was clear that this was one part of her past she'd hung on tight to. He liked seeing her in her element. He was glad she actually had a comfort zone, although he'd known intellectually she must, he hadn't seen it for himself before this moment.

They'd been in Nashville for twenty-one hours. They left Memphis after her second concert there last night, and drove through the night, arriving at Liana's house before dawn.

He'd gotten the quickest tour ever of her home before

they tumbled into bed. Sleep came first, but then they spent most of the morning making love.

He knew it wasn't the smartest way to think about it, but there wasn't really any other term for how it felt to be inside her. It just felt right, and boy did that worry him pretty hard.

But he knew that Liana understood where his head was at. And he knew that he'd do his damnedest not to hurt her. It was the best he could promise himself, and silently, promise her.

From across the room, a tall, young, bearded man in a faded chambray shirt waved at her.

She squealed and threw her arms in the air. "Caleb Anderson, you get over here."

Dean took a sip of beer and tried like hell not to react to the way the younger man picked Liana up and twirled her around—and hung on to her hips for a good long while after he put her down, too.

"Tell me we're singing tonight, Li."

Li? Dean's eyebrows shot up.

Liana just laughed. "I'll cheer you on."

"You'll do nothing of the sort, gorgeous. I want you on stage with me."

Gorgeous? Caleb might as well have said he wanted Liana naked, which Dean was sure was about to come next.

He stood up and shoved his hand between the two of them. "Caleb. Nice to meet you. Dean Foster."

Liana gave him a pleased smile. "This is Caleb."

"So I gather."

"He's just a fantastic singer and songwriter. I'm like a one-woman fan club."

Dean gave her a totally understanding smile. He hadn't

realized he could lie so easily with his face. "Cool."

"Hey, there's West!" She waved at her drummer, who shouldered his way through the crowd and shook Dean's hand, then Caleb's.

"Hey, man. You playing tonight?"

"Sure am. Trying to get your boss up on stage with me, too."

"Ah, you gotta, Liana. You guys are magic together."

Dean regretted any and all nice thoughts he'd ever had about West.

She just rolled her eyes and shifted closer to Dean. "Maybe one song, later."

Caleb made a finger pistol and clicked his tongue at her. "I'm gonna hold you to that."

And he did, an hour later, at the end of his set. He announced to the room that she was hiding at the back, and got everyone to cheer for her to join him on stage. After a quick whispering consult, she took the hand mic and he sat on the stool to accompany her with the guitar, another mic on a stand in front of him.

She swayed under the tiny spotlight, an angel in her crisp white cotton dress and well-worn cowboy boots. "This is a song my Mama and Daddy used to sing to each other while makin' dinner, and Caleb and I have done it a few times, once on the stage of the Grand Ole Opry. I hope you enjoy it. It was originally performed by George Strait and the incomparable Lee Ann Womack. This is called, 'Good News, Bad News.'" She smiled and pressed her lips together as Caleb started playing beside her. Her breath-taking beauty, that secret smile, was all Dean could see, so it surprised him when Caleb started singing first.

The younger man had a rich, baritone voice that filled the slower ballad, and as he sang, he became the persona of an older, broken hero looking for a second chance with the woman he loved.

And then it was Liana's turn, and after watching Caleb, she turned to the crowd, just glancing sideways every other line as she confessed that she no longer wanted him. It was a magnificent duet that played back and forth until the crowd was on its feet at the end.

Liana gave a curtsey, set the mic back on its stand, and gave Caleb a quick kiss on the cheek before she hopped back through the crowd to Dean's side.

He raised his bottle in a toast to her. "Wow."

"You liked that?"

"I loved it." He gave her a quick kiss on the temple and lowered his mouth to the curve of her ear. "I'd be jealous if you looked at him like he looked at you, though."

"That's just the performance."

"He's good at it."

"He is." She gave a rueful smile. "I wish I could sing with people like that every day."

"Why can't you?"

She waved her hands. "Complicated label stuff."

"Ah."

She laughed. "That's the least convincing *ah* ever."

"Well, I don't get it." He gave her a half-smile and tipped his beer up. "I say, you should do what you love."

"I do, most of the time. And I'll get to do a lot more of it by next year. Anyway, tonight is all about cutting loose, so let's not worry about that."

"Cutting loose, eh? What exactly did you have in mind?"

— —

DEAN'S EYES crinkled as he asked that, and Liana forced herself to tamp down the heady wave of arousal that washed through her. This was about showing him the good parts of her life. The normal, "maybe we could do this together" parts. Not lusting after him so much she dragged him back to her bed until they had to get back on tour.

So she took a deep breath and leaned back against the bar beside him. "Do you want to ride a mechanical bull?"

He laughed out loud, his head tipping back, and she tried not to get too distracted by the roll and bunch of his shoulder muscles, and the way he restlessly moved his thick arms as the laugh rolled down his long body.

"What? That's cutting loose."

"That sounds like a broken neck waiting to happen."

"Chicken?"

"Not even a little. But I thought you meant like tequila shots and karaoke or something."

She giggled. "Do you sing?"

"Nope."

"But you'd do karaoke with me?"

"I'd do anything with you, princess. Okay. First we'll do it my way." He caught his lower lip between his teeth and waggled his eyebrows. "Then once we've got some liquid courage in us, we'll do it your way."

"I don't need tequila to ride the bull," she protested as he spun around and slapped the bar.

"Maybe not. But I do."

"We can do something else."

"Oh no. You've challenged me. I'm a competitive man."

"Well…that's silly. Let's do what you want."

He leaned in close. "I want to impress you."

Her breath caught in her throat. He didn't need to do that. Maybe…

But the bartender was in front of them and Dean was ordering two shots for each of them before she could say anything. He picked up the shot glasses and handed her one before lifting his own in the air. "To cutting loose."

She raised hers to meet his in a gentle clink. "Alrighty."

After they tossed back the shots, they headed next door to a club with a mechanical bull and a decent-sized dance floor. There was a sign-up form for the bull, so Dean put his name down, then they did some line dancing. He had zero problem following the choreography, and when a slow song came on, and she raised her eyebrows at him, he held out his arms and she folded into his embrace.

"You don't mind doing this here?"

"Unwritten law in Nashville—nobody's going to pay any attention to me having a social life."

"No videos currently being taken of you slow-dancing with Arm Guy?"

"Not likely."

He turned her effortlessly. "And if there are?"

"I'm okay with that." She waited a beat. "Are you…?"

He slid his hand from the small of her back to her waist and spun her around before answering. "Yeah." He tugged her hard against his body. "I am if you are."

Well, that was an unexpectedly easy conversation. She rolled her hips against his as he led her through the dance, trusting that he had her.

Around and around they went, their bodies moving in unison as he moved them across the dance floor. And when he finally stopped, they were along the wall, near the back, and there was a private nook right there.

Without letting herself think of all the reasons not to, she grabbed his hand and pulled him into the shadows.

He loomed over her, big and warm and perfect. The first brush of his lips against hers was hard and fast. A test. Were they really doing this here?

Yeah. She twisted her arms around his neck and pulled him against her.

Kiss me. The simplest, neediest of thoughts, and it was all she could manage. She couldn't breathe, couldn't speak.

Slower this time, he lowered his head. His lips pressed hers open, his tongue questing right away. His hands squeezed at her waist, then curved around to cup her bottom through her dress.

He could tug it up. She was wearing the skimpiest panties underneath. He could touch her and she could touch him. He'd be so hard in her palm, so hot…

With a growl, Dean broke away from the kiss and jammed one of his forearms against the wall beside her head. He leaned against it, breathing heavily.

She tried not to feel such a thrill at the effect she had on him, but it was hard.

Hard.

She giggled.

"What?"

"I was thinking it was hard to resist you," she whispered, modifying her answer a bit. "And you know. Hard. It's a dirty word."

He stared down at her. "Oh shit, you're drunk."

That just made her laugh harder. "Well, yeah. We've been drinking all night."

"Okay, princess. Let's take this party home." He pushed away from the wall and turned to steer her out of the nook.

"But the bull!"

"I'm sure it'll be here the next time I visit."

That made her smile. "Next time?"

He just patted her hip and pointed to the alley door.

"I'm not that drunk," she protested under her breath.

"Then let me take you home because you said my cock was hard, and now I want nothing more than your hands on it," he growled in her ear.

Oh. Okay, then.

She behaved herself in the back of the hired car, just tangling her fingers with his on the seat in between them. But as soon as Dean let them in the side door of her house and turned on the alarm, she slid her hand down the front of his jeans and gave his still-hard erection a good squeeze. "Hello, officer."

He grunted and grabbed her wrist, tugging her hand away from his body and spinning her around at the same time. His palm slid up her side, hot and heavy even through her shirt. "You want to play, princess?"

She twisted her head to the side, trying to catch a glimpse of him. "Maybe."

"You think you deserve the white glove treatment, Ms. Hansen?" His breath brushed against her ear as he leaned in and nudged her feet apart with his foot.

"I don't know what you're talking about."

"We got a report that you were drinking tonight."

She smiled and pressed her forehead against the wall. "I'm not sure if I should be answering any questions."

"Could you pass a sobriety test, ma'am?"

She gasped. "What did I tell you—"

He cut her off with a swat against her bare thigh that stung just enough to send a shiver up her spine. "Apologies, *ma'am*. Just doing my job."

"I may have been drinking. But I didn't drive."

"And how did you get home?"

"In a hired car."

"What company?"

"I don't remember. My bodyguard organized it."

"Likely story." He rocked his erection into her bottom, his hand sliding up the front of her leg at the same time. Trapping her. "And where is this bodyguard now?"

"I don't know."

"Just you and me, princess. And now I need to search you."

She whimpered as his fingers slid under her panties and found her soaking wet, ready for anything he might want from her. She rocked into his touch, trying to rub her clit against his fingertips and keep pressing against his erection behind her at the same time.

"What's this?" He nipped at her ear as he jerked her panties down her thighs.

"What did you find?" She tried to kick off her boots, fully intending to spin around and climb him like a tree, but he clamped his hand down on her hip.

"Leave the boots on."

"Oooh, officer." She swivelled her head the other way, catching her lower lip between her teeth and batting her eyelashes at him. "Are you sure we couldn't work something out? Since you like my...boots so much."

"I don't see how you're in a position to be negotiating anything." He cupped her sex, his entire hand covering between her legs. "God, you feel good."

She gave up the role-play then, rocking shamelessly

against his touch, and behind her he fumbled with his jeans, then shoved a condom into her hand.

"Open that and we'll call it even."

She giggled as she ripped the foil, then passed the slippery latex back to him. But her laughter died as he quickly thrust into her, fast and hard and deep, and she scrabbled at the wall. Oh, yes.

His arms wrapped around her, one sinking low across her hips so he could roll his thumb over her clit as he fucked her from behind. The other crossed her chest and wrapped around the side of her neck, holding her in place and shielding her from the bump of the wall as he increased his speed.

She pressed her hands against the wall, too, but he had her, so she reached behind her and slid her fingers into his hair. "Dean," she breathed, panting and desperate already.

"I've got you," he growled. "Come on."

He was so thick inside her, hard and solid, each thrust a threat and a promise at the same time. Her body sang as he surged into her and protested when he retreated, every nerve ending licked in both directions so she was spinning hard toward a climax before she realized it.

It was too much.

It was just enough.

"Almost there, oh my God," she breathed, and he grabbed her hand off the wall, shoving it under her dress.

"Get yourself off. Make yourself come on my cock," he growled, and she closed her eyes, letting the feelings wash over her.

This was hot and out-of-control.

But it was perfect, too.

He was wrapped around her, holding her tight. It was dirty, but oh so loving. And that was the best fantasy of them all, that Dean was a forever guy, her forever guy, and this wasn't a fling that had a definite end date on it.

Because even though it was and it did, how she felt for him wouldn't just turn off at the end of the tour. *I love you,* she let herself admit as she stroked herself into a freefall. *Tumble with me,* she begged in her mind. And as he growled his own muttered words, filthier than hers, she imagined he was right there with her in more ways than one.

Bittersweet and filthy, it was the best orgasm of her entire life.

CHAPTER TWENTY-ONE

HE'D SEEN a lot of sides to Liana already, but when she pulled a pair of reading glasses out of her bag he did a double-take.

"What?" she asked as she tucked a lock of glossy hair behind her ear.

"Nothing," he said, trying to swallow his tongue. "You don't look like a librarian pin-up or anything."

"Shut up." She grinned. "I just wear them when I'm writing."

"I'd like to watch you write more often."

Just then the door opened, saving him from making more of a fool of himself.

They were in a converted house at the end of Music Row, the offices of a group of songwriters that Liana apparently worked with when she was in Nashville.

Her idea of a few days off and his were pretty different, not that he was complaining. She'd explained that it was good for Track to hear she was working Music Row, that she wasn't scared. Yes, he controlled her next record. But he didn't control the songs she might write for someone else. And frankly, she was to the point where she might just give away a song to make a point.

Plus it was pretty cool to see the inner workings of the music industry—especially a side that made her light up from the inside out.

When Caleb Anderson walked through the door, Dean's enthusiasm dimmed for just a second, but he kicked himself. Liana only had eyes for him this summer. It was fine.

The younger man wasn't alone, either. Behind him was West, and an older woman who looked vaguely familiar. When she introduced herself as Karen McAster, he realized she'd had a couple of hits in the late 90s—which dated himself as much as her.

Interesting.

She took charge of the writing session, flipping on the monitor on the production board. A dizzying array of colours and lines of recorded music filled the screen. With a few taps on the keyboard, a bit of a song started playing.

Everyone nodded along, making notes or grabbing an instrument.

Dean was surprised—again, he really needed to check all assumptions at the door—when Liana picked up a guitar. "How about this lick instead?" she said, singing back some of the lyrics, changing the melody a bit as she played along.

She kept playing as Caleb took over the vocals, and her fingers flew over the strings. They worked on four songs, finishing one, and it was an impressive flow of work.

Dean kept his question about the guitar to himself until they took a break two hours in. "You never play on the road," he said when they were alone.

She shrugged. "I have. Not this tour."

He didn't push the inquiry further, because his curiosity didn't trump her right to privacy. *Maybe later*, he found himself thinking, knowing he meant after the tour, when he'd be gone.

When the other songwriters came back, he took lunch orders and headed out to make himself useful.

But he didn't get that far, because he ran right into Track Gantley at the bottom of the stairwell heading back to the parking lot behind the house.

The singer sneered at him. "You look lost."

Dean stared past him, projecting an air of *get the fuck out of my way*. "Excuse me." *Do not engage. Do not—*

"What are you doing here, besides panting after Liana?"

"At the moment, I'm in charge of fetching lunch." He dragged his gaze lazily up to Track's face. "You're in my way."

"You're a bad influence on her."

Well, that was direct. And wrong. Dean cleared his throat. "I have no idea what you're talking about."

"It's not going to work."

Dean shook his head. "I really need to get lunch, so if you'll excuse me."

"She's refused to meet with us while she's in town. Her latest album is unacceptable and—"

"I'm going to stop you there and remind you that I'm not someone who's privy to the contractual details of your agreement with Ms. Hansen, and as such probably should not be told your opinion of her work that is under said contract." Dean bit down, hard, to keep any other, choicer words from spilling out.

That didn't stop Track from continuing his bizarre

attack. "You don't know what you're doing. What you're messing with."

"I'm not doing anything other than being a good friend to Liana."

"You keep telling yourself that. But I see how you look at her. You're no better than any other shark out there."

Whoa. Dean didn't like how he got his back up to that one. He exhaled roughly, slowly, trying to maintain control. "Takes one to know one, Gantley."

"You and I are nothing alike."

"That's for damn sure." Dean knew he was treading on thin ice, but he couldn't help himself. "Why are you so hung up on her still?"

Track gave him a look of pure derision. "You think I still want in her pants? I had the frigid bitch—"

White hot rage propelled Dean's fist forward, connecting to Track's jaw with a serious crack.

Shit.

Their ragged, heavy breaths filled the hallway.

Track slowly stood up and rubbed his jaw, fire lighting up his eyes. "That was a mistake."

"You gonna tell anyone that you took a punch?" Dean leaned in and rolled the dice. "You got hit because you're scum. You got hit because you're weak. And small. And pathetic. But most of all I hit you because you insulted a woman, and I don't think that flies in Tennessee or anywhere else you might make noise about this. Don't underestimate me, Gantley," he growled. "Don't play games with me. And don't even think about messing with Liana."

Then he shoved past the singer and threw himself into the hot, humid afternoon sun.

So much for staying in control.

———

HE MADE it halfway to the restaurant they'd called in an order to before he pulled over and parked so he could call his brother.

Jake picked up on the third ring. "Hey, how's life on tour?"

"I punched Track Gantley."

His brother let out a harsh exhale. "Wow. I'm assuming he deserved it."

"Yeah."

"Any witnesses?"

"No, but Homeland Security might be listening to this right now."

That got him a laugh. He hadn't been kidding.

"How's everyone back home?"

"I'm currently reading a book about home births."

Shit. That was…real. "I don't know what to say to that."

"Me neither. But what Dani wants, Dani gets." Jake didn't sound disgruntled about that at all. If anything, the softness in his voice was enviable.

And for the first time ever, Dean kind of understood it.

Not that he loved Liana, of course. It wasn't like that.

Exactly.

But it was something. He didn't punch other men. Ever.

And he'd called Jake for a reason. Not Matt or Sean, or even one of the Minellis, because only Jake knew what it was to grow up a Foster and still be capable of a healthy relationship. Although it wasn't like his relationship with

Dani was logical or practical or anything else Dean valued in his own friendships.

Jake had fallen for Dani when she was still an off-limits teenager. And he'd waited for her, through college and other relationships, until they were on the same page.

Dean didn't have that kind of patience. He couldn't imagine watching Liana with someone else.

But he would, wouldn't he? Once the tour was over. He'd go home. And she'd move on with her life.

His gut twisted.

Jake cleared his throat. "Did I lose you with the pregnancy talk?"

"Nah." Dean made a fist and bounced it lightly off the steering wheel as he winced. "I just…"

"How's the singer?" Jake offered when Dean trailed off.

"I think I might be falling for her."

Stunned silence was his brother's only response.

Dean knew the feeling. He groaned.

"Does she…know?" Jake cleared his throat. "Do you need Zander to come and bail you out?"

"Fuck off. Yes she knows. I guess…we're in a relationship."

"You don't sound impressed."

"I am. With her. Not with myself. I don't know. She's…" He thought about her with that guitar. "She's amazing. She's got so many clever layers that nobody ever sees. And she's talented, too. Holy fuck, man, you should hear her sing. On stage, or just off the cuff. There's nothing like it. But she's tough, too, because this is a crazy town. And it's hard to be in the public eye like that. I could never do it. They've given me a nickname—"

"Oh yeah, Olivia said something about that. Army Guy?" Jake laughed.

"No. Uh…" No, Dean wasn't going to correct him. "Yeah. It's weird."

"But you don't mind it." Another laugh. "Hey, I get it. Prenatal books, and weird nicknames. This is the stuff they never tell you about."

"I didn't see this coming."

"You never do. Hey, I gotta go. Dani's on the other line."

"Later. Thanks, man."

He sat there looking at his phone for a few minutes longer, thinking about what his brother had said—both deliberately and inadvertently. And when he pulled up at the restaurant, he was smiling.

CHAPTER TWENTY-TWO

LIANA WAS in the middle of singing the same line, over and over again, trying to find just the right end note, when an angry rap on the window of the writing room interrupted them.

Caleb and West were both on their feet, but it was Karen who opened the door and stood bodily in the way of Track coming into the room. "We're in the middle of a writing session."

"With one of my signed talent."

"Liana has every right to be here." Karen glanced over her shoulder and gave Liana an understanding looking. "But if you'd like five minutes with Track, we can break."

She pressed her hands, clammy and cold, against her yoga pants. Oh, Dean, hurry back with lunch. Instead of standing, she waved Caleb and West back into their seats. "We're in the middle of a song. But maybe if you wait five minutes, we can wrap it up?" She took a deep breath as an even better idea came to her. "In fact, come in. Sit down."

Karen's eyebrows hit the roof, but she stepped out of the way. Track couldn't refuse the invite, although he looked like he wanted to, so in he came. He stood against the far wall, and the icy blast radiating off him would normally have killed her creativity, but this song was good, and more to the point, it was essentially done.

She picked up the guitar again and looked to her drummer, then to Caleb, and finally to Karen. "From the top? It's down to you and it's down to me. I like that version best."

West hit play on the drum line he'd already recorded into Pro Tools, and grabbed a shaker to add some depth. She starting strumming, a fast, steady beat, and then dropped into the off-tempo, unexpected accompaniment for the melody.

Caleb gave her a fast grin before they started singing together.

I T'S gonna be what it's gonna be
And it's gonna hurt like it's gonna hurt
But there's no doubt
Can't have doubt
Cause it's gonna circle back circle back
And in the end it's down to you and it's down to me
The way it's gonna be
You and me
Circle back
Gonna hurt
You and me

THEY STRETCHED out the last two words, then she played another few bars before letting it fade. It was good. It wasn't her, not a song she'd ever want to record, but being a part of creating it was a massive thrill.

And even better, Track was stunned silent.

Another knock came at the door, this one gentle. Dean held up two bags of takeout food, and she gestured him in.

It took him a single stride to realize Track was in the room. Another to get between them, and turn his back on the other man long enough to make eye contact with her. *You okay?*

She nodded and he navigated his way around the stand of guitars to the long table against the window, leaving the food there before returning to stand next to her, feet wide and arms crossed.

Track stood, and so did West and Caleb.

Too many standing men.

She rolled her eyes at Karen, then joined them. "West, Caleb…you guys start eating. Don't touch my salad. Karen, could we use your boardroom?"

"Can I join you?"

She gave the older woman a curious look, but shrugged. "Sure." She held up her hand when Track started to protest. "I'm on her dime today, Track. You can deal."

She let her hand brush against Dean's as she turned, hooking her fingers around his for a quick squeeze. *Come with me*, she told him, and he followed. Maybe because she'd invited him, maybe because wild dogs couldn't keep him from her side when her ex was in the room.

Either way she didn't care. Kind of liked the latter reason, really. Hoped it meant something more than she should really hope for. But wanting Dean felt good, so she let her heart stay there, in the safe-for-now embrace of hope.

Once they were all in the boardroom, Liana decided not to sit. She wasn't wearing heels today, so she didn't have a height advantage, but being able to pace felt freeing.

"Okay, Track, what is so urgent that you needed to interrupt our writing session, and that you needed to ignore my request that you go through my management for these conversations?"

"If we go through management, you're going to lose the contract." His words were thunderous, and unexpected.

She froze, her heart stopping too, mid-slam against her ribcage. "What?"

"We can only produce what we can sell, and you aren't young enough anymore to write an edgy album."

"What the actual fuck?" Those four words had echoed in Liana's mind, but they came out of Karen's mouth. "What the actual serious fuck does that mean?"

Track opened his mouth, but Liana's new hero—heroine—wasn't having any of it. She stood up and crossed the room, slinging her arm around Liana's shoulders. "Either produce the album she delivered to you or sell it to me," Karen said smoothly, as if one of country's biggest stars wasn't seething in front of her. "I'd love to bring Liana in house as more than an occasional songwriter. She's an incredible talent."

"Thank you," Liana whispered, still shocked at Track's real reason for rejecting her album.

Too old?

She was thirty.

Track stood as well, swore under his breath, then glanced back and forth between Dean and Liana before throwing his hands in the air. "Good riddance, then."

He swung the boardroom door open so fast it slammed against the wall, and she jumped.

No, it wasn't that easy, was it?

She turned to look at Karen, who shook her head. "No, not that easy."

"Did I say that out loud?"

The other woman nodded. "But it's the start. You've got a witness." She pointed at Dean.

He winced. "Track hardly accepts me as a neutral third party."

Karen shrugged. "Doubt that would matter to a judge."

Liana felt faint. "Surely it won't go that far."

"Depends on if his label partners want to hang on to you. I'm serious, I'll buy your contract out from them, but if they don't want to let you go, then you need to be prepared for a breach of contract fight."

"I just want to make music. Why would they sue me?" But she knew why. Because it was a business at the end of the day, and that was how cold, ruthless business people dealt with problems like her. "What do I need to give them to avoid that?"

"If they don't let me buy out your contract, then I think you should give them right of refusal on all the songs you've written."

A frisson of fear skittered down Liana's spine. "All of them? What if they want them all?"

"That's not going to happen. So play their game. They didn't like this album you delivered? Give them another. And another. Be careful that you get it all in writing. So you'll email your coordinator at the label, someone low level, and let them know you had a meeting with Track today. An unexpected one, and you think he wanted to see more songs. Did he? Can she confirm what he wants? And then worst case scenario, if they backtrack, then tell them you've recorded a few more songs than you expected, and can you present some at the originally scheduled meeting, and maybe set up a second one to fill in the gaps of the album based on what they like from the first meeting?"

"So I can control the spin on the second set of songs," Liana said slowly, the pieces falling into place. She glanced over at Dean. "Sorry. I think we're going to be here all night now."

He just shrugged. "Doesn't bother me. You're the boss." He hesitated. "But I need to tell you about something that happened earlier."

"Something bad?"

He winced. "Depends. Given what just happened, maybe not. But I had a run in with Track before he found you and I lost my cool."

Her eyebrows hit the roof. She didn't know that was possible. "What did you do?"

"It may have come to blows."

"Blows, plural?"

"Nah. I decked him."

"Oh, honey. No, that's not a problem in the least." She hesitated and looked at Karen. "Do you have security cameras?"

The other woman gave her an innocent look. "I don't think they're on today."

— —

BY THE TIME they fell asleep, Liana was seriously blissed

out from the possibilities she'd never imagined before, and her dreams reflected that.

But morning brought reality with it. It was back to work later today, with an afternoon into evening drive to Tulsa. She was playing at a festival there the next day, and the soundcheck was first thing in the morning. And since she didn't like to sleep on the road, they were leaving mid-day.

Her plan.

She scowled. What a terrible idea that had been.

Beside her, Dean roused. "Morning," he murmured, his voice sleep-rough and husky.

Terrible, terrible idea.

"I never want to get up," she whispered, snuggling back into the hard warmth of his body.

"Not even for a delicious kale smoothie?"

She snorted. "You really want me to take you out for a diner breakfast, don't you?"

"Of course."

"I know a place."

"Smoothies are fine."

She smiled. No, they'd go to a diner. He'd put up with her food for three days. She knew a good one that could do a vegetable hash for her.

They drove, because it was a hot morning already, and after breakfast she wanted to swing downtown again. She felt a pang of guilt as they passed Jackie's house. "Do you mind if we invite Jackie and Andrew? She just lives there —" She pointed back down the block.

"Of course not." He frowned. "Why would I?"

She shrugged. "Don't know. Okay." From the driver's seat, he squeezed her left hand as she typed out a quick text message with her right. Then she remembered he didn't know where they were going. She should have driven, but he looked really good behind the wheel. Strong and capable and the way his arm curved against the wheel, with the sun glinting in the hair on his forearm… If he was more of a social media person, she'd totally have Instagrammed that with the hashtag #ArmGuy. He was drool worthy.

"We almost there?"

Oh right. She'd been thinking about that, too. "Next block. It's on the corner, but we'll have to go past it to find parking."

"You're distracted this morning."

"It's possible I have a crush on you." She grinned.

He just laughed, deep and rich, and that didn't help the situation. Her heart fluttered in her chest. *Fluttered.* Oh boy.

— —

THERE WAS a small crowd in front of the Sky Blue Cafe as they cruised past, so Dean turned onto the next block and found a free parking spot on the side street.

When he came around to her side of the car, she took his hand, and he lifted their clasped fingers so he could brush a quick kiss to her knuckles.

He liked holding her hand.

It was a little thing, really, but three days of being together, really together, had shifted something inside him.

And when they arrived at the restaurant, and that crowd had gone inside, so they were waiting at the outdoor "Please Wait To Be Seated" sign by themselves, he didn't want to let go.

"When we get back on the bus," he said in a rush. "We can…people could…"

She smiled up at him. "You trying to ask me something?"

The real strength of what he wanted to say needed to be saved for another time and place. "I don't want to stop holding your hand."

"Then don't."

He ducked his head and kissed her gently. Her mouth was so soft, it undid him every time.

She smiled again, this time against his lips.

"This is interesting," someone—Andrew—said from behind them. Dean gave the bassist a slow up and down look as he turned around, because he and Liana weren't the only ones holding hands. Andrew and Jackie had made up from their fight in a big way.

Liana didn't look surprised, though. Secrets, eh? Not his to know, Dean guessed. So he just shrugged. "Who's hungry?"

A young woman in high-waisted jeans held up by suspenders over a Dolly For President shirt came out to seat them, saving them from any further awkward relationship conversations.

Inside, the cafe was stuffed to the gills with hipsters. Jackie recognized someone, so she took a detour to talk to a couple covered in gorgeous tattoos.

The rest of them followed the waitress to a table at the back. "Drinks?" she asked.

Liana ordered a coconut milk latte for herself and one for Jackie as well. Dean wanted his coffee black, and Andrew shrugged. "Sounds good to me."

She left them with menus, which looked like the place catered to both Liana—egg white omelettes—and Dean's tastes, too. A south-west omelette covered in chili with a side of sourdough toast? Holy shit, that made his stomach growl.

Jackie joined them a minute later, and she reached across the table to grab a box of Trivial Pursuit cards tucked against the wall. Dean watched in amusement as the three bandmates all moved in synch with each other, shuffling through the randomized deck to find the music trivia questions, passing sugar to Andrew when their coffee arrived, Jackie collecting the menus like a bossy older sibling as the waitress took their orders.

He liked it all. He liked that Liana had this. Hope worried about her, but she had a pretty good little family going on here.

She had a blood family, too, but she didn't talk about them much. Her parents were divorced, had been since she was a kid, and she'd left her mother's trailer at eighteen, never to return. She'd told him she saw them every few years. She'd been closest to her maternal grandmother, but her MeeMaw had died when she was a teenager.

He couldn't imagine not seeing his father. Even though the old man was a bastard, they still did a regular-ish family dinner.

On the other hand, Hope also had a difficult relationship with her mother, and no relationship with her father. So it wasn't a surprise they'd found each other, and found others. Family could be chosen. And sometimes that was for the best.

He'd chosen Zander as a brother in kindergarten. And now they were brothers through marriage, too. He thought of Jake, and Dani, and he pulled out his phone to take a picture of the restaurant. Dani would love it. Maybe after their baby arrived, they could come down for a visit.

And visit who? Liana?

He'd told her he was going home. He told her he wouldn't be able to stick around after the end of the tour.

But he liked holding her hand.

As if she could sense he was thinking far too heavy thoughts for so early in the morning, Liana found his hand with hers under the table and gave his fingers a quick squeeze.

"Hey, can we ask about yesterday?" Jackie said, leaning in and lowering her voice.

Liana glanced around, then shrugged. "I guess. Did West fill you in?"

Jackie nodded. "That's crazy."

"Well, that's…" She trailed off and glanced at Andrew.

He just laughed. "That's Track."

"I know you like him."

"I like his music. And he doesn't even write it. He's a great stylist, but fuck him. He's not a great person. I'm on Team Liana, all the way."

"I don't want there to be teams." She groaned softly, and now it was Dean's turn to squeeze her hand. She took a sip of her latte before continuing. "It's a small town in so many ways. I just want to keep my nose clean and make music."

"Do you think Track is really cutting you loose?" Jackie asked.

Liana shook her head. "No. I mean, I get that he wants to. He wants to threaten me with that. But my sales are good. My fan base is solid and I sell out concerts. I'm struggling to get songs that rise to the top of the charts, but that's because of them, not me. As a songwriter, I've got that number one spot, so I can get it as a singer, too."

Dean didn't know that. Had that been in his research on her? Maybe he hadn't understood enough about her job when he'd done his reading.

"You owe him an album, right? And then you're free?" Andrew frowned. "Can you not just...make the album he wants?"

Both Liana and Jackie shook their heads at the same time. "It's more complicated than that," Liana said. "A bad release is almost worse than not releasing at all in terms of getting another deal."

Andrew frowned. "But what if you don't need another deal?"

Liana laughed. "Well, it would be hard to keep paying you if I didn't have a new album to tour on."

"Why do you need someone else to necessarily release your next album?" Andrew held up his hand. "Hear me out. I'm not so naive to think just fuck the labels, as nice as that would be. But what if you could drop an indie album soon after the label album."

Jackie sat up straighter in her chair, then did another look around before leaning in. "That's a good question. If you had another album ready to go..."

"Oh my gosh." Liana tightened her grip on Dean's hand and bounced in her seat. He bit his lip to keep from laughing. This was better than Christmas, even if he didn't really follow it completely. He could already see Andrew's idea getting better as she rolled it around in her glorious, clever mind. "You guys are geniuses."

Andrew shook his head. "I wish I could take the credit. It was something that West said at one point, about giving up on the dream of getting picked up by a label, because—"

"Because he can get the best of both worlds with me. Oh, you clever man." She let go of Dean's hand and launched herself at her bassist, peppering his cheek with kisses before she leaned across the table to high-five Jackie.

Now it was Dean's turn to do the lazy look around the restaurant, but nobody was giving them a second glance. And then it was his turn to get her appreciative kisses, although he hadn't done anything to earn them. He still tangled his hand in her hair and held her close for a second.

"You're happy?" he whispered.

"Very."

"Good." He kissed the tip of her nose as he gazed down at her clear blue eyes. "I like that sparkle in your eyes."

Beside them, their waitress cleared her throat.

He still maintained that grown men didn't blush, but Dean's cheeks felt suspiciously warm as he leaned back and accepted his monster plate of food.

CHAPTER TWENTY-THREE

THE TOUR RESUMED with an outdoor festival in Tulsa.

And like in Louisville, Liana found it too much. Too chaotic, too intense. It left her feeling too vulnerable, and she couldn't crest that wave. Couldn't get on top of it and ride it like a queen.

The fact that she'd had such a good break in Nashville and had finally confronted Track made it even worse. So much for finding her inner warrior goddess.

She finished the last song on auto-pilot, which of course wasn't good enough and sent her even further into a spiral of negative self-talk.

How was that? Was that good enough? It wasn't, not really. The crowd wasn't really into it. Should I have sat down on the stool? Would that have been more authentic?

Her head started to spin, just a little. Not like she was going to pass out, but something more subtle than that. More concerning. Like she was starting to see what was happening around her from an odd, detached angle.

"Great job," one of the roadies said. Chris, her brain reminded her.

Detached.

Yeah. That was the word for it.

"Thanks, Chris," she heard herself say, then felt herself give a little fist pump in the air.

"You want water?" he asked, holding out a bottle.

"I'm good." She clenched her hands into fists to keep them from shaking.

A large, male body stepped in front of her. "I'll take that," Dean said to Chris, grabbing the water. Then he set his arm around her shoulder and propelled her forward. "Come on."

He walked them across the wing of the stage, letting her stop at the top of the stairs to sign autographs, then again at the bottom, but he kept her moving past the tent, down the carpeted path to the makeshift hallway of curtains that led to the tour bus parking. Behind her, she could hear her band veer off into the VIP tent, and then they were, for a split second, alone.

"I'm fine," she whispered under her breath, to herself as much as him. And she fought for that control, wanted to believe it, even as her head spun and darkness threatened at the corners of her vision.

"You're just going to get changed," he responded just as quietly, his gaze staying straight ahead. He smiled at the security guard at the other end and flashed his backstage pass.

"Lovely performance, Ms. Hansen," the cop said with a flashing white smile.

On autopilot, she winked at him. "I aim to please."

"And please you did," he chuckled. "You coming back in?"

"Absolutely. Just need to change. Won't be long."

"I'll be waiting for you."

She was still laughing when Dwayne spotted them and opened the bus door for her.

She gave him a more tired but also more authentic smile. "Thank you."

"You have a good show?"

"I did, thank you."

"Good to hear."

"I'm just going to get changed." The words spilled out of her. Thanks to Dean for the excuse.

"All right. I'm just going to sit here and finish this level of Candy Crush."

She nodded, her voice sounding more distant now, like she was listening to the conversation through a tunnel. "Have you passed Andrew yet?"

"Not yet."

"You can do it." She patted his shoulder and headed down the aisle, all the way to her room. It was all she could see at the end of the corridor.

Dean was right behind her the entire time, and when she opened the door, he followed her into her private space.

"Can you close the—" she started to ask, glancing back at him over her shoulder, then cut herself off when he'd already shut the door behind him.

"How do you do that?" he asked, staring at her.

"Do what?"

"Go from nearly passing out as you came off stage to… flirting with a security guard and remembering that Dwayne is five levels behind Andrew in Candy Crush."

"Is it five?" She wasn't the only person who remembered stuff. It wasn't a superhero skill.

"Doesn't matter." He pointed to her bed. "Sit."

She sat just in time for everything to fade. "Whoa."

"You're doing it again. What's wrong?" He took her hand and peeled her fingers out of the white-knuckled fist she'd made.

"Nothing," she said quickly.

"You turned white as you came off the stage. I thought you might pass out. And now you just did that again."

"It's hot today."

"You usually have trouble performing in the heat?"

She didn't answer him.

"Here." He unscrewed the lid from the water and pressed it into her hand. "Nobody can see that your hands are shaking."

"Except you."

"But your secret's safe with me, so drink up."

"I need to go back to the tent," she whispered after taking a few shallow sips. She pressed the bottle to her cheek, but that didn't help. She wasn't hot.

"What happened out there?"

"It doesn't matter."

Dean stared at her incredulously. "It damn well does. Tell me."

"Don't yell at me." She closed her eyes and put the cap back on the water bottle. She just wanted to lie down.

"This is what happened in Savannah?"

"Maybe." Her stomach knotted up.

She could feel him moving around her. She blinked her eyes open when he settled beside her on the bed and took the water bottle from her hands.

"I think you need to see someone about this. A medical professional."

She started to cry. It was like a dam burst, and she sobbed against his shirt as he lowered them both so they were flat on the mattress. "That's not the answer I wanted," she sniffled, burrowing deeper into his chest.

"I know. Do you want to talk about what you were thinking on stage? Would that help?"

She shook her head. Not if she was going to have to talk about it over and over again with a doctor. And when was that going to happen? She was just kicking off the Western leg of the tour.

"We can fly ahead of the buses and meet someone in Denver," he said quietly into her hair, his voice steady.

"That'll mean telling people."

"People already know. That's why you brought me on tour, remember?"

She frowned. No, she'd forgotten that. And it had been a non-issue.

"We can go out and do some shopping while we're there. I'll roll up my shirt sleeves and everything. Start some Arm Guy rumours."

"You don't want to do that."

"I want to do whatever it takes to keep you feeling safe."

"Don't let go..." she whispered, giving in to the sleep that was calling for her.

"I won't." *Not ever*, she wanted to imagine he said next, but she was already drifting.

— —

DEAN WATCHED Liana sleep for a while, then pulled out his phone and texted Brad.

He filled the tour manager in on Liana's panic attack. Brad immediately jumped into action, and they had a new travel plan within an hour.

"She wants to keep this low-key," Dean kept repeating, and he was ninety percent sure Brad got that, but there was enough doubt that he stayed in the close vicinity of the bus so when she woke up, he'd be there to stand beside her.

The buses would be hitting the road in a few hours. They'd stuck around after her show so the crew could enjoy some of the other acts, and they had a day in between this concert and the next one in Colorado.

But Dean and Liana would be heading to the airport shortly. Brad already had an appointment lined up for her with a highly-recommended therapist for the next morning in Denver.

He was just climbing back onto the bus to wake her up when his phone vibrated in his pocket.

Dean read the text from Sean twice, blood pounding in his ears.

Leaving for the sandpit in six days.

Damn. For his brother, it would be good news. A show of confidence from his commanding officers that he didn't need the extended workup training. That his knowledge and skill level were deployment-ready.

"Bad news?" He jerked his eyes up. Jackie was sitting quietly on the couch.

"Uh…No."

She pointed to the bedroom. "I hear her moving around."

He nodded. "We're flying ahead to Denver."

Her brow squeezed together and he realized her hands

were fisted so tightly her knuckles were white. "It really hasn't happened that many times before."

"I know. She told me about Savannah."

"We didn't ignore it."

"I know." He shot a quick glance toward the bedroom. The last thing Liana needed to worry about was people talking about her. He grabbed a chair and spun it around so he could sit facing Jackie. "This is new for her. The performance anxiety part. So it'll get nipped in the bud. Don't worry about it."

"I just…" She screwed up her face and exhaled. "I know about things getting out of control."

"And you know about getting them back in control, too, right?"

She nodded.

"Liana's lucky to have you in her corner." He stood again and tucked the chair back against the table. "We just need to insulate her a bit through this."

Jackie started to say something, then stopped. Started again, and he chuckled when she gave up again.

"Spit it out."

"Don't try to protect her too much. Remember she's still a star. She's worked hard for more than a decade to earn her place in the limelight. She hates scrutiny. Embarrassment. But she loves attention. For better or worse."

"Noted."

"Even if that means you end up in the limelight, too."

Yeah, he'd already figured that out. "Doubly noted."

He knocked on the bedroom door.

A muffled "come in" came from the other side.

She was curled up under a throw blanket now, her tablet propped up on a pillow beside her. She was responding to fan messages.

He recounted the travel plans to her, underlining that so far, Brad and Jackie were the only ones who knew there would be any change in plans. "And you'll do your show there just like normal. Easy peasy."

His phone vibrated again and he ignored it.

Liana didn't. She glanced to his pocket. He waved her off and she rolled her eyes. "Everything okay?"

"Yep. Do you need help packing?"

"No. Do you?"

He laughed and climbed onto the bed. That deserved a kiss, but no sooner was his mouth on hers that his phone started vibrating and this time, it didn't stop.

So Sean would have told everyone else now. "I'm sorry," he groaned, pulling it out.

Six messages.

He thumbed into the screen with one hand, tucking Liana into his side with the other. "It's family stuff."

She read the messages along with him, her body tensing up and he swore under his breath. "Dean? Is your brother going overseas like…now?"

"Not now," he muttered. "In a few days."

"That's earlier than expected."

"Yeah."

"Do you need to go home?"

"I need to be right here with you."

"It's okay if you do."

"And it's okay if I don't, too." It would be, anyway. He sent out a group message to all of his brothers and the Minelli clan, too, that he was getting on an airplane and would reply once he got to Denver.

Then he turned off his phone and pulled Liana tight into his chest.

CHAPTER TWENTY-FOUR

THE FLIGHT WAS short and uneventful.

Dinner was room service in the Four Seasons, with a view of mountains in the distance.

The entire rest of the day was quiet, too quiet, and calm. By the time it was dark, Liana felt so edgy and restless she wanted to snap at Dean and she had no idea why.

She knew he didn't deserve it. And in the back of her mind, she hated herself for keeping him next to her when his brother was about to head to a war zone and the rest of his family was blowing up his phone about that.

He'd turned the ringer all the way to silent, not even letting it vibrate, but she knew he was still getting messages.

"I'm going to go to the gym," she announced.

He stood, too.

She tried to wave him down, but gave up when she got as far as her suitcase and realized she'd left her running shoes on the tour bus.

Fuck.

She dropped to her knees and hung her head.

"Hey," he said quietly, crouching behind her. "It's fine."

"I don't have my shoes."

"Can you do yoga or something?"

She nodded. It wasn't what she wanted, though. She wanted to run, hard and fast.

"Come here." He pulled her into his arms, rocking her almost, and it was awkward and sweet at the same time.

"I hate being weak," she mumbled into his chest.

"But you really are strong. You are. This is just a normal human breaking point thing."

She shook her head. She didn't feel strong. "I've learned how to act. How to survive. But this has been coming for a while."

"You've been knocked down how many times? Anyone would snap. And you haven't snapped. You're just…done with pretending, maybe? But you've climbed a hard ladder, princess. Hard. I had no idea until I saw you at work in Nashville. How many people try to do what you've done and fail?"

She wasn't sure she wasn't failing at the moment. Darkness crept in closer, cold and clammy, because given what his family was preparing for, that was so weak. "You should go home."

"What? No. I'm right where I need to be."

"Your brother—"

"Has two other brothers. And one of them isn't an idiot. He has best friends and an entire community, including one of your best friends, too. You have me. It's a fair trade."

She laughed, because he was being funny, and he was funny, but it still hurt.

"You're awesome, you know that?"

She shook her head and tried to twist away from him.

He caught her hands in his and held her still. "Listen to me. Listen. Stop and hear me."

"No, don't do this." When she realized he wasn't going to let her get away, she tried to kiss him instead, but he rolled her onto her back.

"I'm doing this." He gave her a soft smile, his eyes crinkling at the corners.

Her heart was going to explode. Was it wrong to feel happy and sad at the same time?

"I'm telling you how awesome you are, and you're going to hear it."

Swallowing hard, she forced herself to be quiet. Forced the voices in her head to stop arguing and let him do this, even if it was a lie.

I've made him think these wonderful things. I've manipulated him somehow and he'll realize it soon enough. She didn't feel the tears on her cheeks until his fingers wiped them away.

"Is that so hard to hear?"

"Maybe," she whispered.

"Damn it, Liana." He stared down at her, then shook his head. "What am I going to do with you?"

"Yoga?"

Instead, he kissed her, and that was better.

— —

THE NEXT MORNING, a therapist came to the hotel for a private session.

To her eternal relief, Liana liked the guy right off the

bat. His name was Howard, and he wasn't a big fan of country music.

She laughed when he told her that. "That's an interesting introduction tack."

"I don't want you to be surprised when I don't know any of your colleagues, or anything like that. The context, relationships, etc. My wife likes to watch Austin City Limits, though, that's a good time."

"It is." She gave a little shrug. "I've been on that, you know."

"That's neat." But he said it like one might comment on bright purple argyle socks. And where someone else might get uppity about that, Liana just relaxed.

This guy didn't care at all about her job. Which meant she could trust him to do his. She took a deep breath. "Okay. So. Where do we start?"

"Why don't you tell me what's been going on with you."

"I'm on tour." She hitched her shoulders and tightened her knees together as she thought about how far back to go. "And twelve years ago I moved to Nashville to be a country music star. A lot happened in between."

"Well, start with that and we'll see where it takes us."

"How much time do you have?"

"As much as you need."

She told him...everything. Writing River Bed Lullaby and playing it at an open-mic night just off Broadway, on a stage that nobody famous ever climbed on to, that was more about being a tourist attraction than a real showcase of up and coming talent.

But at that point, she hadn't been up and coming yet. She was young and sexy and she knew how to play a guitar, so she didn't need a band. She could get on any stage, anywhere, and she did.

Over and over again for almost ten months, which was nothing, really. She knew that now. But it had felt like a lifetime. And then one day, that day, there'd been a guy in the crowd who'd liked her enough to mention her to someone else.

Three weeks later, she was in a studio.

Four weeks later, she met Track.

She started crying at that point in the story, and Howard gave her tissues. She apologized and he waved her off.

"You want to tell me about this tour?" he asked, but she shook her head and kept going.

It took her an hour to finally get to the tour. When she did, it seemed…like not such a big deal, in the grand scheme of things.

"Why is this happening now?" she asked him, because that didn't make any sense. There were so many points in her past when an anxiety disorder could have, maybe even should have, reared its head. Why now?

Howard just shrugged. "Triggers are weird things."

"And after finally having it out, and knowing that I've got options, no matter what? Shouldn't I be relieved now, not more scared than ever? But I'm finally moving forward. I've been locked in an awful contract for years and now there's an end in sight."

"Freedom is something that people die for." Howard let out a slow breath. "The closer we are to it, the harder we'll fight to get it, but also the more we'll fear losing it. That can be overwhelming."

She nodded, reluctantly. She didn't want that to be true, but it was.

"You may experience more panic attacks, even after the contract is done and over." The way he said it was level, like it wasn't that big a deal. Except when she looked up at him, he wasn't being dismissive. Just not judgemental, either. Which was probably a good thing in a therapist, but hard for her to truly accept.

"You aren't making me feel better."

He nodded. "It's not my job to make you feel better. It's my job to help you see how you can make yourself feel safer."

"Oh." Well, that sounded good. "How do we do that?"

"I'm going to give you a couple of tools. And we're going to meet again."

"I'm only here for two days."

"Planes travel all over the country, they tell me. And there's this magical device that lets us talk over great distances."

She laughed. "Point taken."

"Is there anything else you want to talk about today?"

When she hesitated, he gave her a look that told her he knew she knew better. She sighed. "Do you know anything about overseas deployments? My…" Bodyguard sounded wrong. "My boyfriend's younger brother is going to the Middle East. Kind of unexpectedly. And I don't know how to support him through that. He's a soldier himself, and he's being all tough and stoic about it, but… I'm scared, and I've never met the kid."

"That's a big topic. We can talk more about that tomorrow. When is he leaving?"

"In a week." The guilt of that weighed against her again, still heavy.

Howard frowned. "And your boyfriend is here with you?"

She winced. "He's also my bodyguard."

Howard laughed.

"Is that funny?"

"It's not *not* funny. So he's an ex-soldier, security professional. And his relative—"

"His baby brother. That he raised."

"Ah." Howard shrugged. "Tell him to go home."

"I did."

"Was that before or after you had another panic attack and someone hired me on an emergency basis?"

She hung her head.

"Hey, Liana. I'm going to tell you something that I don't know if you hear enough. Cut yourself some slack."

She jerked her head up. "What kind of therapist are you?"

"A pretty good one. Do you think you can trust me with your mental health long enough for your boyfriend-slash-bodyguard to go bid his brother a fond farewell?"

— —

DEAN DIDN'T like this plan at all. But Liana wasn't wrong. He'd feel like shit knowing he could have gone to say goodbye and he didn't. So he got on a plane after she left Denver. He'd rejoin the tour in Salt Lake City.

He had a connecting flight in Chicago, and after he landed and checked in with Liana, he called Matt. "Hey, bud."

His brother was somewhere busy, from the roar in the background. "Dean! How's the high life?"

"Pretty ordinary. How's everything at home?"

"Same old. What's up?"

"Do you know what Sean is doing tomorrow?"

"Packing, probably. Why?"

"I'm on my way back. Just for a day."

"What?" Matt muttered something in the background, then the dull roar faded. "Sorry, I was…occupied. No, don't come back. You've got a thing to do. It's all good."

"It's not. I need to…" Dean heard his voice catching and he swallowed that down. "I want to see him off."

"You're such a sap." Matt laughed. "Okay. Cool. I'll make sure he doesn't disappear into the woods."

"Thanks."

"No worries, man. When do you arrive?"

"I'm in Chicago. Getting on a plane for Toronto in a couple of hours."

"Cool." Dean listened as Matt headed back into the fray of whatever he was doing. "See you soon!"

He killed the time before his flight in a sports bar, then grabbed a news magazine to read on the plane. He didn't mind all the air travel, actually. He could do this regularly. He needed to talk to Zander about what that meant for the business.

Not that he wanted to play bodyguard much. Protecting Liana was one thing, but he wasn't really cut out for being in the public eye with celebrity after celebrity. But now that he'd done it, he could sub-contract that more easily. Recruit the right kind of guys. He knew enough reservists who would leap at the chance, and still keep their heads about them when they got nicknames and fangirls.

Who would he trust with Liana?

He gritted his teeth. Nobody was the short answer.

When his flight landed in Toronto, he made his way to customs. Nothing to declare, other than an overactive sense of big brotherly guilt and a weird ache in his chest where he held all his feelings about Liana.

The border agent wasn't interested in either, he assumed, so he kept his thoughts to himself.

He stopped before going through the last security gate to pull out his car keys and parking stub, then shouldered his backpack again.

Time to go home.

But as the sliding doors opened into the arrivals terminal, he slowed to a stop, because there in a row were his three brothers, each holding a sign.

Jake's said, **FOSTER**.

Matt's said, #**ARMGUY**.

And Sean's said, **BRO**.

"You little bastards," he said, hopping over the barrier to join them.

"You're not the only one who gets to surprise people, you big softie." Sean held out his hand, and Dean took it. He didn't miss that his brother's grip was stronger than usual. Point made.

Then he pulled his baby brother in tight for a crushing hug. "When did you grow all the way up?"

"No clue. Happens to us all at some point, eh?"

"I guess." He stepped back far enough to look the kid —the man—in the eye. "It's so good to see you."

"You too. You look fucking happy."

"Sure am. Even more so now that I've seen you. You want to ride back with me?"

Sean shook his head. "Let's have dinner."

"What?"

"We've been talking." Sean pointed to Matt, who pointed to Jake, who shrugged.

"He's doing nothing but packing and shopping and working out for the next few days. Meanwhile…"

"What?" Dean really didn't get it.

Matt rolled his eyes. "There's this woman that you've got a limited amount of time with on the other side of the continent…it's kind of a no-brainer, man."

Sean nodded. "And I want to take your truck back for you, because you're an idiot to pay for another month of parking fees. So we'll eat, then we think you need to get back on a plane."

"I don't. I've got a couple days." But his heart had already leapt at the thought of surprising Liana with an early return. He could feel a goofy grin spreading across his face and his brothers hooted and hollered at him.

It was official.

Grown men blushed.

"Come on. Let's go find some steaks to demolish and you can tell us what it's like to join the Old Man Club with Jake."

"I think if there's a club, maybe it's a Responsible Older Brothers Association."

"Wishful thinking. It's definitely an old man thing, and there's a Hopelessly in Love waiver, too."

He coughed and Sean rolled his eyes. "Come on, you can't even say the L-word, can you?"

"I can. I do. I…I love you guys."

"Sure. But you don't say it."

"I just did."

"That might be the first time ever."

"Well, I love you. There. Not a big deal, right?"

He thought about that exchange as he followed Jake down Dixie Road to a restaurant Matt had picked out. As the waitress took their orders and his brother teased him about Liana and the nickname and the ridiculous number of images of him now on Google, all some variation of the one where he was mooning over her just a few weeks earlier.

That was it. No time at all, really.

And in that short window, everything had changed.

His brothers weren't the only ones who deserved to hear all that was in his heart. It might be too soon to expect her to feel the same way back, but Liana had done this to him. Somehow, she'd cracked through his decades-old crusty exterior and let loose the guy-with-feelings trapped inside.

CHAPTER TWENTY-FIVE

THE IDAHO FALLS Super Eight wasn't the nicest hotel Liana had ever stayed in, by a long shot, but after two days on the road and a muddy-ass, rainy day at an outdoor festival outside of Mountain Home, it felt like paradise. She was beyond thrilled to have a hot shower and a warm bed that didn't sway beneath her as she tried to sleep.

Liana didn't care if it was uncool. She was ready for bed at nine at night. She braided her hair, put on her jammies, and curled up with a paperback Dean had left on the tour bus. She was tired, so she pulled out her writing glasses to make it easier to focus on the pages, yellowed from age, and worn from a fair bit of re-reading. She rubbed a dog-eared fold and wondered how his trip was going.

She hadn't talked to him since his stopover in Chicago. He'd texted when he arrived and said he was with his brothers. That had been just before she'd gone on stage the night before in Bozeman.

Idaho and Montana were two of her favourite states—

mud not withstanding—and she was a bit sad she wasn't sharing this with Dean. One of the realizations she'd come to over her first few sessions with Howard was that while she loved performing for large crowds, she was also quickly coming to hate it.

That had taken her by surprise and thrown her for a loop.

Hate might be too strong a word, but it definitely wasn't a sure-thing positive experience. And the more anxious she got about who might be watching her and what they might be thinking, the worse her odds got for a show going well.

It was time, once this tour came to a close, for her to take a break.

She'd write and sing and still be a musician in every other sense of the word, but it would be a while before she got back on a large stage again. And that decision brought her just as much relief as running to Pine Harbour had the month before. Maybe more, because it gave her a bit of space to think about maybe visiting that little town again, without any need to leave for a while.

Maybe convince an emotionally-reluctant ex-cop to keep dating, and see where they might end up if they just didn't stop.

She flipped back to the page before the one she was trying to read.

She hadn't absorbed any of what she'd just skimmed over. Her thoughts were too all over the place and what she really wanted to do was call Dean, but she didn't want to be needy or interrupt his family visit.

A quiet knock at the door made her roll over, but not get out of bed. She really didn't want to be social. It came again, and she looked up. A curious prickle skated over her skin and she swung her legs out of bed.

She was mid-yawn as she swung open the door, but any fatigue she'd been feeling flew away when Dean leaned into the open doorway, a tired grin on his handsome face. "Can I come in?"

"Can you…" Relief and shock and pure, unadulterated excitement coursed through her. She leapt into his arms as he tossed his bag against the wall and kicked the door shut behind him. "What are you doing here?"

"I came back," he said with a low chuckle, burying his face in her neck.

"But your brother…"

He groaned and carried her to the bed, sitting with her in his lap. He gave her a rueful look as he tugged on her braid. "I went to Toronto. He met me there. They all did, actually. And all I could talk about was you. All I could think about was…you. I had to go and see him, and then I had to come back. To you."

"Oh." She was pretty sure she was going to cry, and she wasn't sure why. She pressed her lips together and blinked her eyes, big and wide, refusing to let tears fall.

"How was your show today?" he asked softly, rubbing his knuckles along her jaw, then drifting his fingers down the line of her throat. "I had like four connections to get here. I didn't get a chance to call, I'm sorry."

"It was muddy. And good. I missed you. Is that crazy? It was just two days."

"I missed you, too." He cupped the back of her neck and groaned under his breath. "More than I realized. It was hard to fly away from you."

Her heart hammered against her ribcage as he tugged them together, brushing his lips against hers, soft at first, then more insistent. She touched his cheek, now mostly covered in a light beard, then slid her fingers into his hair, no longer quite so short on the side.

Still a little too long on top. Perfect to hold on to while making out. Her head started to spin as he kissed her thoroughly, devastating her with each erotic slide of his tongue. She opened for him, wanting more, *needing* more.

His kiss deepened as she pressed closer, and he tugged her hair. Yes. More. Harder.

"Dean…" she breathed as he pulled back.

"There's something I want to tell you first."

"Later."

"Now."

"Kiss me."

"I love you."

She froze, and he searched her face, his eyes flashing from her eyes to her mouth and back up again.

"And if that's too soon, just put it away until you're ready to hear it. I just want you to know. You deserve to know that someone loves you."

He gave her a lopsided grin that made her tingle. "I mean, thousands of people love you. But I…I love *you*, exactly as you are. Hair in a braid, reading glasses on. I love every inch of you, from the way you worry about your band to the way you sing to the heavens and everything in between. I love that you run like you're being chased by hell hounds and how you look when you're concentrating on getting a lyric just right. I love being on tour with you and—"

"I don't. Love being on tour. Not anymore." She reached out and touched his cheek again. "Not like that's the most important thing you just said, but…I don't want you to think I need to tour."

"Whoa, when did that happen? Because I'm easy, princess. I'll take what I can get, and wait for you."

"I've been doing a lot of thinking." She took off her glasses and, leaned in and pressing her forehead to his. He was blurry, but she could feel his warmth and his breath and his smile. She could feel that to the depth of her soul. "About us, too, but me and writing and performing. It's been an intense couple of days."

"Whatever you want, we'll do. If you want me."

"I want you." So much. She kissed him again, hungrier this time. She scraped her teeth lightly on his bottom lip, tugging it into her mouth. "Here, in Nashville, in Pine Harbour. I get that you've got a big family and they need you."

He shrugged. "They'll survive. And they've got my back, too. They were all very much in favour of me racing back to you. Turns out I've been selfish in how I've handled them." He shook his head. "But that's a whole separate side thing. Right now I just want to hold you."

She slid her arms around his neck. "Is that all?"

"What were you thinking?" He tightened his grasp on her, sliding his hands under her shirt and up her back.

She rubbed her nose against the tendon running down his neck. He smelled so familiar and good and comfortable. He smelled like home, her home that she'd been running in search of for thirty years. "I want you naked."

"God yes."

He tumbled her to the side and leaned over to get his boots off, but she scrambled off the bed and knelt at his feet. "Let me."

He unbuttoned his shirt, slowly, his hot gaze never leaving her as he watched her strip him down. Boots and socks, then she reached for his belt buckle at the same time his hands reached the bottom of his shirt, baring his chest and abdomen for her. She leaned in and kissed the small trail of hair that led south from his navel and disappeared into his jeans.

He loved her. It was more than she'd ever let herself really hope for. And it was everything she wanted. Her chest was full, so full, and she wanted to show him how she felt, too.

His hand smoothed over the top of her head and she twisted into the touch. Her fingers were shaking as she unzipped him, but the heat of his body was what she wanted, needed, and as soon as she took him in her mouth, the rest just clicked into place.

Because he was thick and hard, and all hers. She took her time worshiping him, alternating between sucking him deep into her mouth and backing off, teasing him with little licks and the head and down his shaft. And the whole time, he watched her, his thighs flexing beneath the soft denim. She stroked her hands up and down his heavy, solid muscles, pushing his legs wider for her. And as he started to groan and grunt, she needed him all the way naked. It wasn't enough.

She tugged those jeans down his legs, then stood in front of him and peeled off her shirt, her pj bottoms, her panties…

"I love you, too," she whispered as she climbed onto his lap and straddled him. "I missed you and I love you."

He kissed her as she sank onto his erection, welcoming him into her body. He filled her up, all the way to her heart, and she rose up, just a bit, so she could sink down and feel that stretch again. He was hers. She was claiming him, forever and ever, because he loved her just the way she was, and she loved him with her entire being.

She cried out his name as he palmed her ass, pulling her tight so he could pulse inside her, and he kissed her neck, rough and wet. "Say it again," he growled.

"Dean…"

"No. Tell me you love me."

"I love you." She smiled and gasped as he surged into her again, causing her to say it twice more, the last one more of a cry than actual words.

And when she shattered into a million pieces of pure, blissed-out wonder, he held the shell of her until they all fell back into place, and then he was the one to say it in, in a whisper against her skin.

CHAPTER TWENTY-SIX

LIANA'S last concert of the summer was in San Diego, at an outdoor amphitheatre. Fighter jets flew overhead as they waited for her turn to do her sound check, and Dean took no small pleasure in holding her in his lap and correctly identifying each aircraft she pointed at. It was a cool city for a service member to visit, for sure. They were going to stay in the area for a few days, so he'd rented a car and while she was busy, he took off for the afternoon to tour the USS Midway, permanently docked in the harbour.

He took a picture from the flight deck and emailed it to Sean. He hadn't heard from his brother in a few days. **Miss you, kid**, he added to the photo.

A reply came in as he was getting out of his cab at the amphitheatre.

Yeah, you look real sad. How's your woman?

That was the easiest question in the world to answer. **She's great. We're both looking forward to heading home. Can't wait to introduce her to everyone. She'll probably be there when you get back.**

Dean pictured Sean on his laptop, maybe on his cot

or bunk, his boots kicked off and his uniform shirt balled up behind his head like a second pillow. Thank God for the technology that allowed them to fire messages back and forth like this. It didn't take long for his brother's reply to pop up. **Sounds good. I'm thinking of hitting Ibiza for my leave in a few months. Maybe I'll find a girl there. Good to have goals, right?**

Dean chuckled to himself, then took his time re-reading the message before firing off one last reply. **Definitely. Stay safe. I love you.**

He found Liana in her dressing room. She was sitting cross-legged on the couch, her eyes closed, and she was listening to a white noise track on her phone. He leaned against the door and watched her for a few minutes, until she opened her eyes and gave him a smile.

"You ready for tonight?"

She nodded, her face soft. "I want to say that I'm going to miss it, but that would be a fib of magnificent proportions."

He laughed. "You'll still perform."

"Exactly. I look forward to a long run of small stages and crowds that don't expect me."

"Hey, Zander emailed me while I was at the Midway. He's lined up a bunch of work for the fall. Security installs, a big Christmas event, and if I can find a reason to go to Nashville, he thinks we can start sub-contracting more bodyguard work."

"Oh, well it turns out I've got friends in Nashville," she winked. "And a nice house that I don't spend enough time in."

"Hey, that is convenient." He grinned.

A knock at her dressing room door interrupted them,

and he got out of the way so she could pull her wardrobe for the show that night.

When she found him again, he was holding one of Jackie's guitars as the lead guitarist was adjusting the other.

"Hey cowboy," Liana said with a glint in her eye, and he glanced down at the instrument in his hands.

"You like this?" He went to strum it and Jackie cleared her throat.

Liana laughed. "Maybe we'll get you a hat when we get back to Nashville. And boots."

"I like my boots just as they are."

"Yeah, but cowboy fantasy."

They were going boot shopping, apparently.

Jackie shook her head wordlessly and took her guitar from him, probably afraid he was going to violate it or something.

— —

LIANA PLAYED three encores that night. She'd done a WhisperSnip earlier that day and confirmed this was her last planned tour for…a while. Never say never.

"I'll be back," she promised the sold out San Diego crowd. She had an entire lifetime, after all, and it really felt like her career was just beginning.

And when the lights finally went dark, she went backstage and they had an epic after party.

The next day she slept in, and Dean woke her up just

before noon with a skinny hazelnut latte and a slow, sweet kiss.

"Today's the first day of the rest of your life," he whispered. "What do you want to do?

— —

IT TOOK them almost a month to get back to Pine Harbour. California had been so much fun, they ended up renting a place for two weeks and just kicking back. And in those days of exploring and nights of making love, they talked about crazy things like kids and future travel plans and whether or not to take kids on adventures like hiking the Italian coast or sailing around the Caribbean.

"I didn't get on my first airplane until I was nineteen," Liana admitted on their last night in California, as they walked along the beach.

An unexpected melancholy washed over Dean. "I went to England with my mom when I was six. I don't remember much about it, but there are pictures somewhere in my dad's attic. That was the only real vacation as a kid, although the Colonel took us camping at least once every summer. But that was more boot camp prep than a holiday."

"Hope's going on location next summer and she wants to bring Ryan and the kids."

"Zander told me. We'll make sure they're safe."

"Maybe I'll come along and be the nanny."

He grinned. "The kids like you."

"I like them."

And that was where they left it, but when they tumbled into bed, he couldn't shake the image of Liana holding a little girl or a little boy of her own. Of making that baby with her, and for the first time in his life, it didn't scare him to his core.

The next morning she had a conference call, so he went shopping for some last minute souvenirs.

When he got back, she was sitting very still on the couch.

"What's up?" he asked, careful not to assume something was wrong, but his heart hammered in his chest.

"Well…" she said slowly, blinking up at him. "I've been released from my contract. My lawyer says the agreement is pretty generous and there's no limitation on what I do with the songs that I'd put forward for the last record."

He dropped to his knees in front of her. "That's great."

"And…" She laughed a little. "And Karen wants it. Exactly as it is. She has an idea for two more songs, so she wants me in the studio for that, but…it's pretty much a go." Her smile started in her eyes and transformed her entire face as she let the laughter take over and turn into the most amazing, celebratory cheer. "How awesome is that?"

Pretty fucking awesome. "Oh, angel. Good fucking job, you." He cupped her face and kissed her sexy, talented mouth with everything he had.

She returned the embrace, peppering hungry, appreciative kisses on his mouth, along his jaw, down his neck.

"Whoa there, tiger," he said with a laugh, tugging her into his lap. He laid another soul-stealing kiss right on her lips to reward her a little, then pinned her hands in her lap. "I'd love to celebrate naked, but we're getting on a plane in four hours and we haven't packed yet."

"Drat."

He laughed as she peeled herself off him and sprinted to the bedroom.

——

LIANA HAD STEPPED into the recording booth more than a hundred times, at least, but this time it felt different.

This time she didn't have any fears about what would happen to the song once they cut it. If she'd face backlash or repercussions. She wouldn't, because behind the producer stood Karen, and she had a big ass grin on her face.

Watch out, Nashville. The women have a plan.

Liana had stopped at her favourite boutique and picked up matching Dolly for President t-shirts for them to wear today. It seemed fitting.

Karen leaned in and pressed a button on the control panel. "Ready to do this?"

"Am I ever." She flashed a quick thumbs up and pulled on her headset.

——

NERVES RIOTED through Dean's gut as Zander parked his truck in front of the small two-bedroom house one block off Main Street. His wife Faith and their son Eric were waiting on the porch swing.

Dean had been proud of that swing when he'd bought it last year. He thought it made the house look cute, but now it just looked small.

Because he was bringing Liana home, to his home, and suddenly he feared it didn't stack up. It wasn't anything like her bungalow in East Nashville, freshly renovated and magazine perfect.

It wasn't even anything compared to his friends' homes.

It was clean and neat and fine for a bachelor, but now through the eyes of a man who very much didn't want to be a bachelor anymore, it was…lacking.

He helped Liana out and introduced her to Faith. Then he busied himself carrying their bags onto the porch.

"Dani's making a big group dinner tonight," Zander said. "It's not exactly a command appearance, but she is seven months pregnant, so if you don't show up, then pretend I didn't tell you, okay? I don't want her wrath."

Dean wasn't sure what to say to that. *Thanks for driving five hours to pick us up at the airport, now go away? I can't handle the thought of people right now, I just want to get through showing my famous girlfriend my embarrassing little house, thank you very much.*

Liana gave Zander a beaming smile. "That sounds awesome. Can we bring something?"

Shit. He didn't have anything to bring. He hadn't been home in two months and Matt said he'd cleaned out the fridge, but did he trust the standards of a twenty-nine-year-old man who didn't have any life plans beyond the expiry date on his next jug of milk?

"Just bring Dean." Zander winked and hoisted Eric up

onto his shoulders. The kid was getting a bit big for that, but neither of them seemed to care. Faith murmured her own hope that they'd come and then his partner was gone.

"So this is your place," Liana said, looking around with big eyes.

"It's not much." He stuck the key in the lock and turned the handle. He wanted to step in first and make sure his brothers had in fact not had a party, but that was rude, so he stepped back and gestured for her to step over the threshold.

She gave him a little smile as she moved past him, then a surprised sound as she stepped inside.

His heart stopped. What?

He followed her in—and found flowers on the table.

"Those are so pretty!" She turned and squeezed his hand. "You have the nicest friends."

He was going to have a heart attack. This had been a terrible idea. He stepped outside and sucked in a big, deep breath that did nothing for his nerves, then he picked up their bags.

He found her looking at his bookshelf. With a happy sigh, she wrapped her arms around his waist and rested her cheek on his chest.

He patted her back. Fuck. He was messing this up.

She glanced up at him. "Are you okay?"

"I'm…" He stroked his fingers through her hair. The long dark waves were loose today. God, she was so pretty. And his. And he was fucking nervous about that, not the house. "I'm fine."

"You seem a bit tense."

"I am."

"Why?"

"Stupid shit. Want a tour?"

She grinned. "Okay."

It didn't take long. The living-slash-dining room was where they stepped into, then the kitchen was behind it, and two bedrooms and a bathroom were off a short hallway. Someone had left flowers in his room, too, and he was thankful he'd been caught up on laundry before he left. The last thing he needed was Dani or Olivia washing his socks to help him make a good impression on Liana.

"Nice big bed," she whispered, climbing onto a duvet cover he'd never seen before.

Okay, maybe he did need their help.

"I want to ask you to marry me," he blurted out. "I've got a ring, and it's nice, too. But then I brought you here and I don't know what I was thinking, honestly."

"Honey."

"So let's put that in the same category as when I told you that I love you. Good to know, save it for later."

"Sweetie."

"And I don't have anything to take to Jake and Dani's tonight."

"Babe."

He just stared at her.

She stared right back. "Dean…" She laughed.

Laughter wasn't good, right?

"Are you freaking out because you want to ask me to marry you? Or are you freaking out because you brought me home?"

"Uh…" He swallowed hard. His throat was too damn dry. "Do you want some water?"

"I want to marry you." She reached out her hand and gave him a beseeching smile. "Come here."

He took it, but he felt like shit. "This is the worst proposal in the history of proposals."

She just shrugged. "You've done a lot of sweet and romantic things for me already. This is a way better story than the usual blah blah blah down on one knee."

"I was gonna do that."

"You would have rocked that. You can try again if you want."

"I'm sorry my house is so small."

"Because there isn't enough room for you to get down on one knee?" She looked around in confusion. "There's lots of room."

"Because it's not big enough for…" He trailed off. He wasn't sure anymore. "Because it's not big."

"But you're just one guy. I mean, you're a big guy, but what do you need a big house for?"

"You."

"Oh." Her face softened and she swayed against him. "That's pretty sweet right there."

"I want to be worthy of you."

"You are," she whispered, brushing her lips against his. His legs bumped against the bed and he wrapped his arms around her to keep from knocking her over. She giggled. "See? You've got me. Always. That's what I need. Just you. Isn't that what you said when you came to Idaho? You love me just the way I am. Warts and all. And I love *you*, I want to marry *you*. Not some fancy house, although this place is super cute. Can we turn the other bedroom into a recording studio?"

"No." They were going house hunting tomorrow. "Wait." He wound his fingers into her hair and held her close, kissing her until she was breathless and his nerves finally settled.

Then he stepped back and lowered to one knee. He pulled the ring out of his pocket and held it in front of him. "Liana Hansen, you're the most amazing woman I've ever met and the only woman I've ever fallen in love with. I want to fall in love with you over and over again, every day for the rest of our lives. Will you marry me?"

She nodded through what looked like happy tears, a stupid grin all over her face, and this time when she reached for him, he let her pull him down onto the bed. Sometimes he needed to be her stable rock, and sometimes he needed to let her tip him sideways and make his life crazy.

Just before they headed to Jake and Dani's that night, he took a selfie of the two of them on his front porch. Liana coached him how to frame it just so, showing off the ring but in a subtle kind of way.

"You're an Instagram natural," she promised as he added a filter and a border to the picture.

But instead of posting it online for the world to see, he just emailed it to the one brother he wouldn't be able to tell in person.

Hey kid. So I'm getting married. Gonna go house hunting. My place is too small and she needs a studio. Should be in a new place by Christmas, or the spring at the latest, depending on how much work we need Jake to do to whatever I buy. Your welcome home party will be fancy-ass. Love, Dean (and his future bride)

THE END (FOR NOW)

*Want to see who's coming to town next? Keep reading for **a bonus epilogue**! But be warned...it'll have you screaming for Sean's story...*

If you aren't ready to read it, join my VIP mailing list and I'll remind you when Sean's book, *Love in a Sandstorm*, is coming out.

If you enjoyed this book, please leave a review on your favourite book retailer sites! Reviews help readers decide to give new authors a try.

EPILOGUE

Nine months later

"I CAN PISS BY MYSELF," Sean growled, and Dean held up his hands, backing away slowly.

"Of course you can," he said, reminding himself to be fucking patient with the fucking jackass, because he'd been fucking injured while at fucking war. Concussion, brain-bleed, vertigo…a long list of things that added up to the fact his brother had gotten his bell rung, a fucking good one, and it was a miracle he'd walked away without any more serious injuries.

Acquired Brain Injury. Traumatic Brain Injury. Dean had heard both of them, over and over again. Sounded pretty fucking serious.

Expletives didn't make it any easier, really. But they didn't fucking hurt, either.

Sean slammed the door in his face and Dean stood there, forearm braced against the door frame, listening as his brother slowly moved through the bathroom—then stumbled, crashed, and fell.

He waited, hand poised on the door knob.

"Go away!" Sean yelled. "I fell down. It's not the end of the fucking world."

Dean wasn't the only one trying out the expletive-laden coping strategy. And Sean was right. If he needed to crawl to the toilet, so be it. Dean sighed and nodded at the door, lifting his voice to travel through it. "I'm gone, man."

"And stay gone for a while. Fuck. I'm not a fucking invalid."

Except he was, at least temporarily.

And Dean and Liana were his roommates, for better or worse. Nobody else could do it. Jake and Dani's son was still pretty little and woke often in the night. Matt's apartment wasn't set up for a guest who wasn't sharing his bed. And their father…well, that was a non-starter.

So when Sean came home, it was to the new house that Dean and Liana had bought. They'd barely had a chance to christen it before Sean was hurt. But Liana hadn't missed a beat, and when Dean brought it up, she didn't even let him finish the ask before she wrapped her arms around him and said his brother was welcome to stay as long as needed.

If only Dean had that same level of patience. He'd give anything to make Sean whole again. To heal him. But they were butting heads, constantly, and it was wearing on them both.

He counted backwards from ten, slowly, and headed downstairs. He found his woman curled up with a scratch pad, a couple of coloured pens, and a hockey puck stress ball.

She was working that thing over like nothing else.

He'd be lucky if it didn't resemble a soccer ball when she was done with it.

"Not going well?" he asked quietly, dropping a kiss on her head.

"Mmm," she mumbled, not looking up. But then she paused, her eyes still glued to her notepad. "Love you."

He grinned. "Love you, too. Hungry?"

"Mmm," she said throatily.

"Sandwich?"

She blinked up at him, a slow, suddenly aware look. "I was thinking…hungry for you."

His dick pulsed, thickening against his fly. It had been more than a week since they'd had sex, because of Sean, and these new song ideas that were pouring out of her. "Where do you want me?"

She laughed her her breath and glanced toward the stairs. "Will we disturb His Grumpiness if we go upstairs?"

Dean didn't want Sean hearing them have sex. "I'd rather *he* doesn't disturb *us*."

"Studio it is, then." She leapt her feet, notepad firmly in one hand as she wiggled the fingers of the other at him. "Come on."

"Dare I ask what brought this one?" he asked quietly as she led him down the half-flight of stairs and across the family room to the converted sunroom she used as a recording studio. It was insulated to be soundproof, had a fantastic wide couch against the far wall, and a lock on the door.

Perfect.

"I wrote you a song," she confessed, her cheeks turning pink. "Lyrics, really, although I can hear the bridge in my head." She hummed a bit, then sang a line of notes, her voice clear and teasing.

He tugged her close as he flipped the lock. "And do I get to hear the lyrics?"

Her eyelashes dusted her cheeks. "Maybe."

"Do I need to bribe you for them?"

"Yes, please."

He swept her into his arms, the way they folded together now familiar and comforting. Still thrilling though. He was sure he'd never lose that shiver that went up his spine when she sighed against his skin. Never stop getting hard at the press of her breasts against his chest, the feel of her ass under his palm. He kissed her thoroughly, until she was turned on and moving against him. Then he peeled her out of her clothes and spread her out on the couch before dropping to his knees and dipping his head between her thighs.

His woman. His life.

He might have to be the rock for everyone else, but she was his secret support. Always there to hold his hand and tug him to bed. When he found out about Sean being injured, when it wasn't clear what had happened or what the outcome would be, he'd cried. And she'd held him. The next day, she'd told him he was her Superman, her hero.

God, he loved her.

And now she'd written him a song.

He licked along the seam of her sex, sliding his tongue against her sensitive nub for just a second before easing away. "What's the song about?" he asked as he breathed on her most intimate place.

"A hero," she breathed. "My hero."

How did she know that had been what he needed,

again? He kissed her then, a dirty kiss, a secret just for them. He kissed her until she writhed beneath him, then he reared up and filled her, hard and fast.

— —

AN HOUR LATER, Dean jogged back upstairs to check on his brother. He found him fast asleep, face down on top of his covers. Some of the happy ease in his chest was pushed out by a now-familiar worry.

In the distance, a gentle knock broke through his thoughts.

He glanced back down the stairs.

Liana was still in her studio.

Anyone else who could be here—anyone who would be helpful and non-stressful—had a key and could let themselves in.

Another knock.

He caught his lower lip between his teeth as he headed for the door, ready to tell whoever was there to go away.

When he opened the door, though, he didn't find a salesperson or someone preaching gospel. Didn't even find a well-meaning town busybody.

Instead there was a nervous looking stranger. A woman, tall and slim, with golden-brown hair hanging loose around her shoulders and wide, grey eyes, unadorned with makeup. Behind her was parked a nonde-script silver rental car—he could make out the sticker.

She hitched her bag up on her shoulder and swung her hands at her sides. She wore jeans and a cargo jacket.

There was nothing about her description that should set off his internal alarm bells, but he couldn't turn off his cop brain. "Can I help you?"

She nodded slowly. "I'm looking for Sean Foster."

"I'm his brother, Dean."

Another nod. Her eyes flicked up and down his face, searching for more information.

That was all she was getting. If Sean had gotten into trouble, or owed this woman something…

"Is he here?"

Dean crossed his arms and lifted his chin. "What do you want with him?"

She swallowed hard. "I asked at Mac's. The diner?"

Was that a question? He gave an equally dense response. "I'm familiar with it."

She coloured. "Of course. They said he was staying here."

No point in lying to her. "He's asleep right now."

Her eyes flicked past Dean's shoulder, tightening in confusion.

Yeah, Sean was sleeping in the middle of the day. What was it to her? "Maybe it would be best for you to come back another time."

"Right." She licked her lips, her tongue darting out in nervous, quick movements. "Maybe we should talk, anyway."

"Us?"

She fluttered her hands again, this time in a weak gesture inviting him out onto his own porch.

He glanced behind him into the empty front room and the staircase. Yeah, probably best. He stepped outside and closed the door. "What do we need to talk about? If you're looking for Sean, you should know he's not in great shape right now."

Her face blanched and for a second, Dean felt badly for dealing her that blow. But a second was all it took for her to square her shoulders and tighten her mouth. "Then it's all the better that I'm here."

"And why is that?"

She shoved her hand back through her hair and glanced to the side. "I guess he didn't tell you."

"Tell us what?"

With a sigh, she held out her hand and looked him right in the eye. "I'm Jenna. Sean's wife."

THE END

ACKNOWLEDGEMENTS

aka The People Who Get Me When I'm Silly

The first acknowledgement for this book has to go to my sister, who has worked in radio for almost twenty years (which is impossible, because she's still a kid), and it's through her stories that I learned enough about performers and concert tours to want to tell Liana's story. She also didn't blink when I told her we needed to go to Nashville for last minute fact-checking. Thanks, Pan!

Next nod is to my developmental editor, Kristi Yanta, who saw two frustrated early drafts of this. This is the third Pine Harbour novel we've worked on together, and to say she's supportive and understanding is an understatement. I love how she sees the heart of what I'm trying to do and encourages me to smooth everything else out around it, letting the core of it shine. It was hard for me to explain in my first (second, third, fifth) draft what story I wanted to tell, and I'm glad I kept trying until the pieces clicked into place.

Sadie Haller gets all the thanks for talking me off many

ledges. She's so good at pointing out all the little things I just don't see when I'm dreaming about the bigger picture.

Lori Carter, the best assistant ever. She notices a lot of the little details, too. And I think she loves Pine Harbour more than anyone else possibly could. It's good to have a super-fan in house.

Dana Waganer, for her thorough proofreading. Without her, internal thought would be depicted in at least four different ways in each book. Also, hyphens.

Nancy Stopper also caught some typos in an advance copy. I always appreciate the heads up!

Maria Rose helped me with an early conversation about running; some of that ended up on the cutting room floor, but all back story is important for the writer, and I like to get things right.

To my readers who didn't complain when I bumped this release back, and then back again. Who pre-ordered the book even after I said I was struggling with it. Who wrote me the most amazing, encouraging notes to get Dean's book done…thank you so much from the bottom of my heart.

As always, my family, for being so chill about takeout —again—and the ever-growing laundry mountain. My muse appreciates the understanding.

And finally, to the country music singers and song-writers in Nashville who inspired this book, and gave me so many of the little details—my hat is off to you. You make incredible art. Thank you for never giving up.

With love and a few unexpected tears,
Zoe

ABOUT THE AUTHOR

Zoe York lives in London, Ontario with her young family. She's currently chugging Americanos, wiping sticky fingers, and dreaming of heroes in and out of uniform.

www.zoeyork.com

www.ingramcontent.com/pod-product-compliance
Lightning Source LLC
Chambersburg PA
CBHW020913060726
47591CB00004B/1229